The Other Alice

Also by Michelle Harrison

The Thirteen Treasures
The Thirteen Curses
The Thirteen Secrets
One Wish

For older readers
Unrest

MICHELLE HARRISON

The Other Alice

SIMON & SCHUSTER

First published in Great Britain in 2016 by Simon & Schuster UK Ltd
A CBS COMPANY

1 3 5 7 9 10 8 6 4 2

Simon & Schuster UK Ltd
1st Floor, 222 Gray's Inn Road
London
WC1X 8HB

www.simonandschuster.co.uk

Simon & Schuster Australia, Sydney
Simon & Schuster India, New Delhi

A CIP catalogue record for this book
is available from the British Library.

PB ISBN 978-1-4711-2427-3
eBook ISBN 978-1-4711-2428-0

Typeset in the UK by M Rules
Printed and bound by CPI Group (UK) Ltd, Croydon, CR0 4YY

MIX
Paper from
responsible sources
FSC® C020471

Simon & Schuster UK Ltd are committed to sourcing paper that is made
from wood grown in sustainable forests and support the Forest Stewardship
Council, the leading international forest certification organisation. Our
books displaying the FSC logo are printed on FSC certified paper.

For Julia, who loves stories,
and for anyone who has ever wished
a fictional character could be real.

Once Upon a Time . . .

ALICE SILVER HAD NEVER MET ANYONE WHO had killed before, but that changed on the day Dorothy Grimes walked past the window of Alice's favourite coffee shop.

Alice had been sitting at the smallest table, staring anxiously at her notebook. It was open on the table next to her coffee, which had gone cold, because she'd forgotten to drink it. She turned the notebook's pages, reading over her work.

Words swam before her eyes, the same words she had written weeks, months ago, and had read through many times since. She didn't even know if they made sense any more.

She was tired. Her head ached, her neck ached, even her eyes ached. Irritable, she flicked to the pages at the front. The writing here wasn't quite as dense: it was mainly lists and diagrams, and snippets she had stuck in, such as photographs or pictures from magazines. One of these, a news article, had come loose over time and slipped out on to the table. Alice picked it up, scanning the headline she knew by heart.

YOUNG KILLER
LOCKED UP FOR LIFE

The cutting was over two years old now, but Alice still remembered all the details. They had shocked her deeply – and everyone else in the country. The thought that someone her age – just sixteen – could murder five people in such horrible ways was not something that could be forgotten easily. In fact, the killings were what made this case an oddity. Most murderers use the same method to kill each time. This one was different. There had been one strangulation, one bludgeoning, a stabbing, a drowning, and a house fire that had been set deliberately.

She turned the cutting over. On the back was part of another story about a teenage girl who had won a prize for keeping a diary for a year. Alice remembered how she had been holding the cutting to the light, allowing the words on the other side of the thin paper to show through. How words from the two different articles had combined to form 'kill ʏɪɒiḃ'.

Kill diary.

That was how she'd got the idea to combine both articles to make a truly memorable character for the story she was working on: a killer who kept a written log of her murders, framing each one as a piece of fiction.

Alice shivered. Sometimes the best ideas came about by accident, and this was one of them. A few tweaks here and there, a new name, a few different murder methods. It was surprisingly easy to think it all up. Alice wondered, not for the first time, if she were a wicked person for imagining such terrible things, but she supposed that all storybook villains had to come from someone's imagination. After all, what was the point of a villain if they were not scary?

She put the cutting down and closed her eyes, massaging her temples. Words floated in the dark space behind her eyelids. Even when her eyes were shut, there was no escape. They surrounded her like a prison, but she knew the only way she would get free was with more words. The *right* ones. The trouble was she didn't know them. She'd written herself into a corner and she had no idea how to finish the story. And now she was starting to worry about what would happen if she didn't. Not just because all her hard work would be wasted, but what would happen to *her*.

Alice had spent the last few months telling herself that what had happened last time hadn't been real. That she'd imagined it, that it had been the lack of sleep, the stress. Whatever it was, it had started up again in the past few days. The shadows, like someone moving just at the edge of her vision. The footsteps behind her on an empty street. The whispering.

She was afraid.

She opened her eyes, letting out a slow breath. The coffee shop was within a bookshop, up on the first floor. She did most of her writing at home, but had thought that a change of scene might help the words to flow. It hadn't. If anything, being around so many other stories, all finished, was like a quiet form of torture. Instead of inspiring her, she imagined the other books were taunting her. She leaned closer to the window, looking out. A sharp winter draught crept in and prickled her face as she watched people moving about on the street below, unaware they were being observed.

And then it felt like all the hairs on her body were standing on end as she caught sight of a slight figure that was looking in the window of a shop opposite.

It can't be, it can't be, it can't be . . .

The words pounded in Alice's head, each one accompanied by a sickening thud of her racing heart. She stood up without even meaning to, knocking into the table. The untouched coffee slopped over the sides of the cup, speckling the notebook and the newspaper cutting. She pressed her hands to the glass, barely aware of the *drip, drip, drip* of liquid hitting the floor and splashing on to her boots.

She snatched her notebook up and lurched away from the window. The newspaper cutting floated to the floor, but she didn't register it or the strange looks she was getting from other customers.

'Not again,' she whispered, the words catching in her throat. 'Please, not again!' But she still had to know for sure. She stumbled out of the coffee shop and rushed for the

4

stairs, arriving outside the bookshop moments later. Her breath came in fast gasps, each one puffing in the frozen air.

The girl had gone. Alice turned this way and that, searching the street. Had she hallucinated the whole thing? Fallen asleep perhaps? She hadn't slept properly for a while now—

There. Alice just caught sight of the back of her, vanishing round a corner. She followed, a chill wind making her teeth chatter. Only then did she realise she'd left her coat behind, but if she went back now she'd lose her. She caught up and drew level, trying to get a proper look at the girl's face.

When she saw it, a small cry escaped her lips, but it was whipped away by the wind.

It *was* her.

She had changed her appearance since leaving the hospital. The dull brown hair that had hung in limp rats' tails was gone and so was the dowdy hospital gown that made her look young and helpless. To anyone else she would have been almost unrecognisable ... but not to Alice. She stumbled, bumping into someone nearby, but was too full of shock and horror to react to the cross words that were spat at her. She had read about a person's blood running cold in many books, but now she actually felt it: the warmth draining from her toes and an icy chill working its way through her entire body like a wave.

What is she doing here? Alice thought. *Does she know? Is she looking for me already?*

And, almost as though Alice drew her like a magnet, the girl turned and stared at her. There was curiosity in her expression, but nothing to suggest she recognised Alice. Nothing to say she was aware of their connection although, as Alice stopped walking and became frozen to the spot, something stirred behind the girl's eyes. Malevolence and a different kind of awareness.

She can see I'm afraid of her, Alice thought. *And she likes it.*

Slowly, Dorothy Grimes strode up to her, a small smile curving her lips. It became wider as Alice backed away, not even realising she was doing so until she came up against a wall.

Dorothy finally stopped, too close to Alice. So close Alice could feel her breath on her face. The sensation of it turned her stomach.

'Have we met?' Dorothy asked. Her voice was soft, but there was nothing gentle about it. It was soft the same way a pillow could be as it smothered you.

'N-not . . . in person.' The words came out as little more than a croak.

'But you know who I am, don't you?'

'Yes,' Alice whispered. 'I know who you are.'

'And you know what I've done.'

A wave of dizziness threatened to overwhelm Alice then. She swayed lightly, managing to steady herself, trying to blink away the awful images that had come to mind. Images of Dorothy striking a match, of squeezing someone's throat, and of scratching crusted blood that wasn't her own off her cheeks. Yes, Alice knew exactly what Dorothy was capable of.

'Did you read about me in the news?' Dorothy asked. She lowered her voice. 'All the naughty things I've done?'

Alice shook her head weakly. 'Not exactly.'

'Then how do you know me?' Dorothy asked.

'I know everything about you,' Alice whispered.

Dorothy rolled her eyes. 'Oh, not you as well. Do you know how many doctors I've had to listen to, spouting that sort of rubbish? We know all about you, Dorothy,' she mimicked. 'You must have experienced some kind of trauma, Dorothy. We want you to keep a dream diary, Dorothy, Dorothy, *Dorothy*.' She was getting worked up now, getting that glaze over her eyes. 'Repeating my name over and over to make me think they're my friends.'

'I know,' Alice said.

'Oh, you *know*, do you?' Dorothy said, her eyes gleaming.

'I told you. I know everything about you.' Alice sagged against the wall, her knees trembling. She wanted to run now, but felt like she was stuck in one of those dreams where, if she tried to, she'd be going in slow motion. 'How . . . how did you get here?'

Dorothy laughed. 'Well, if you don't know that, you don't know everything about me, do you?' she mocked. 'I followed someone. Someone who took something of mine and I want it back.'

'Ramblebrook,' Alice muttered.

The smile left Dorothy's face. 'How could you possibly know *that?*' She leaned further in to Alice's face. 'You'd better start talking.'

So, in a few brief words, Alice told her.

Afterwards, Dorothy stared at her for a few seconds before erupting into giggles.

'Oh, that's good,' she said finally, clapping her hands together. 'Bravo! Even I couldn't have come up with *that* and my plots are pretty . . . *twisted*, shall we say?' She shook her head, still chuckling. 'You actually believe that, don't you?'

'No . . . I *know* it.'

Dorothy gave a low whistle. 'And people say *I'm* dotty.' She looked impressed, envious even. 'Girl, you are *mad*. You are one *craaaaaazy* cuckoo!' She clucked sympathetically. 'I don't have to worry about you talking to anyone about me. You sound far too bonkers for anyone to believe you.'

She pushed her face even closer to Alice's and, with that, something inside Alice snapped like a spell being broken. She lashed out with her notebook, catching Dorothy on the side of the face.

'Get away from me – stay away! Just . . . *just go back to where you came from!*' Her voice erupted from her, shrill and desperate. She hit out again, missing this time, for Dorothy ducked out of the way, and the notebook flew out of Alice's fingers, landing with a whack on the pavement.

She threw herself towards it at the same time as a cackling Dorothy did. Panic gripped her as Dorothy

8

reached it first, her eyes fixed on the open pages. With a gasp, Alice wrenched it away.

Without another word, she ran, swerving to avoid tripping over a black cat before fleeing into a side street. Her breath came in ragged sobs that burned her throat, but she didn't stop. She felt as though Dorothy Grimes's eyes were still on her, but when she looked back she saw no one except a scattering of strangers staring at her.

Alice ran, and ran, and didn't stop until she reached her house, slamming the front door behind her and locking it. She caught sight of herself in the hallway mirror and stared. Her hair was a tangled mess, stuck to her cheeks with snot and tears. Her face was a deathly grey. But it was her eyes that were the worst. They were wild, haunted-looking. *Mad*-looking. And no wonder, with what she had just seen.

'It's not possible, it's *not* . . .' she wailed to the empty house. Her voice jarred in the silence, like a puzzle piece that wouldn't fit.

She sank to the floor and huddled with her back to the door. Dorothy Grimes was mad; Alice knew that better than anyone. But then what did that say about *her*?

Could Dorothy have been right?

Was Alice even crazier than she was?

1

The Storyteller

EVERY DAY, HUNDREDS OF PEOPLE SIT DOWN AND begin to write a story. Some of these stories are published and translated, and sold in bookshops all over the world. Others never make it past the first chapter – or even the first sentence – before they are given up on. And some stories are muddled, and half-written, and struggled with until eventually the writer stuffs their creation under the bed or into a drawer. There it lies, forgotten for months or years . . . or perhaps for ever. Even if it could have been the most magical adventure that anyone would ever read.

But what happens when a tale with *real* magic, that was supposed to be finished, never was?

This is a story about one of those stories. It begins a long time ago when I was just eleven years old, back when I was known as Midge. Back when my biggest worry was whether I'd be picked for the football team and when one of my favourite things was to hear the latest story written by my older sister, Alice.

Alice had a thing about stories. Not just an amazing talent for making them up and writing them down, but also a strange and firm belief that every story started should be finished. She said an unfinished story was a terrible thing: an unfulfilled dream and unlived lives for all the characters within it. So, every story she began, she finished, no matter how rubbish it might have been or how silly the ending. They all had to have one – an ending.

Until the day one of them didn't.

My sister disappeared on a Friday in February, the day school finished for half-term. It was ordinary in most ways, except that it happened to be the day before the Summoning. On the walk home from school, I was on the lookout for Likenesses: little dolls fashioned from straw or cloth, each made to resemble someone. I'd already noticed a few in the morning, but during the day more had appeared in windows and on doorsteps of the houses I passed.

I stopped to stare at a Likeness propped next to a flowerpot in a nearby garden. It always struck me how strange it was that, each year, everyone in the town made these dolls and put them on display.

'No weirder than dressing up as ghosts and vampires and everything for Hallowe'en on one night of the year,' was Alice's view.

'But that happens in loads of places,' I said. 'The Summoning is just here in Fiddler's Hollow.'

'Lots of towns have strange old traditions,' Alice had replied. 'But they're usually things like cheese festivals or maypole dancing, not something creepy like ours.'

I had to admit the Summoning *was* a bit creepy. On this one night of every year, someone, either living or dead, could be 'Summoned' by the creation of their Likeness. It was said that if the person who made it wanted it badly enough, and the Likeness was good enough, it would work and the maker could then ask the Summoned a question. Just one. After that, they could never Summon that person again.

Of course, no one ever seemed to know anyone who had successfully Summoned another person, although there were plenty of tales of it happening to somebody's uncle's third cousin's son.

In the evening, there was always a huge bonfire in the market square when all the Likenesses were burned. Lots of people came just for this part, even if they hadn't made a doll, because there were stalls selling toasted marshmallows and roasted nuts, hot chocolate and warm, spiced apple juice.

It was a game of mine, every year, to try to recognise who the dolls were meant to be. Some, like the ones made by the lady who worked in the knitting shop, were excellent – but I still couldn't tell who they were. Others, like Tommy Parker's from my class, looked barely human – but his was recognisable by the numbered shirt and football strip of his favourite player. Then there were the mad: a grey felt dog called Fenchurch who'd been missing for more than a year; the bad: Jack the Ripper made by Mr Sherwood, the history teacher, who spent his spare time working on theories to try and unmask the killer's identity.

I reached the white painted gate of a cottage set back from the road. Next to the front door was a small figure of straw. This was one of the sad: the same little figure made every year by the old man who lived in the cottage.

It was a boy, with fair hair and glasses. Every year it wore the same clothes, and the same little pair of old-fashioned spectacles, but every year its features were a little wonkier, as the old man's eyesight grew worse.

No one really talked to the man, so people didn't know who the boy was. Some said that it was his son who had been taken away by the man's wife and never seen again; others said that the boy had died, and once I'd heard a horrid story that it was a little boy unknown to the man whom he had knocked down and killed in his car by accident. So many stories and none of them happy ... except one.

Alice said she thought the story went like this: the man was a time traveller and wanted to use the Likeness to speak to himself as a little boy, asking him questions about things that he had long forgotten about. To Alice, everything was a story and hers was the one I wanted to believe.

I moved on past, pulling leaves from the hedge, trying to decide whether to make a Likeness or not. Alice usually did, but she was the creative one, not me.

By the time I reached Cuckoo Lane, the street where we lived, the sky was dark and a thin slice of moon dangled above the little shop on the corner. Our house was number 35, a short way down. It was an old house, which looked tiny from the front, but was surprisingly large inside, stretching back much longer than it was wide. When I went in, the house was warm and the smell of something delicious was wafting from the kitchen.

I hung my keys on the hook in the hallway and went through to the living room, where a fire had been lit in the grate. A basket of logs and a bucket of coal sat on the hearth, and our cat, Twitch, was sprawled out asleep in front of it, her black coat gleaming in the firelight. I held my cold fingers up to the heat. I could hear a little tune being hummed in the kitchen. I followed it and found Alice leaning over the cooker, stirring a large pot.

'What's for tea?' I asked, my tummy rumbling as I sniffed deeply. The humming stopped and Alice turned to me with a smile.

'It's stew.' She covered the pot and put plates in the oven to warm. 'Stop sniffing it; you'll steal all the flavour.'

I grinned. Alice was always saying silly things like that, mostly to amuse me – and herself – but also, I think, because she couldn't help it. She saw magic in everything: a trail of drips from a teacup were elf footprints; garden statues were people and animals that had been enchanted and turned to stone. Storytelling was in her blood; blood that we shared, though Alice's was a little different. She

15

didn't have the same father as me. Hers had left her and our mum when Alice was just three years old. She had seen him only a handful of times in the thirteen years that had passed since then.

I watched as she set the table, noticing a plaster on Alice's finger. 'What happened?' I asked, nodding to it.

'Hmm? Oh. My finger decided it wanted to be a carrot and got in the way of the knife.'

'You're so daft,' I said, giggling. Then I stopped as I saw that she had only laid the table for two.

'I thought Mum was here for tea tonight?' My voice came out all whiney.

Alice laid cutlery on the table and began to slice some bread.

'She was supposed to be, but she called to say she had to work late.'

'Again?'

'Someone's off sick and Mum has that book fair coming up. She's snowed under.'

'She's always snowed under,' I said sulkily.

I sank into my usual seat. I'd been looking forward to this evening. Mum had been working much later recently. She was the manager of a rights team for a big publisher, which meant that she sold books to lots of different countries. It was over a week since we'd last eaten a meal with her. In fact, it had been more than a week since I'd had a chance to say much to her at all, during mornings of uniforms being ironed and bowls of cereal being gulped down in the rush to get ready for school. We hardly saw my dad, either. He worked away on an oil rig and sometimes he was gone for months. Since Alice had left school in May, she'd taken over a lot of the cooking and household chores. She wasn't just my sister, she was like a second mother.

'It won't be for ever,' Alice said. 'Things will calm down after this book fair.'

She ladled stew and dumplings on to our plates and I wolfed mine down, but Alice only picked at hers. By the time the subject changed to the Summoning and the Likenesses I'd seen on the way home, Alice had put her spoon down and abandoned her stew. She listened, her eyes clouding at the mention of the old man and his little-boy doll, and I wondered if she'd ever write down the story of him using the Likeness to speak to himself as a child. She often based characters on people from real life, if there was something about them that interested her.

'Are you making one this year?' I asked.

'A Likeness?' said Alice. She gave a vague shake of her head. 'I've got other things to be getting on with.'

I was half relieved, half disappointed. Relieved because if Alice wasn't making one then I wouldn't feel I had to to, either. And disappointed because Alice always chose interesting people, like her favourite authors – or even characters from their books. One year, her teacher had made a project of it, and Alice been told off in front of the whole class for making a Likeness of someone who wasn't a real person. Alice had replied, 'They're real to me.'

I loved her for that.

Later, we ate rice pudding in front of the fire. Shortly before nine o'clock, Alice went outside to get more coal, and I shivered as fingers of icy air crawled in through the back door and found their way to my neck. Alice stirred up the embers with the poker and heaped on more coal, then settled in the armchair.

I put down my maths homework and yawned. Alice wasn't as strict about bedtime as Mum, mainly because half the time she didn't realise what hour it was herself.

I stretched out on the rug next to Twitch and watched my sister. She sat with a notebook open on her knees, legs curled underneath her and her long fingers wrapped round her favourite pen. Her hand was still and she was staring into the fire, though I guessed she wasn't really seeing the flames. I knew better than to ask what she was thinking about. Being interrupted while daydreaming was one of the few things that made my normally mild-mannered sister lose her temper. Daydreaming, she said, was how she made up her stories – and interruptions meant lost ideas.

Judging by the way she was nibbling her top lip, this story wasn't going well. Once or twice, she began to write, but then ripped out the pages and threw them into the fire. Then, suddenly, she lifted her pen and began to scribble quickly, lines and lines, without pause. As she did so, she began humming the strange little melody again, the one I'd heard when she was making dinner. Now and again, she crossed words out, but continued until she must have filled an entire page. Finally, she stopped, looking over her words with a slight smile. So I was surprised when she tore out the page and screwed it into a ball. Then, like the ones before it, she aimed it at the fire. It hit the back, just below the chimney opening, but somehow bounced out and landed somewhere on the hearth. Alice leaned forward to pick it up, but a sound distracted her.

She glanced up. The nine o'clock news had just started on the TV. She snapped her notebook shut. 'I hadn't realised it was that late. Go and have a bath. You should be in bed by now.' She got up, propping the fireguard in place, and went into the kitchen to put the kettle on. Her mood had changed – she seemed worried again.

Instead of going upstairs, I followed Alice to the kitchen, hovering in the doorway. The coldness of the kitchen tiles seeped through my socks. Alice was barefoot, but it didn't seem to bother her, or perhaps she just didn't notice. She had a tea bag in her hand, but made no attempt to put it in a cup, seemingly lost in thought.

'Everything OK?' I asked. 'You hardly ate any dinner.'

'I wasn't very hungry,' said Alice. 'Food never tastes as good when you've cooked it yourself.'

'What were you writing about?' I asked, shifting from one foot to the other to stop my toes from cramping.

'Just this story,' Alice said softly.

'Can you read it to me?'

She shook her head. 'It's not ready yet. It wouldn't make much sense to anyone but me.'

19

'What's it about?'

'It's a secret.' Alice finally put the tea bag into a cup. 'It's been in my head for months. But now I'm ... well, stuck. I can't figure out where it goes next, or how it ends.' She sighed, her next words a mutter. 'Maybe it's not even supposed to.'

'Then you'll have to give it one of your silly endings,' I said. 'Every story has to have an ending, right?'

'Right.' She smiled faintly. 'But a silly one wouldn't be right for this. This story's different ...'

I eyed the notebook poking out of her pocket. 'What else are you working on? Any detective stories?'

'Only this story,' she said. 'There's nothing else.'

'Not even a little one?'

'Not a bean.'

'Beans aren't to be sniffed at, you know,' I said. 'Just look at what happened with Jack and the beanstalk.'

'True,' Alice said. 'But I'm all out of beans – magic ones, baked ones, or otherwise.' She lifted her hand to her forehead and massaged it. 'This story ... it's taking everything. All of me.'

Something about the look in her eyes then was different. She'd struggled with stories before, but tonight she really meant it. There was only one other time when I'd seen her like this.

Last summer. No one except her knew what that story had been about, and she swore no one ever would. She'd destroyed the entire thing without finishing it. But, before she had done that, she'd told me something that had scared me a great deal, because I'd seen that Alice herself was terrified.

The kettle came to the boil. She poured the steaming water into her cup, staring into it.

'If only it were as easy to brew a story.'

'You'll figure it out,' I said. 'You always do.'

'Not always.'

Our eyes met in an uneasy silence. I guessed then that she, too, was thinking of last summer. Of the unfinished story . . . and of the things she had told me.

Alice went back into the living room. I followed and we sat side by side in front of the fire, saying nothing. She took a few sips of her tea before setting it on the hearth and gazing into the fire. I could tell she was thinking, brooding about storylines and characters. She didn't pick up her cup again and I didn't remind her. I'd known all along that it would go cold before she remembered to drink it.

The same way I also knew that, whatever this story was about, it was going to lead to trouble.

2
The Magpie's Nest

I WOKE IN THE NIGHT, SHIVERING. THE BEDCOVERS had slipped off and, as I pulled them back over me, the comic I'd been reading when I'd fallen asleep slid out and fell to the carpet. I turned over, noticing a soft glow through the bedroom door. The landing light was off, but yellow light filtered down from the attic room.

I listened. At first, I heard nothing, then came a faint rustle of paper. Alice was still up.

I got out of bed and crept on to the landing. In the ceiling, a square hatch lay open and a fold-out ladder hung down from the attic. I placed a hand on each side and began to climb, the ladder creaking lightly under my weight.

I poked my head up into Alice's room. She was hunched over her desk with her notes in front of her, wearing her fluffy dressing gown, slippers and a pair of blue fingerless gloves. She was humming that same little tune again, over and over, hardly pausing for breath. I said her name softly, but she jumped anyway.

'Midge.' She turned and rubbed her eyes. 'Why aren't you asleep?'

'I was. I'm not sure what woke me up.' I pulled myself through the hatch and sat on my knees on the thick rug. 'What's that tune you keep humming? Did you make it up?'

'No, well . . . yes. Sort of.'

'Sort of?'

'One of my characters made it up. It's his tune, not mine.'

I didn't say anything. I was used to answers like this from Alice. Most of the time I loved them, but sometimes, like tonight, they worried me.

'What time is it?' she asked.

I shrugged. 'Why are you still up?'

'I can't sleep.'

'You look like you need to.'

'It's chilly up here.' Alice blew into her hands. 'Come on.' She got up and went to her bed, still clutching her notebook. We both got in, her at the head and me at the foot, as usual.

'You forgot,' I said.

'Forgot what?'

'To ask a riddle.'

There was a game Alice and I played when we went into each other's rooms. To be allowed in you had to answer a riddle. We spent hours making them up and solving them, so I'd got pretty good at them.

'Well, you're up here now so there's not much point.'

'Ask me one anyway.'

Alice sighed. 'All right, here's one: I've an endless vocabulary, I'm known for being sharp and disliked when blunt. Yet I'll never speak a word. What am I?'

'Ooh. That's a tricky one. A dictionary? No, that can't be it. Hmm ... Let me think.' I snuggled down under the blankets, even tucking my nose in.

Cold air swirled round the tips of my ears. It was a lot cooler up in the attic. There was no proper heating like in the rest of the house, only a couple of plug-in oil radiators that just about took the chill off. But Alice never complained; she loved her attic room. If it were possible, I loved it even more.

You can tell a lot about a person from their room.

Alice always said that writers are hoarders like magpies – hoarders of ideas. If Alice were a magpie, then her room was her nest. Stuffed with odds and ends that, to an ordinary person, might seem as worthless as a wooden bead. But Alice had the power to string a row of wooden beads together and transform them into jewels.

Above her desk was what she called her 'inspiration wall'. Here she pinned all sorts of bits and bobs: newspaper stories, postcards, photographs. Things that someday might hatch into a story. Notebooks were arranged in neat piles or were spread across her desk – depending on how well her work was going, the messier, the better. She wrote her stories by hand before typing them on to a laptop that had pride of place on the desk. Next to it was an old Woodstock typewriter that Dad had found at a car boot sale for just a few pounds. It probably weighed more than the desk, and the 'A' key was missing, but Alice thought it was the best gift ever.

In the corner was a smaller table with a kettle, cups and an open carton of long-life milk. Used tea bags sat wetly on a saucer, but it looked homely, not messy. There was no tap up here, but Alice could fill the kettle in the bathroom on the landing below, rather than having to go all the way down to the kitchen.

Books lined the walls, the gaps inbetween them stuffed with unusual trinkets: an old key, a framed postcard of a stag, a jewelled frog with a hidden mechanism that opened its mouth to reveal a place for treasure, or secrets. Alice had always liked knick-knacks, and many of her stories had been inspired by some object or other. Even the quilt was a patchwork of fairy tales: a glass slipper, a spinning wheel, a clock striking midnight. Tales Alice had told me when I was small, the tales almost everyone knew.

The only clear space was the floor. Alice was under strict instructions from Mum that nothing, *nothing*, was to be left on it. Ever. Not a book or even a biscuit. The rule had been put in place just a few weeks after Alice had first moved into the attic room. She had tripped on a cold cup of tea next to the bed, sending it through the hatch and almost falling through it herself. Mum had threatened to lock the attic and make her share a room with me again if ever this rule were broken.

I heard Alice write something in her notebook, then sigh and scribble it out again.

'You should go to sleep,' I said, my voice muffled under the covers. I'd warmed up now and my eyelids felt heavy.

'You should take your own advice,' came her moody reply. 'In your own bed.'

'It's cold down there.'

'It's colder up here.'

'I'm comfortable now,' I murmured. I knew she wouldn't really make me go to my own room. I often sneaked up here when I couldn't sleep, or if I'd woken after a bad dream.

I peered over the covers. Alice had flopped back on the pillow with her arm half across her face. Only her mouth was visible. In her hand, she still clutched the notebook.

'Go to sleep,' I repeated.

'Not until I've figured this bit out.'

'Maybe the answer will come in the morning.'

'I've been telling myself that for a week now.'

I felt an odd little twist in my stomach. 'Stop it,' I whispered.

'What?'

'You know what. What happened before, when you thought that ... What happened last time when you got like this.'

'Nothing happened.'

'Don't lie.'

'All writers lie.' Her voice was sing-song. 'It's what we do.'

'That's not what I mean and you know it.'

She laughed, but there was nothing funny about it.

'You were ill!' I said fiercely. I sat up, wide awake now. 'And you'll get that way again if you carry on like this.'

'I won't. And anyway it was just the flu.'

'No, that's what you told Mum and Dad,' I argued. Alice's arm was still over her face and her lips were set in a stubborn line. 'But I knew different. And if you make yourself ill again I won't cover for you this time. I'll tell them the truth, and then Mum will make you share with me again. You won't be able to sit up here writing all day and night.'

Alice lifted her arm and glared at me. 'You wouldn't.'

'I would.'

She pursed her lips and threw her arm back over her face, but not before I saw her eyes glistening.

'Why do you do it?' I asked, my voice softer now. 'Why do you keep writing? I mean, you're brilliant at it. Your stories are the best ever.' I hesitated. 'But sometimes, when you get like this, it just makes you so sad.'

She swallowed noisily. 'But when it goes well I feel like I'm on top of the world.'

I had no reply to that, because I knew it was true. So I said the only thing I could think of to try to distract her.

'Tell me about your dad.'

She sniffed. 'You've heard it a hundred times.'

'Tell me again.'

She paused and took a few deep breaths. When she spoke again, her voice was steady and clear. I felt the usual thrill as she said the next words, so familiar that I knew them by heart.

'He was a traveller, a water gypsy. A group of them stopped on the canal on the day of the summer fete, mooring their narrowboats near the bridge. Mum was there with some of her friends, looking around. Most of the stalls were selling cakes and pot plants, but the travellers were selling things, too. Little wooden carvings, paintings, caged birds with feathers that had been dyed in exotic colours.

'She didn't notice him exactly; it was more that she saw *him* noticing her. He wasn't handsome, but he wasn't unpleasant to look at, either. She found that the longer she looked, the more she liked. His nose was a little too long, and his lips too thin, but it was his eyes that captured her. They were such a pale shade of grey they were almost silver, like moons under the thick black clouds that were his eyebrows.

'He didn't say anything at first. Just crooked his finger and beckoned her closer. "I've got something for you," he said and opened a wooden box. Inside, it was packed with scrolls of paper, each one tied with ribbon.

'"What are they?" she asked.

'"Stories." He pulled one out. "And this one I wrote for you."

'She felt her cheeks reddening, and heard the whispers and giggles of her friends behind her. "I suppose you want paying for it?" she said. She thought about putting it back in the box, but curiosity wouldn't allow it.

'He shrugged. "Have to eat, don't I?"

'"How much?"

'"Tell you what." He picked a blade of grass and chewed it with bright, almost perfect teeth. Almost perfect but for the bottom row where the front four stood at angles to spell out a 'W'.

'*W for words*, she thought. *W for writer . . . water gypsy, wandering.*

'"Read it," he continued, "then pay me what you think it's worth."

'So she took it and stood away from her friends to read it. Before she even reached the end, his words had worked a spell on her and she was already falling in love with him.

'*W for weakness, W for wishing . . .*

'And so love was the price she paid for it. A high price, because he loved his stories more than he loved her. Four years later, he was gone. And she found that W was for weeping, and wretched, and woe, too. But, even though he'd left her, he hadn't left her alone.

'Their baby was called Alice. It was an easy choice, because that had been the name of the girl in his story.'

Alice paused as she often did at this part of the tale. Sometimes it was clear she didn't want to go on, but she always did in the end. 'Alice grew up barely remembering or knowing her father, but with his love of stories and the same gift for telling them. As she grew, so did her curiosity. One day she decided to look through her mother's things and she found something which led her to him. So she went.

'He seemed happy to see her. They spent a day together, talking and learning about each other. They caught fish in the river and ate them for supper, and they told each other stories. When the day ended and she had to leave, they made plans and promises. But they, too, were stories – for when she returned next he was gone.'

Alice went quiet then. The story was finished, but every time she told it I wondered what she had left unsaid, what she had held back.

I remembered the day that Alice had gone looking for her father. It had felt like an adventure at first, like one of Alice's stories. The two of us whispering as I kept watch on the landing and Alice filled her small suitcase: clothes, a packed lunch, a book, notepad and pencil, and her best story – tied with a silver ribbon – for him.

I was only small, but old enough to recognise the panic in Mum's voice, and know something was really wrong, when she discovered that Alice hadn't arrived at school that day. I'd finally cracked when Mum started to cry. As soon as I'd given up Alice's secret, I was left with a neighbour while Mum went looking for her. It was late when she returned with a red-faced Alice. Both of them wore the silvery streaks of dried tears on their cheeks.

We were sent to bed straight after supper that evening. It was early, and I was too upset to sleep, but Mum had said we weren't allowed to talk. Alice was at the desk, looking at a well-thumbed book of fairy tales. The page was open on Sleeping Beauty. Her finger rested lightly on the spindle in the picture.

We jumped when the door opened and Mum looked in. Neither of us had heard her come up the stairs.

'Don't you think you two are in enough trouble already?' she snapped. 'Lights off, books away and no talking.'

'Mum?' Alice said in a small voice.

'What is it?' Mum's voice was brisk. She'd calmed down now, but was still cross enough to be scary.

'Do you believe in curses?' Alice asked.

The room was very quiet. Then Mum's voice sliced through the silence.

'No.' She walked over to Alice and took the book out of her hands, closing it. 'And neither will you, if you've any sense.' She put the book down and placed her hand on Alice's cheek. 'I can guess exactly what your father's been saying to you. Filling your head with stupid ideas.'

'But what if—' Alice began.

'It's rubbish,' Mum cut in. 'I should know, because he told me the same rubbish, too, once.'

Alice said nothing, but she turned her face away from Mum's hand.

'I know he's your dad, Alice,' Mum said, sighing. 'And I know you want to get to know him. I won't stand in your way – but I will say what I think, even if you don't want to hear it. Be careful of who you believe and what you believe in. Belief can be good, but it can also be dangerous. If a person thinks they're cursed, then they are.'

When Mum had gone back downstairs, I couldn't help but pester Alice in loud whispers to tell me more about the mysterious curse. But Alice refused to say, and to this day she'd kept that particular part of the story to herself.

'Alice?' I said now, using my toes to prod her elbow. 'Do you believe in curses?'

'If a person thinks they're cursed, then they are,' she said, repeating Mum's words.

'Do you think you're cursed?' I asked.

'Go to sleep, Midge. It's too late to be talking about this. It'll only give you nightmares.'

'Alice?'

'Mmm?'

'The answer to the riddle . . . is it a pencil?'

'Yes, well done. Now go to sleep.'

I closed my eyes, happy I'd scored one victory at least. As for the curse, I made up my mind to ask her again in the morning.

Only I never got the chance, because, when morning came, Alice was gone.

3
Black Cat

WHEN I CAME DOWNSTAIRS INTO THE kitchen the next morning, I found the house empty. There was no sign of Alice or Mum, but someone had pulled out the rainy-day boxes from the cupboard under the stairs and left them on the kitchen table. Alice loved them – they contained all sorts of craft materials to keep us busy when the weather was too wet for us to go outside.

There was a note stuck to the fridge under a magnet. I took it off and read it.

Alice and Midge, it said, *I won't be long. Don't eat breakfast – pancakes when I get back! Love, Mum. PS Got the rainy-day boxes out to make Likenesses for the Summoning.*

Pancakes! Now, in the light of day and with pancakes on the horizon, last night's talk of curses with Alice seemed no more than a bad dream. I called her name, wondering if she could be upstairs in the shower, but there was no answer and none of the usual gurgling of pipes when someone was in the bathroom.

I'd woken alone in Alice's bed which wasn't unusual – if I slept up there, she'd often get up without waking me; she was as quiet as a mouse. But what was strange was that the room was freezing cold. The heaters hadn't been switched on, which was normally the first thing Alice did.

I poured a glass of orange juice and sat down. Something warm and furry slithered past my ankles under the table, and then a dark shape slunk away through the kitchen door. 'Morning, Twitch,' I called after it, peering into the nearest box as I drank my orange juice in one go. Inside was a jumble of wool and fabric scraps. A black paw shot out of the tangled contents to swipe playfully at my hand.

'Ouch!' I pulled my fingers back. A bead of blood swelled on my thumb. The box on the table rustled, and then a mischievous black face popped out of it with ribbon looped over one ear.

'Oh, no,' I muttered. *This* was Twitch.

I went into the living room and had a quick look around. We'd had problems before, with other cats coming in through the cat flap and stealing Twitch's food, but there was no sign of any intruder now. Perhaps it had sneaked out again. I went back into the kitchen and was about to sit down when I heard a distinctive *bleep*, and something buzzed next to the toaster.

Alice's phone.

It had been left to charge, but, typical of Alice, she had

forgotten to switch on the plug. The *bleep* was the warning tone for low battery. I went over to it and turned on the power.

I frowned. Alice never left her phone behind – but she hadn't been in bed, either. Or had she? Suddenly, I doubted myself. Could she have been still asleep under the covers when I got up and I just hadn't noticed? It would explain the heaters not being on. I decided to go and check.

I took the stairs two at a time, then scrambled up the ladder into the attic. I hadn't been mistaken. The covers were thrown back as I'd left them, and Alice's single bed definitely had no Alice in it. It wasn't empty, though.

'How did you get up here?' I said, puzzled. 'You were in the kitchen a minute ago.'

Twitch blinked at me from within the folds of the rumpled bedclothes, then deliberately turned her back on me and started to lick her sleek, black coat. I turned away, ready to go back down the ladder, but noticed something.

The skylight in the roof was open, just a crack.

'No wonder it's so cold in here.' I climbed on the bed and pulled it closed, then looked round the room and back to Twitch. Something glinted within the cat's fur: a golden pendant on a deep purple velvet collar. Twitch didn't have a collar as posh as that; hers was green and tatty.

'Wait,' I said, stepping towards the cat. 'You're not Twitch, are you?'

The cat stopped licking itself and leaped on to Alice's

desk, sprawling across her notebooks. It regarded me lazily as I approached.

'Who are you then?' I said. 'We'd better get you out before Mum gets back.' I kept my voice soft so as not to scare it, but the cat seemed at home. I reached out and gently ran my hand along its back. It purred and lifted its tail. Up close, I could see that there were small differences between this cat and ours. Its coat was longer and sleeker than Twitch's, its tail less bushy and, where Twitch's eyes were a very feline shade of green, this cat's were golden.

I scratched its neck, my fingers finding the small, jewelled pendant on the collar. I turned it over, looking for an address or a phone number on the other side. There was none, although three letters were engraved in the surface.

T. E. A.

I frowned. *T. E .A.* ?

'Come on,' I said, sighing. I moved my hand under the cat's chest to try to lift it up. The cat rolled on to its back and swatted me away playfully. The undersides of its paws were black, too, and its nose. Twitch's were pink. This was the blackest cat ever.

'You really are beautiful,' I said, stroking it again. 'But you can't stay here.' I had a quick look round the attic, sniffing. A tomcat had got in once and peed upstairs, but I couldn't smell any evidence of that. 'At least you haven't done anything.'

'*Done* anything?' the cat enquired. 'Do you take me for

36

a common alley cat? I know the difference between inside and outside, you know!'

I staggered backwards in shock, colliding with Alice's bedframe.

'Huh?' I whispered.

I squeezed my eyes shut, shook my head and opened my eyes again. The cat was still there.

'Did you just … what did you say?'

'I said I do know the difference between inside and outside.' The cat stared at me for a long moment, then licked its paw and started to wash its face. I dropped to my hands and knees, peering under the bed, in the wardrobe, then down the hatch to see if there was someone on the landing. There was no sign of anyone, no Alice. No one that could be playing a trick on me.

'Say something else.' I felt sure it wouldn't and that I had some kind of fever.

The cat carried on washing its face with no sign that it had heard me. Just as I was starting to convince myself that I had imagined it, the cat sat up and looked straight at me.

'I miss soap and water,' it said.

'Wh-what?' I stuttered.

'Soap … and … water,' the cat repeated slowly, as if it were speaking to someone stupid.

Still disbelieving, I moved towards the cat and sunk a finger into the warm, soft fur. There had to be batteries, or some kind of remote control. The cat batted my hand away again.

'Do you mind? How would you like it if someone poked you?'

This time I felt the warm hiss of its breath on my skin.

'You *are* real,' I whispered. 'What are you doing here?'

'I got in through the cat flap,' the cat drawled, like it was obvious. For the first time, I realised that its voice was female.

'Yes, I guessed that,' I said. 'But, um ... what I meant was, why did you come here? Where are you from? And how can you talk?'

'So many questions.' The cat yawned and spread herself over Alice's notebooks once more. 'Too many questions make me sleepy.' She half closed her amber eyes, but still watched me through the narrow slits. It was a sneaky look.

'One at a time then,' I said. 'Where are you from?'

'The Crowstone Marshes,' she replied. 'It's cold there. Next?'

'I've never heard of that place,' I replied. 'It must be far away. How did you get here?'

'That I can't answer,' said the cat. 'Because I don't remember.'

'What's your name?' I asked.

'Perhaps you shouldn't be asking me all these things,' the cat said. 'Weren't you ever warned about talking to strangers?'

'I don't think talking cats count.'

'Fine,' the cat replied. 'My name is Tabitha. Tabitha Elizabeth Ashwood.'

'So you're *T. E. A.*,' I said, remembering the initials on the pendant.

'Yes,' said Tabitha. 'Speaking of which, I'd love a cup. Would you mind?' She glanced at Alice's little tea-making table.

'Tea? You don't want milk?'

'Oh, no,' said Tabitha. 'Tea would be lovely, thanks. Milk and two sugars.'

I put a tea bag and sugar into a cup and switched the kettle on.

'Why did you come into our house?' I asked.

'I needed somewhere to stay,' said Tabitha. 'Somewhere I hoped I wouldn't be noticed while I figured out what to do.'

'And so when you saw Twitch in the garden you decided to follow her through the cat flap?' I guessed. 'Because you look alike enough to be mistaken for her?'

'Yes,' said the cat. 'Although that part didn't exactly go to plan, did it?'

'No,' I said. 'But it would have if I hadn't come up here to ...'

To look for Alice.

All the excitement and weirdness of the talking cat had distracted me from wondering where my sister was. I wanted so badly for her to be here that I actually felt an ache in my throat. A talking cat, in Alice's room. It was just so, well ... *Alice.* Exactly the sort of thing she loved and would write about ...

The thought sat uneasily in my mind as I remembered

the things Alice had been saying the night before and what had happened last summer.

I made the tea and put the cup in front of Tabitha. She lapped at it in neat little licks that made it look like she was trying not to wet her whiskers.

'How long have you been a cat?' I asked. 'And who turned you into one?'

Tabitha didn't answer straight away. She drank all the tea in the cup, then a second after I refilled it. When it was licked clean, she settled down, purring, her tail curled over the keys of Alice's typewriter.

'What makes you think someone turned me into a cat?' she said finally. 'And that I haven't always been one?'

'Because you can talk,' I said.

'All cats talk,' said Tabitha. 'But not all people understand them.'

'Twitch definitely can't talk,' I said.

'But you can still understand her, can't you?'

'Yes, but that's different. She just stands around and meows, but you talk. You really, actually *talk*. And you drink tea. Normal cats don't drink tea.'

'It's more refreshing than milk,' said Tabitha.

For the second time, I got the feeling that the cat was being sneaky and more than a little unhelpful. Then I remembered something.

'You said something a minute ago, when you were washing yourself. You said, "I miss soap and water."'

'Did I?'

'Yes,' I said. 'And that proves it – you were a human once. Cats don't use soap and water to wash, and missing it means it's something you *used* to do!'

Tabitha's tail twitched. 'Cleverer than you look, aren't you?'

I was clever enough to know that that wasn't much of a compliment.

'So who are you?' I knew I sounded huffy now, but I couldn't help it. 'Or who *were* you?'

'Have to be careful about who I tell that to.' Tabitha tucked her paws underneath her.

'Why? Are you hiding from someone?'

I didn't get an answer. The front door rattled and a moment later Mum called up.

'I'd better go downstairs,' I said, still staring at Tabitha. I didn't care about pancakes for breakfast now. I wanted to stay and quiz the mysterious cat, but it seemed she had had enough of my questions, because she'd gone to sleep.

I climbed down the ladder, hesitating when I reached the bottom. All it would take was two quick folds of the ladder and the hatch would swing back in place, trapping the cat in the attic. Eventually I decided not to. She wasn't my prisoner and, besides, she seemed in no rush to leave. There would still be time for questions and Alice should be back soon. She'd know what to do.

Mum was pouring the pancake mixture into the frying pan when I got downstairs and the table had been cleared of the rainy-day boxes and set for two.

'Where's Alice?' I asked.

'I haven't spoken to her,' said Mum, slicing a lemon into quarters. 'But I saw her in town just before I came back.' Her forehead crinkled. 'I waved, but she didn't seem to see me.'

I sat down at the table. When the pancakes were cooked, we sprinkled them with sugar and squeezed wedges of lemon over them, digging in. But each mouthful of pancake stuck in my throat. I washed it down with a slurp of tea, unable to shake the feeling that something was wrong. It wasn't like Alice to go out so early on a Saturday, especially not without telling anyone where she was going. And she'd been in such a weird mood last night.

A buzz by the toaster broke the silence. Mum looked up.

'That's Alice's phone,' she said. 'Strange that she'd go out without it.'

'Do you think she's all right?' I asked.

'She looked fine when I saw her,' Mum said. 'Why wouldn't she be?'

I shrugged. Alice didn't talk to Mum like she did to me. I knew things about Alice that Mum didn't, and wouldn't ever know, because Alice had made me promise. Sometimes I didn't know if this was a good thing.

'No reason.' I glanced at the phone. 'She's just forgetful, I suppose.'

'Have you decided who you're going to make a Likeness of?' Mum asked.

'Not yet. I was hoping Alice would help me.'

'I can help you,' Mum offered. 'Or we can get it started

anyway, but I need to pack this afternoon, I've got an early flight tomorrow.'

My head snapped up. 'Flight? To where?'

'Brussels, Midge. It's the book fair – I did say.'

'Oh. That,' I said, making a face. 'How long will you be gone this time?'

'Only for three days. Don't look so gloomy! You'll be fine with Alice. I know how she spoils you when I'm away.'

It was true. Alice *did* spoil me. We stayed up late, watched bad TV and ate too many sweets. On the good days, Mum wasn't around enough to notice the bad ones. The ones when Alice forgot to wash her hair, hardly spoke, and dinner was beans on toast that I'd have to make myself.

I'd just finished my last pancake when I caught sight of the tip of a black tail sailing past the table behind Mum. In an instant, I knew it wasn't Twitch, because she was on Mum's lap, sniffing her plate. I jumped up, knocking the table.

'Midge, be careful!' said Mum. 'What's the matter?'

'Thought I saw next-door's cat,' I blurted out. I ran for the back door, hearing the squeak of the cat flap, and looked through the window just in time to see a black blur vanishing over the garden wall. Quickly, I unlocked the back door and ran to the gate, unlatching it and stepping into the alley that ran between our house and next door's. At first, I thought the cat was gone, but then I caught a small movement towards the front of the house. I crept out of the alley and into the street.

Tabitha was sitting on next-door's front wall, totally still except for her tail, which swished from side to side in a figure of eight. I approached and was about to speak when I saw what she was looking at.

On the other side of the road near the corner shop was a girl with long, blonde hair who had a notebook tucked under her arm. She wore a black leather jacket that I didn't recognise, but I *did* know *her*. Relief rushed through me.

'Alice!' I called, waving. 'Mum's made pancakes – still some left!'

Alice looked behind her, then back at me, but didn't return my wave.

'Alice!' I shouted again.

She continued to stare blankly in my direction. Weird. Mum said she'd waved at Alice, too, and she hadn't seen her . . .

I crossed the road and went towards her, not caring that I was still wearing my pyjamas and slippers. 'Alice,' I said again. 'Are you all right?'

She looked at me with a puzzled expression. There was something odd about her eyes. They looked different to normal, but I couldn't figure out why. She appeared prettier somehow: her cheeks and lips pinker and her hair glossier, with tiny plaits woven in here and there. I'd never seen her wear her hair like that before. I waited for her to answer, but instead she took out a pen and wrote something in the notebook. She held it up to show me.

I'm not Alice, it said.

'Very funny. Why aren't you talking? Do you have a sore throat?'

Alice gave a strained smile and wrote something else.

I don't know who Alice is. You have the wrong person.

I waited for her to laugh or wink, but she didn't. I stared into her eyes and finally saw what was different about them: Alice's eyes were blue, like mine. This girl's were bright green.

I backed away from her, gasping as my foot slid off the kerb and into the road, almost tripping. The girl grabbed at my hand to steady me, but I brushed her off and got my balance, my skin crawling where she'd touched me.

A squirmy, knotted-up feeling had started in my tummy, the sort of feeling I'd had at my granddad's funeral when I was just seven. Of not fully understanding what was going on, but knowing it was something bad and that things would never be the same again.

My gaze was fixed on her face. Everything about her was almost *exactly* like Alice. It was only the eyes that were *really* different, but it was enough to convince me. The girl underlined something and held the notebook up again.

I'm not Alice. She turned away from me and began to walk off. I watched her round the corner and vanish into the next street, now certain she wasn't my sister.

But if she wasn't Alice then who was she?

4

The Museum
of Unfinished Stories

WHEN I GOT BACK TO THE HOUSE, MUM WAS sniffing around in the living room.

'Was it next-door's cat?' she asked, coming into the kitchen.

'Oh, er . . . yeah,' I said.

Mum picked up the water-spray bottle that she used to mist her pot plants. 'Well, I can't smell anything. But if you see it again give it a squirt with this.' She went into the living room with her cup of tea, leaving me alone.

I stood for a moment, trying to calm down. My breath was coming too quickly, like I'd just run really fast, and my knees felt all shaky. I put a hand out in front of me and saw it was trembling. Who was the girl I'd just seen, the *not* Alice?

After a minute, I went into the living room. Mum

was sitting down with Twitch curled up on her lap. I blinked, remembering the reason I'd gone outside in the first place – Tabitha – and wondered if she would come back, half wishing I *had* shut her in the attic. I pushed the thought away. Talking cat or not, this was more important.

'Mum?' I said. My voice came out thin and squeaky. I coughed. 'Mum, something strange just happened.'

Mum dunked a biscuit in her tea. 'What's that, love?'

'When I went outside just now, I saw Alice. Only it *wasn't* Alice.'

'Is this one of your riddles?' Mum said through a mouthful of biscuit. 'Because you know I'm hopeless—'

'It's not a riddle.' My hands were clammy with sweat. 'There was a girl standing on the corner by the shop who looked like Alice. Exactly like Alice. Except for her eyes. They . . .' I hesitated.

Could it have been a trick of the light? I'd been so sure of what I'd seen a few minutes ago, but now I was starting to doubt myself.

'They what?' said Mum.

'Maybe I imagined it.'

Mum waited, saying nothing.

'They were green.'

Mum rolled her eyes. 'People's eyes don't change colour, Midge. Maybe it was someone who just really looked like Alice.'

I shook my head. 'You don't get it. She *was* Alice.

47

Everything about her, except her eyes. Her hair colour, the way she frowned. But . . . it wasn't her. She didn't know me, didn't recognise me. And she said she wasn't Alice.'

'Oh, Midge, don't be daft. Of course it was her,' said Mum. 'Playing a trick, or doing some sort of weird research for whatever story she's working on. She'll come whizzing through that door in a minute and shut herself up in the attic, writing for hours. You know how she gets.'

'But her eyes—' I began.

'Contact lenses,' said Mum. 'Although she shouldn't be messing around with those when her vision is perfectly good. I'll be having words with her about that.'

Mum took another biscuit out of the tin and crunched it, dropping crumbs on Twitch's head.

Perhaps Alice was just messing about. I wanted to believe what Mum was saying, but she hadn't seen Alice last night. I went upstairs, chewing my lip as I looked at the ladder up to the attic. Then, before I really knew why, I started to climb it, pulling myself through the hatch.

I went to Alice's desk. On it were college prospectuses, with some pages bookmarked. Mum had been on at Alice for months to pick a course, but so far Alice had hardly looked at them. She'd decided to take a year out between school and college to write, and I knew Mum was worried that she might not go at all.

I reached for a stack of notebooks, flicking through a few. Some were dog-eared and grubby, filled with pages of character notes, story settings, spidergrams, flow charts and stories, each with Alice's trademark 'THE END' printed and underlined where a story finished. A few were blank and unused. I put them back and lifted up a folder. The knot of worry tightened in my tummy when I saw what was underneath it.

Alice's purse. I picked it up and opened it. There was some money, her bank and library cards, and a little photo of the two of us that was taken a couple of months ago.

I put it down and looked round Alice's room. Maybe it was because I wasn't used to being there without her, but I felt her absence more strongly than ever. I was surrounded by her things and yet without her the room was so hollow that it seemed as though a loud noise would echo.

A memory of a story Alice had written last year came back to me. I looked over my shoulder, uneasy, but the attic was empty, of course.

What if, I thought, *the girl I'd seen was one of those things Alice had written about in that story? Those people who look exactly the same as someone else.* It was a funny word, one I'd never heard before that tale. Alice said everyone has one, somewhere in the world. Not a twin . . . a *doggle* something? Wait, no. A *dopp* . . . doppelgänger.

That story had stuck in my head. It had been about a boy who started seeing an exact version of himself in the town. At first, he'd wondered if he had a long-lost twin, but it turned out to be his doppelgänger. Slowly, the doppelgänger took over his life, worming its way in and stealing the boy's family and friends. In the end, the boy had saved himself

49

only by the use of a clever riddle proving that he was his real self.

At the time, I'd loved it. Now, though, the thought of another Alice – an *almost* Alice – walking around was just creepy. Who was she? And did she know anything about where the real Alice was?

I turned the doppelgänger story over in my mind, picking at the threads of what Alice had told me. It still didn't make sense. If it was a doppelgänger, then surely it'd be pretending it *was* Alice, not that it *wasn't* . . . unless it was trying to fool me. Playing a clever game before it moved in. Because, if it wasn't Alice playing a joke and it wasn't a doppelgänger, then what else could it be?

There was another possibility. Something I'd been trying to push out of my mind, but which kept pestering me like a gnat . . . and it wasn't so much the strange girl that was making me think it. It was the cat. A talking cat . . . just the sort of magical creature that would come from Alice's imagination. The fact that they had both appeared on the same day told me that somehow they must be connected.

A draught whistled round my ankles and my eyes went to the skylight. It was closed. I'd been the one to pull it shut when I came up here earlier, looking for Alice. At some point during the night, or this morning before I'd woken, Alice must have opened it.

Could she have seen something, or someone, that had made her leave the house in a rush? Someone she'd wanted to speak to . . . or hide from?

I climbed on to Alice's bed and opened the window. A chilly breeze flew in as I peered out across the rooftops. There was a clear view of the street, all the way down to the corner shop.

Had Alice looked out and spotted the girl standing there?

I'd seen the girl well enough from the street. Enough to think it *was* Alice. Now Alice was gone without telling anyone where she was going, without her phone, or even her purse. I tried to imagine how I would feel if I saw someone who looked exactly like me. Excited? Confused? Afraid? Probably all three. I didn't have to think about what I would do – I already knew that. I'd follow them.

The problem was that the girl was gone. She couldn't be followed. But there was a chance she'd gone into the shop and, if she had, there might be a clue to where she was now. If I could find the girl, perhaps I might also find Alice.

I started to pull the window closed, my gaze drifting to the bushes at the front of the garden. A memory hovered at the edges of my mind. A figure skulking behind those bushes in the dead of the night . . . and Alice cowering in the corner of the attic. Wide-eyed, terrified, whispering, 'You do see him, don't you?'

I shuddered, pushing the memory away, and clambered down. My toes nudged something within the folds of the bedclothes. I fumbled through them, already guessing what it was. I found it hidden in the pillowcase: Alice's notebook. The one she'd been writing in last night. I picked it up. It was

51

heavier than I expected it to be, like there was a secret within its pages. I hesitated. Alice would be furious if I peeked.

But she doesn't have to know, I told myself. If I just had a quick look, it might offer a clue as to where she could be. Sometimes Alice did things to research whatever she was writing about, or went to certain places. Once she'd made Mum shut her in the boot of the car when she was writing a story about someone being kidnapped and driven off, just to see if she'd fit. We'd had some odd looks from our neighbours after that.

Another thought was untwisting in my head like fraying rope. I wanted to get a look at the characters in case . . . just in case . . . I shook the thought away, then lifted the cover and looked inside.

My sister's curly, black writing covered the first page from top to bottom in a numbered list. It went up to number seventeen and each number had something written after it, a word or short phrase. Could they be story titles?

On the next page, I found what I was searching for. I was looking at a character description. It was about a page long, with a chart of likes and dislikes and longer passages with more detail. As I read it, the skin on the back of my neck began to tingle.

Tabitha, an enchanted black cat that was once a human. Talks, fond of tea and riddles. Six of her nine lives remaining.

I turned the next page and found another one, and at this my hand froze.

I stared at it, then read it again.

*Gypsy, a sixteen-year-old storyteller. Unable to speak, uses
a notebook to communicate. Blonde hair, green eyes.*

So I hadn't imagined the girl's eye colour.

The girl and the cat were characters from Alice's story.

I collapsed on the bed, feeling squirmy and shaky. There
was no holding it back now. The memory flooded into my
head like an unwelcome guest turning up unannounced.

*The memory of climbing up into the attic last year, the roof
space stifling hot and airless as it always was in the summer.
It was dimly lit, so dingy that I heard Alice before I saw her.
The crackle of papers being shuffled, over in the corner of
the room.*

'Alice?' I whispered, snapping on the light.

*A figure flew at me, teeth bared through tangled, damp hair,
hissing.*

'Turn the light off! He'll see!'

*The sour smell of sweat filled my nose as she reached past
me and snapped the light off, before scuttling back to the corner
like a beetle hiding under a stone. I ducked down and crawled
towards her, my heart drumming hard.*

'Who?' I whispered. 'Who's out there? Should we call Dad?'

*'No!' Alice's fingers dug into my arm, bruising my skin.
'Don't call anyone! Just shut up, I need to think.'*

*I shrank into the corner next to her, stung. It wasn't often
Alice spoke to me that way. Most people that I knew with
brothers and sisters fought all the time, but not us. We were
a team.*

I watched her in the faint glow of a single tea light on the desk. Her face was sickly white, and her forehead and upper lip were beaded with sweat. Her eyes were glazed and staring, and her hands shook as she fumbled through the pages of a notebook.

'Alice?' I whispered, even more quietly than before. 'I'm scared. Who's out there?'

'Someone who shouldn't be. But you don't need to be scared. It's me he wants, not you.' She paused, then her voice rose, becoming more panicked. Her breath was stale as it carried to my nostrils. 'But then he could still use you to get to me . . . to force me to give him what he wants!' She turned to me, grabbing my arm so hard it felt like her fingers were bruising me. 'If anyone ever approaches you, Midge, anyone you don't know that asks you about me, don't trust them. Do you hear me? They'll say anything . . . just get away from them . . .'

'Stop, you're hurting!' I prised her fingers off my arm. 'Alice, please . . . you're frightening me!'

She bent her head over the notebook, her pen almost touching the paper, but unmoving. 'I need to think, I need to think . . .'

My head was fuzzy with confusion. What was she doing with her notebook if she thought there was someone coming after her? My fears shifted, from the worry of a stranger outside in the night to the far more likely possibility of Alice having a fever.

'Alice, you're not making any sense. You don't look well,' I said. 'I think you should lie down.'

'I can't. Don't you see? I have to make him go away, I have to . . .'

'When was the last time you slept?'

She shook her head, impatient. 'I don't have time to sleep, I—'

A whistled tune, like a short burst of birdsong, floated through the window. But there were no birds around at this hour.

'It's him,' Alice whispered. 'He's still out there.'

Slowly, I crept out of the corner and climbed on to the bed. The window was wide open, but the night air was almost as still and sticky as it was in the attic.

'Don't,' Alice moaned, wide-eyed with fear. 'He'll see you!'

I raised myself on to tiptoes and stared out through the darkness, across gardens and houses and parked cars that I saw every day. In daylight, all these things were familiar, but at night, and from so high up, it was like looking out on an unknown land. Everything was still, too warm even for foxes and cats to be on the prowl. Then, out of the corner of my eye, I saw something shift down by the lavender in the hedge. Such a slight movement in the deep shadows, but the spell was broken and I could see him now.

He was thin and tall, but stooped, with long hair that hung past his shoulders. He glared up at the attic window with one eye; the other was hidden beneath a ragged bandage wound round his head. Even though it was dim outside, I could see it was stained with a dark mark. A streak of blood? Something was thrown over his shoulder. A long, thin rope. A noose.

55

Despite the suffocating heat, I shuddered and, at the jerking movement, he tilted his head sharply, bird-like. He whistled again, long and low, then slid further behind the hedge, out of sight.

I dropped to the bed, heart thudding. There was something incredibly eerie about the man, like he had stepped right out of a horror movie. He didn't belong on our nice, normal street.

'You saw him, didn't you?' Alice whispered. 'You saw him, too.'

'Who is he?' I kept my voice low, even lower than Alice's. The night was so still that I imagined each word carrying down to the stranger in the shadows.

Alice shrank back further into the corner. 'The Hangman.'

The words sent a horrified shiver down my spine. 'The Hangman?'

'No one knows his real name,' Alice said hoarsely. 'But he knows your worst secret. The thing you're most ashamed of . . . the thing you would die before you let anyone find out. That's how he does it. How he kills people.'

'K-kills people?' I stuttered. 'Is that what the rope he's carrying is for? He hangs you with it?'

Alice shook her head, her eyes glassy. 'By the time he's through with you, you do it yourself.'

'But why?' I asked. 'What would this person want with you, Alice? How does he even know you?'

She gave a short laugh, more of a bark. 'Because I made him up.'

I stared at the film of sweat glistening above her eyebrows.

56

She had to be in the grip of some kind of fever, although that still didn't explain who the man outside was. 'Alice,' I said gently. 'I think you need to—'

She shoved the notebook at me, scrabbling through the pages. 'You don't believe me? Look. It's here! It's all here!'

And it was. The word jumped out of the pages, over and over again; at first, neat and tidy, like a coiled rope, and then, later, pushed into the paper, breaking it like a neck as Alice's writing changed, as the story went beyond her control.

'The Hangman is a character from your story?' I said incredulously.

Alice nodded, her greasy hair veiling her face like a curtain. 'He's not the only one. There are others. I've seen them. They're looking for me . . . looking for this!' She brandished the notebook.

'But . . . what do they want?' I shook my head, bewildered. 'They want to know how it ends?'

'That's just it,' Alice whispered. 'There is no ending! That's why they're here. Because I don't know how to finish their story.'

'So . . . they want to . . . ?' I struggled to understand.

'To take control of it. To make their own endings . . . unless I can figure it out first.'

I blinked the memory away and found I was holding the notebook very tightly. A different notebook, a different story, but with one similarity: it was long, just like the story with the Hangman had been. I began leafing through it.

Pages and pages of Alice's writing. Months and months of work. This was not a collection of little stories like Alice usually wrote: it was one big story and the list at the front was a list of chapter titles.

It was a novel. A proper, full-length book ... although it wasn't yet finished.

Unexpectedly, a lump came into my throat. 'I knew you could do it,' I whispered proudly. 'I knew you'd write one someday.' I could almost see it now, a fat hardback with Alice's name on the cover. I had no doubt that at some point she would get her stories published. That they would be in bookshops everywhere. That Alice would be famous and I'd be the luckiest brother anyone had, because I'd get to read all her stories first.

I flicked to the start, past the character notes and a few pages in. There it was. Chapter One: *The Storyteller*.

I began to read.

Every day, hundreds of people sit down and begin to write a story. Some of these stories are published and translated, and sold in bookshops all over the world. Others never make it past the first chapter – or even the first sentence – before they are given up on. And some stories are muddled, and half-written, and struggled with until eventually the writer stuffs their creation under the bed or into a drawer. There it lies, forgotten for months or years . . . or perhaps for ever. Even if it could have been the most magical adventure that anyone would ever read.

But what happens when stories with real magic, that were supposed to be finished, never are? What becomes of the story's heroes . . . and its villains?

And what would happen if they were disturbed from their dusty hiding places, woken from their slumbers? And collected and put on display for the world to see?

This is the tale of a museum.

The Museum of Unfinished Stories.

I stopped reading, the warm feeling from moments before slipping away. The pancakes in my stomach suddenly felt stodgy and unwelcome and there was a bitter taste in my mouth that I knew wasn't from the lemons I'd squeezed over them.

My talented, brilliant sister, who was obsessive, almost *scared*, about leaving a story incomplete, was writing about unfinished stories. Now she was gone and somehow at least two of the characters from that story had been unleashed. They were here, in our world . . . but were they heroes or villains? What would they do to Alice, the creator of their story, if they found her? Could they have found her already?

'Alice,' I whispered to her empty room. 'Where are you? What have you done?'

5

The Other Alice

I LEFT ALICE'S ROOM AND DRESSED QUICKLY, pulling on my smartest jeans and the least scuffed trainers I could find. I emptied my rucksack and placed Alice's notebook and purse inside it and, after hesitating, a pair of Dad's old glasses that had no lenses. I'd had them for years, and started out by wearing them when I was playing dressing-up games, like being a doctor, or a detective. I didn't wear them now, but carrying them somehow made me feel smarter, like they were a good luck charm. Alice had always told me that if you looked clever, people would treat you as if you were clever, and that was what I needed to be now if I was going to find out what had happened to her.

I went downstairs through the living room, where Mum was laughing at something on the television.

'Mum, I'm going into town,' I called, heading into the kitchen. 'I need a few things for my Likeness.' The room was still warm with the scent of sugar and lemon. I rooted around under the sink and found a pocket torch and stuck it in my rucksack, then unplugged Alice's phone and put that in, too.

'Shall I come with you?' Mum answered, appearing in the doorway, still in her dressing gown, with a guilty look on her face.

'No!' I squeaked. The last thing I wanted was for Mum to tag along, not before I really knew what was going on anyway. 'I mean, you stay here and relax. Catch up with your soaps. I won't be long.'

'You don't mind, do you?' Mum asked. 'We'll all go again later for the Summoning.'

'I don't mind,' I said. 'You should enjoy your day off.'

Mum yawned, not noticing anything was amiss. 'Well, don't be long.' She turned and shuffled back into the living room. 'I'll have a nice cup of tea in a minute, I think . . .'

I mumbled a goodbye, then zipped past her into the hallway, snatching my keys from the hook and shrugging into my coat before stepping outside. It was a crisp, bright morning. My breath misted the air as I walked, trying to put my thoughts in order. At the moment, there was no evidence that Alice was definitely missing. All I knew was that she had left in a hurry, and that it must be linked to the story, which meant one of two things. Firstly, Alice could have gone somewhere to hide until she figured out what to do. She had vanished a few times in the past after arguing with Mum, sometimes for a few hours and once for an entire night.

The other possibility was that one of the characters had caught up with her. I felt a nasty little twist somewhere deep inside and pushed this thought away. I had to stay calm and use my head. I had to treat this like it wasn't Alice I was trying to find, like it wasn't someone I cared about. Like I was a real detective.

The first thing that a real detective would be thinking is that, when someone goes missing, the first two days of the investigation are the most important. This is because any clues are still fresh, witnesses can still remember things, and the missing person might still be close.

Missing. The word made me feel a bit sick. Missing people belonged on the television or in newspapers. It couldn't happen to someone like Alice. It couldn't happen to a family like us.

I reached the shop on the corner of our street and stopped outside. This was where I'd seen the girl, Gypsy. Finding her might also lead me to Alice, and I was hoping that she might have gone into the shop before I'd spotted her.

A bell jangled above the door as I went in. Gino, the shopkeeper, was stacking tins on a shelf near the counter. He looked up and smiled. He was a large, red-faced, friendly man, though Mum said he was a gossip.

I got a bottle of lemonade out of the chilled cabinet, then took it to the counter. A moment later, Gino got up, ringing up the drink on the till. A straw Likeness with black hair in a little bun and button eyes was propped next to the charity tin.

'Who's this?' I asked.

'Is my mama,' Gino said, patting the doll with a beefy hand. 'She die many years ago without sharing her best lasagne recipe.' He rubbed his tummy wistfully. 'I try to make myself, but is never the same. If she come tonight, I ask her secret! And who do you make?'

'I haven't decided yet,' I said.

Gino wagged his finger. 'You'll run out of time!'

'I'll get my sister to help me,' I said, hoping the mention of Alice would jog his memory of the other girl. 'She's always got good ideas.' I pointed to some jars behind the counter. 'Can I have a pound's worth of rhubarb and custards, too, please?'

Gino beamed and weighed out the sweets, giving me an extra one 'for luck' as he always did. 'Your sister, she is in here earlier,' he said, his smile fading. 'I ask her who she make for the Summoning, but she act like she don't know what I'm a-talking about. Like she never hear of the Summoning before.'

My heart quickened. The real Alice knew all about it, as did everyone else who lived in Fiddler's Hollow. It had to be Gypsy.

'Then she ask me directions,' Gino continued. 'Very strange.'

'Directions to where?'

'The library,' said Gino. 'So I tell her, then I ask if she is a-feeling all right.' He scratched his beard. 'She say yes and give me a funny look, and that she just got lost. And the strangest thing is, she don't speak. She write everything in a notebook and show me.' He shrugged. 'And so I think to myself that maybe she is playing a trick on me. And I have a busy morning, so I forget about it until you come in.'

I paid him and left, turning out of Cuckoo Lane. If I hurried to the library, perhaps I could find her. I headed for the town centre. Saturdays were always busy, but the weekend of the Summoning saw it packed out, the square near the town hall especially. The library was at the back of the town hall and, as I neared its huge doors, I slowed a little. They were shut and the board displaying the library's opening hours confirmed it had closed fifteen minutes ago.

I felt a little of the wind leave my sails. My first lead and I'd lost it! I shrugged the bag higher up my back. There were still other clues and my biggest one was the notebook. If there were anything else I needed to know about Gypsy, I'd find it there. Plus, I had another place in mind that I wanted to go – but there, instead of Gypsy, I would be looking for Alice.

I cut through the centre of town to the church, taking the path that wove through the gravestones. At the back of the churchyard, there was an overgrown mass of trees and shrubs. I stopped, taking a quick look about to make sure no one was watching me, before pushing through a gap in the greenery. Twigs and leaves brushed against my cheeks as I crawled between them, the winter ground dampening my hands and knees.

The Den was a short way in and a bit of a scramble

through what appeared to be a dense thicket. Once you were through, though, there was a hollow space like a leafy cave beyond. It was completely hidden from view and, if you were quiet enough, no one would ever know you were there. Alice had shown me the spot a couple of years ago, but made me promise not to tell anyone.

I came to a halt and spat out a leaf, searching the ground for any sign that someone had been here recently. Last year, Alice and Mum had argued and Alice had stormed out of the house. She hadn't returned until the next afternoon and wouldn't say where she'd been, but the next time I came to the Den I found Alice's name traced over and over in the soil. Later, she told me she'd been there all night.

Now, however, there was no sign of her at all. I reached into my bag and popped a rhubarb and custard into my mouth, then took out Alice's phone and notebook. I tried the phone first – perhaps there was a message on there, or maybe a call from someone Alice had gone to meet? I was quickly disappointed, for the phone was locked with a password to stop anyone from looking at it. I put it back in the bag, frustrated, then opened the notebook.

It was hard to see in the gloom, but I remembered the pocket torch and shone it at the paper. There were three pages of character notes on Gypsy, mixed in with doodles, diagrams and even little pictures of outfits that had been cut out of fashion magazines. At the top of the page, a word had been written in capital letters: CURSED.

'Just like Alice,' I whispered to myself.

A flowery doodle had been drawn heavily round two words: *Gypsy Spindle*. I traced it with my finger, remembering the night Alice had first mentioned the curse. The day she'd come back after going to search for her father. She'd been looking at the book of fairy tales: Sleeping Beauty about to prick her finger on the spindle of the spinning wheel. About to fall under the spell. Alice had always liked using weird names, and Gypsy Spindle was straight out of a fairy tale. I read through the notes. Some of it was very familiar: her mother was a Romany traveller and her father had worked with a bookbinder. It sounded a lot like our mother, who had worked in a bookshop before going into publishing, and Alice's father.

I continued reading, discovering more. There were lots of notes about Gypsy's favourite music and books. She had a tattoo of a scorpion on her neck, just below her ear. She had been betrayed by a boy she once loved. She had lived with her curse, which was Silence, for six years.

'That's why she didn't speak to me,' I murmured aloud. 'She *couldn't*.' I reread the profile, lingering over the scorpion tattoo. It seemed such an odd choice for a young girl. Had Alice secretly got a tattoo? She couldn't have – it would be too difficult to hide from Mum – and besides I was sure she would have told me if she had. The more I looked, the more convinced I became that Gypsy was a mixture of who Alice really was and who she *wanted* to be. Even the curse tied in with it all. She had never told me what her own curse was, but I knew it must be something to do with her father. It made sense that part of the story would be about Alice's character finding a way to undo her own curse.

I scanned the rest of the notes, and then I saw something that made my heart hammer: *Lives on a narrowboat called* Elsewhere. I snapped the notebook shut and put it back into the bag, squeezing out of the Den. If I hurried, perhaps I could still find Gypsy.

The canal ran just on the edge of the town, behind the shops and alongside the train station. I left the churchyard and went along Buckle Lane. From there, it was a five-minute walk down a couple of side streets, then the canal was in front of me. Green, sludgy water glugged at its sides, moved only by a flock of swans. There were a couple of narrowboats moored further up. I headed for them, the air damp on my face.

The two boats were on the other side of the canal just past a bridge. Was one of them Gypsy's? I wasn't close enough to see the names yet. I crossed the bridge, but hesitated as I drew nearer. What would I say to Gypsy if she were there? I had no idea how much Gypsy was aware of. *I* knew that she was a character from Alice's story, but did *she* know that? I doubted it.

Gypsy probably thought she was a real person. If she discovered she wasn't, what would she be capable of? She'd be afraid, confused, unstable even. A shudder rippled over me. All those things could make her dangerous. One wrong word from me might blow it ... and if there was a chance

Gypsy could lead me to Alice then I couldn't afford for that to happen.

I took out the notebook again. Perhaps if I could skim some of the story and get more information it would help me know what to say to her. I looked past the notes on Gypsy and the cat. There were several other characters: a boy named Piper who was some sort of street performer, two other girls listed on the same page – Dorothy Grimes and Dolly Weaver – and another character called Sheridan Ramblebrook: the curator of the Museum of Unfinished Stories. I flicked past these. I could come back to them later. For now, I needed to get to the actual story itself . . .

I never got the chance, though. I looked up as a moorhen started to squawk and saw that, on the bridge behind me, a familiar figure was crossing the water. I squinted, unsure for just a fraction of a second. Was it my sister?

No. It was *her*. The other Alice. My heart raced again. She was coming towards me, heading for the boats. I watched as she came closer, seeing things I hadn't noticed this morning. Unlike Alice, she walked tall, carrying herself with confidence. She was dressed differently to Alice, too. My sister lived in jeans and shapeless T-shirts, but this girl's clothes were daring and colourful. Under her black leather jacket she wore a long, sea-green dress with a crimson sash tied at her waist. On her feet were scuffed boots that went right up to the knee. The sort of boots that looked as though they had walked many roads and had many adventures.

I was aware I was staring, but couldn't seem to stop. The girl appeared not to notice, barely glancing my way. She looked half in a daydream as she approached, passing the first boat and taking out a chain from around her neck. A silver key dangled from it. She lifted the key, then paused, noticing me. A flicker of recognition crossed her face. I moved closer to her. Sure enough, there it was, painted on the side of the boat: *Elsewhere*. Gypsy opened the notebook she was carrying and wrote something in it, then held it out to me.

Did you find Alice?

I looked into her eyes.

'No,' I mumbled, noticing a leaflet poking out of the pocket of her jacket. I recognised the library emblem. It was a list of opening times.

'I've just been to the library, too,' I said. 'Looking for Alice. But I didn't make it in time; it was closed.'

I didn't find what I was looking for anyway, she wrote.

I saw an opportunity to get her to stick with me a little longer.

'There's a bookshop not far from here. I could show you where if you like?' I offered.

She stared at me just long enough to make me squirm. *Why are you so keen to do a favour for a stranger?* she wrote.

For a moment, I faltered, taken aback, but a plan was forming in my mind.

'Well, I'm going there now anyway, to look for Alice. She loves books, you see.' I tried to read Gypsy's expression, but

69

it gave nothing away. 'Plus, if I help you, perhaps you could help me in return.'

How?

'By pretending to be Alice.'

The girl rolled her eyes.

'I'm serious,' I said. 'This isn't the first time Alice has . . . disappeared. If our mum finds out, she'll be in big trouble. I need to find her, but our mum can't know that she's gone.'

At this Gypsy laughed. *Lookalike or not, there's no way you'd be able to fool your own mother.*

'You think?' I reached into my rucksack and took out the photograph of Alice from her purse. 'You don't realise just how much you look like her.'

Gypsy snatched the photo, blinking. The smirk slid right off her face. Her fingers shook as she wrote two wobbly words.

That's impossible.

'Now you can see why I thought you were her this morning.'

But she looks just like me. She practically is me.

I went to take the photograph from her, but her grip was too tight. I had the horrible feeling I'd blown it by scaring her, but as she looked harder at the picture some of the stiffness dropped out of her shoulders and she released it into my hand.

She's thinner in the face than me, and her eyes are blue, she wrote. *Mine are green.*

'Well, yes. You don't look *exactly* like her. That'd be impossible. But you look enough like her to fool Mum for a few minutes,' I said. 'That's all it would need to be.'

I suppose there's no harm in that. She studied me again, watchful as a bird. *My name is Gypsy Spindle.*

I nodded, pretending the name was new to me. 'I'm Michael Pierce, but everyone calls me Midge.'

Gypsy tucked the silver key around her neck out of sight. *Come on then, Midge,* she wrote. *Lead the way.*

We set off, away from the towpath, and headed towards the town centre. As we walked, I heard Gypsy's footsteps next to mine, heard her breathing, saw her shadow falling across the path, just as solid as mine. I remembered Alice speaking about characters from books and how real they were to her.

I wondered if this was what she had meant.

6

The Likeness

WE WALKED A SHORT WAY IN SILENCE. PARTLY, I supposed, as it would have been awkward for Gypsy to keep stopping to write in her notebook. I wondered how she had lost her voice. Somewhere in the notebook in my rucksack, it was likely the answer was written ... but I wanted to hear about Gypsy from her. I wanted to find out how much she knew, without giving too much away.

'Is it new, the book you're looking for?' I asked eventually. 'Chapters has nearly all the latest releases.'

Gypsy shrugged. I wasn't sure if it meant that she didn't know, or couldn't be bothered to make small talk.

'Well, if it's old, there's a good chance they'll have it, too,' I continued. 'There's a huge section of second-hand books on the top floor. Alice spends hours in there.' I sneaked a sideways look at Gypsy, to see if the mention of Alice sparked any interest in her, but it was difficult to tell. I continued talking anyway. It made me feel closer to Alice, somehow, speaking about our life together.

'One Christmas Eve, we were shopping and we lost Alice. Mum was frantic, running back to all the shops we'd been into and showing them the picture of Alice in her purse. Alice was about eight then. I was so little I can't remember it, but Mum tells us about it every Christmas. In the end, she found her in Chapters in the children's book section. She'd wandered back there when she couldn't find us and had fallen asleep in the reading tent.'

Gypsy gave a slight nod, but her face was still blank. She didn't seem interested in hearing about Alice. Did she really have no idea about their connection, or was she just hiding it well? We walked in silence until we reached the next corner, then turned into Cutpurse Way. 'It's just up here,' I said. We wove round people in a stop-start dance to reach the doorway of the old bookshop. I hung back behind Gypsy as she went in, past the new releases on the tables at the front, past maps and the cookery section. The whole place smelled deliciously of new books. Gypsy went straight to the counter, waiting in line until a fair-headed woman called her over.

I followed, hovering behind her awkwardly. The woman behind the counter had a friendly face, and the name on her badge said SARAH. Gypsy opened her notebook, then laid it on the counter and tapped the page. I couldn't see what it said from where I stood, but I didn't want to look nosy by moving closer.

Sarah peered at the notebook. 'I'm pretty sure I don't have that,' she said. 'And I don't recognise the title, but let me check.' She typed some words into a computer. 'No, nothing. Do you have any other information? The name of the author perhaps?'

Gypsy shook her head.

'Are you sure the title's correct?'

At this, Gypsy nodded, but the bookseller looked unsure.

'It could be tricky to track down with only the title, especially if it's not quite right. Just a minute.' She slipped out from behind the counter and vanished into the warren of bookshelves, returning a couple of minutes later. 'It couldn't be either of these, could it?'

Gypsy took one of the books from her. It was called *The Museum's Secret* and it had a nice cover, with illustrations of gleaming, blue-black beetles crawling over it. Gypsy shook her head and handed it back.

'What about this?' Sarah asked. The second one was called *The Museum of Spells and Sorcery*. It occurred to me that this sounded just the kind of book I'd like to read when the familiarity of it struck me, and my breath caught in my throat. At the same moment, I realised that Gypsy's notebook was still open on the counter, and she had moved aside a little to look at the books.

I stepped closer to the counter and looked at what was written. There it was, in Gypsy's perfect script:

The Museum of Unfinished Stories

My head spun. Gypsy was searching for the story Alice had written. The story to which she belonged and which had somehow brought her to life.

Questions crashed into my head, rolling over each other like waves.

Did Gypsy know she was a made-up character in someone else's story? What did she want with it – a glimpse of what was in store for her? If so, how could she know her future if it was only half-written? And what would happen if she discovered that the very thing she was looking for was right under her nose, stashed in my rucksack?

'There's nothing else coming up that's similar,' Sarah said apologetically. 'But we have lots of old books on the top floor, and not all of them are catalogued on our system. There's a chance it could be there.'

Gypsy nodded her thanks and picked up her notebook.

'Are you going upstairs to look through the old books?' I asked. I could barely meet her eyes, I was so afraid she would see the truth in them, but she was too distracted to notice anything different. She sighed, nodding.

'Where shall I meet you later?' I asked. 'For when ...' I paused, moving closer to her. 'When you pretend to be Alice?'

She dropped her gaze and a sick feeling seeped into my stomach. She didn't want to do it.

'You said you would.' My voice came out harder than I meant it to, and I stared at her until she was forced to look at me again.

I'll be here, at the bookshop, she wrote. *Come and find me when you're ready.*

'You'll be here?' I said. 'Promise?'

She nodded. *Gypsies don't break promises.*

I left her and rushed out of the shop into the cold air, aware of how hot my cheeks were all of a sudden: hot with guilt.

I was the only one who knew the truth: Gypsy's search was pointless. She would never find what she was looking for there, or anywhere else. Only one copy existed in the world, and that was the half-written version bumping along in my rucksack. Until I figured out what Gypsy wanted with the story, the best thing I could do was keep my mouth shut. I needed to think about what to do next, but the hugeness of it all felt too much. I wanted Alice, to help me and tell me what to do. But I was alone. It felt like another one of Alice's riddles . . . only this time none of it made any sense and there was no hope of solving it.

I moved away from the shop, following the trickle of people towards the town square. Things were getting busier now, more crowded than an ordinary Saturday. A bandstand had been set up at the top of the steps to the town hall, and street vendors had sprung up in every direction. At the centre of the square was a towering mass of wood. Even as I watched, people were heaping more on: branches, garden cuttings, broken furniture. It made me think of *Sleeping Beauty*: of all the spinning wheels in the kingdom being burned after the wicked fairy had spoken her curse. But this bonfire was for the Likenesses to burn on.

'Don't you just love a good fire?' a voice said nearby.

I looked round to see a lady standing close to me. Her smile startled me, for her mouth was bright and shiny with the reddest lipstick I'd ever seen.

I shrugged. 'Bonfires are fun, I guess.' I looked at the clock tower. It was time to head back home soon. I started to move off, but the red-lipped woman spoke again.

'You're Alice's little brother, aren't you?'

I turned back. 'That's right.'

'Oh, thank goodness I found you.' She stepped closer, lowering her voice. 'Alice sent me.'

My heart leaped. 'You've seen Alice? Where is she? Is she OK?'

She shook her head and her glossy, black hair swished at her jawline. 'She's in trouble. She asked me to bring her something.'

I felt a stab of fear. 'What kind of trouble? Wait – who are you?'

The woman smiled wider, her lips stretching over her teeth. Her mouth was so red I could hardly look away from it, but when I did I saw that she was more of a girl than a woman, perhaps a bit older than Alice. Her clothes made her look more grown-up. She wore a neat suit, with shiny, pointed, black shoes that had little red bows on.

'I'm a friend of Alice's,' she said.

'Are you?' I asked. 'What's your name?'

'Dolly.'

Why was she still smiling if Alice was in trouble? I didn't like it and I didn't like her eyes. They were blue, but not blue like a summer sky, like Alice's. They were blue like a frozen lake, icy and staring, with no warmth in them.

I heard Alice's voice in my head, a memory of last year.

If anyone ever approaches you, Midge, anyone you don't know that asks you about me, don't trust them. Do you hear me? They'll say anything . . . just get away from them . . .

Could she be another one of *them*? Another character from Alice's story? Before I knew it, I'd taken a step back. I tried desperately to remember the names of the other characters that were written in the notebook, but my mind had gone blank with fear.

'I know all Alice's friends,' I said. 'She's never mentioned anyone called Dolly.'

'Surely you don't know *all* her friends?' Dolly's voice was sweet, but those eyes of hers still chilled me.

'I'm pretty sure I do,' I said. 'She doesn't have that many.' I took another step away, my heart thudding.

'Look, you know she's in trouble,' Dolly hissed, her smile gone. 'Do you want to help your sister or not? She told me she could count on you. Was she wrong?'

I froze, like I'd been slapped. The sudden change in her manner had caught me off guard. My gut was telling me to run and yet . . . What if this girl was genuine and there *was* a chance to help Alice? I'd *never* let Alice down . . . but her warning echoed in my mind. The only way to know for sure would be to set a trap.

'What does Alice want?' I asked.

Dolly smoothed a strand of hair with a gloved hand. 'There's a notebook containing a story she's working on. She wants me to take it to her. Do you know where it is?'

I stared at her, heart pounding, hesitating a heartbeat too long. 'No.'

'Are you sure?'

I nodded, then, as her eyes strayed behind me, realised too late that my hand was resting protectively on my rucksack. I let it drop. 'I – I could go home and look for it,' I said at last. 'But you tell me where Alice is and *I'll* take it to her.'

Dolly shook her head. 'No can do. She told me not to let you – she doesn't want you getting mixed up in all this. I'm the one who has to take it.'

'OK,' I said, thinking hard. 'But Alice warned me something like this might happen. So she set a riddle and only the people she trusts know the answer to it.'

The girl looked at me, her face unreadable.

I swallowed. 'Take half of free, and all of end, with I in the middle, on me you depend.'

'Oh, yes. I remember her mentioning it.' I saw her lips moving silently as she repeated the verse to herself. 'The answer is *friend*,' she said brightly.

'Right,' I said. 'The thing is, that wasn't Alice's riddle. It was one *I* made up. So you're lying.'

Dolly stared at me wordlessly, then grinned again. This time her teeth were tinged red. At first, I thought it was lipstick, but then I wondered if it might be blood. Had she bitten her cheek in anger, now I'd tricked her?

'Listen,' she said softly. 'Why don't you come with me?' Her eyes darted from side to side. 'You're alone, right?'

I didn't answer. A jittery feeling was bubbling up inside me. I badly wanted to run.

'Come with me,' Dolly repeated in a friendly voice. 'I can see you're worried – I'll take you to Alice . . .'

'NO!' My voice came out forcefully, and I was aware of people turning to look. 'I'm not going anywhere with you!'

Dolly's fake smile froze on her lips. Suddenly, it didn't look anything like a smile at all. It just looked as if she were baring her teeth at me. Without another word, I turned and fled through the crowd, weaving this way and that, glancing over my shoulder. Twice I ducked and doubled back, checking to see if she was behind me, but there was no sign. Heart thundering, I hid behind the bandstand and tried to slow my breathing. After a minute or two, I felt calmer. She hadn't tried to follow, and I was sensible enough to know that she wouldn't try to grab me or drag me off with all these people around.

I was convinced now that Dolly – if that *was* her real name – didn't know where Alice was at all. She'd lied, simply to trap me. But why? Was she looking for Alice herself, or did she want the notebook? Or both?

I thought about how I'd caught her out. It was Alice's

doppelgänger story that had given me the idea, where the boy had saved himself with a riddle. The one I'd used wasn't too difficult, not when it was written down anyway. But Dolly had solved it in her head and quickly. She was smart.

Something brushed against my ankle and a lazy voice drawled up at me.

'What is all this fuss about?'

I looked down to see Tabitha sitting at my feet.

'What are you doing here?' I gasped. 'Are you following me?'

'Only for the last few minutes,' Tabitha replied. 'I thought I recognised you, and it's not like I know anyone else here.'

I eyed her suspiciously. All the questions I had about Gypsy, and now Dolly and how much they knew ... the same questions applied to the cat, too. Did Tabitha know about the story? Or was she being truthful about not knowing where she was?

'Why are you following me?'

'I thought I just explained that,' said Tabitha, narrowing her golden eyes. 'You're the only person I know. And, well ... I'm hungry. I've nowhere else to go. I waited at your house, but your cat's a greedy beast. She gobbled up all her disgusting food and didn't leave a thing, although I suppose I should be grateful.'

I bent down and lifted her into my arms. 'Come here,' I said. 'There are too many people about; you'll get trodden on if you stay down there.'

She nestled in the crook of my arm, paws on my shoulder and whiskers tickling my cheek. 'So what is all this?'

'The Summoning,' I said softly. 'It's sort of a custom of Fiddler's Hollow. Some kind of old magic. A bit silly really. It's never worked before, not for me.'

'Magic is never silly,' said Tabitha. 'Only the nincompoops who get it wrong.'

I couldn't argue with that. I'd seen enough today to know that some magic was real. I hesitated, then decided to be bold.

'Can I ask you something?'

Tabitha rested her head on my shoulder sleepily. 'You can. I might not answer, though.'

I thought about different ways in which I could ask the question that was burning inside me. 'If . . . if there were a book of your life, with everything written from start to finish, would you read it?' I said finally.

Tabitha lifted her head and flexed her claws. I heard the sharp scratch of them on my collar and was grateful for the thickness of my coat. 'What a peculiar question,' she said. 'Do you mean a diary? Or a biography? Because, in that case, wouldn't I have to be dead for it to have my entire life written in it? And if I was I'd know everything that had happened anyway.'

'No, not a diary, or a biography exactly. You'd still be alive. It'd be like . . . like being able to see into your future. Everything that was going to happen.'

'I'm not sure,' Tabitha replied. 'What if I found out that

I'd get run over? Or eaten by a dog, or poisoned? I'm not sure I'd like that. Cripes, I could get poisoned, run over *and* eaten by a dog.'

'You'd have to be very unlucky for all three to happen,' I said.

'Not really. Lots of people think black cats are unlucky. And cats have nine lives. Does that mean there would be nine of these books?'

'No, just one,' I repeated. 'Why do you have to muddle things up?'

'I'm not the one muddling things. You're the one asking silly questions.'

'You still haven't answered,' I pointed out.

'I'm thinking,' said Tabitha. She tilted her head to one side. 'Yes, of course I'd look. Curiosity always gets the better of cats; that's where the saying comes from. But then that would alter things, wouldn't it? If you read the story before you'd finished living it. If there were things you didn't like the sound of that hadn't happened yet, you'd try to change them, wouldn't you?'

'Maybe you wouldn't be able to change them,' I said. 'Maybe trying to change them would just lead to making whatever it was actually happen.'

'I don't see how,' Tabitha answered grouchily. 'If I found out that I was to be poisoned by a certain meal and a certain person, at a certain time, then I'd avoid it. So reading it would have to change things, wouldn't it? Besides, who would have written the book in the first place?'

'Oh, I don't know!' I shook my head, half wishing I hadn't asked. The cat had an annoying way of twisting things. 'It was just a question, that's all.'

'Hmph,' said the cat. 'I don't like too many questions. They make me—'

'Sleepy,' I interrupted. 'I know.'

'I'm still hungry, too,' she complained.

'Can't you catch a mouse or something?'

'Yuck.' She shuddered. 'I only do that when I have to. Anyway, I'd have no chance with all these people about.'

I looked around us at the ever-increasing crowd, and realised a small girl was staring at us open-mouthed, tugging her father's arm. I turned away and slid further within the folds of people. 'Perhaps you'd better keep quiet,' I muttered. 'Talking cats aren't normal here. You could get taken away if the wrong person notices.'

She raised her nose and sniffed the air. 'What is that delicious smell?'

'Candyfloss,' I said through gritted teeth. 'Did you hear what I said?'

'Yes.' She sniffed again. 'I'm not deaf. I'll keep quiet if you get me some candyfloss.'

'Cats aren't supposed to eat candyfloss,' I said, exasperated.

'They aren't supposed to talk, either.'

'OK, I'll get you some. Anything to shut you up.'

We wove through the growing crowds of people gathering in the square, passing through the steam of buttery corn on the cob and smoky wafts of roasting nuts, to a stall selling toffee apples and candyfloss. I bought a stick and tore some off, discreetly giving it to Tabitha.

'Oooh,' she said, licking pink fluff off her nose. 'That's good stuff.' I fed her some more, pausing by a stall selling plain little straw dolls. There were tables set up nearby with pots of paint, glue and scraps of fabric to decorate them, mostly occupied by children. I saw little fingers become sticky with glue, collecting beads, paint specks and stray thread. As I watched, I realised what I had to do. My fingers fumbling with excitement, I dug out some money and paid for one of the straw dolls.

I was going to Summon Alice.

'What's that for?' Tabitha asked, her breath warm on my cheek. I caught a whiff of it, a mix of sugar and fish.

I wrinkled my nose. 'It's for the Summoning. The idea is that you make a doll that looks like someone you want to speak to, a Likeness. All the Likenesses go on to the bonfire and a spell is said. If it works, the person is meant to come to you and you can ask them a question. Just one question.'

'Why don't you just ask the actual person?' the cat asked. 'Or write a letter? Wouldn't that be easier?'

'Not if the person is dead, or you don't know where they are,' I said.

'Oh, I see,' said Tabitha. 'Now it makes sense. Who do you want to contact?'

'My sister, Alice. That's if she doesn't turn up before this evening.'

'All those straw poppets look the same to me,' said Tabitha. 'How are you going to make it look like your sister?'

'This one isn't going to be Alice,' I said. 'This is a decoy. I can't let my mum know Alice is missing, so I'll have to make a fake Likeness as well as the real one.'

'How sneaky,' Tabitha replied approvingly. She yawned, flashing her teeth. I caught another unpleasant waft of her breath. 'What if you don't have a question to ask? What if you just fancied a chat?'

'I don't know.' I frowned. 'That's a good point.' What would happen if I didn't ask a question and instead simply let Alice speak? Could she tell me what I needed to know without me asking? It was worth a shot. 'If it even works,' I said under my breath.

'Of course it works,' Tabitha said. 'All these old customs wouldn't exist if they hadn't worked at some point. They would fade out and be forgotten.'

'It's never worked before.'

'Maybe you didn't want it enough.'

'Or maybe I didn't believe in it enough,' I said. 'But after today I have to.'

We pushed our way out of the town square, going against the flow of people coming in the opposite direction. I grunted as an elbow found my ribs, and staggered as someone toppled sideways into me. My rucksack thudded to the ground, almost tripping me. Tabitha slid out of my arms and landed neatly on all fours, her tail spiking up.

'Don't say sorry, will you?' she hissed, glaring at the boy who had barged past.

I shot her a warning look, but the boy, who'd glanced back over his shoulder, hadn't noticed the cat and was staring instead at me.

'Sorry,' he muttered. He looked a bit older than Alice – eighteen, maybe, with shiny, black hair that fell across his face in a long fringe. His eyes were dark and mischievous, and he had thin lips that were curled into a smirk.

'He really looks sorry, doesn't he?' I said, as the boy was swallowed into the crowd. Tabitha shook herself and stalked off ahead of me, a black silhouette in the fading light. The streets became emptier the nearer I got to home and, though I checked behind me a few times and saw nothing, I couldn't shake the feeling I was being watched. Without the bustle of the busy town around me now, I felt it more strongly. Dolly, whoever she was, had rattled me.

Mum was asleep in front of the TV when we got home, and none the wiser when she woke to find me sitting in my room with the contents of the craft boxes spread over the floor.

'Why didn't you wake me?' she yawned, peering through the door with bleary eyes. 'I've been asleep for hours.'

'I tried,' I fibbed. I glued some more fabric to the straw figure in my lap. 'You snored and turned over.'

'Oh,' said Mum, turning pink. 'Who are you making?'

'Peter Pan,' I answered, perhaps a little too quickly. I'd

had time to think about the fake Likeness on the way home.

'Peter Pan?' Mum said, puzzled. 'But he's made up. From a story.'

I shrugged. 'Doesn't matter. If the magic is strong enough, it'll work.'

'I suppose so,' said Mum. 'What would you ask him, if it works?'

'To take me to Neverland, so I don't have to grow up.'

Mum smiled. 'Sounds wonderful.' She stepped over a ball of wool and kissed me on the forehead. 'Sometimes I wish that, too.'

'That you didn't have to grow up?' I asked.

'Well, yes. But more that *you* didn't have to, you and Alice. That you could stay like this, always believing in magic.'

'Do you believe in magic, Mum?'

Her smile faded a little. 'I used to. But not any more.'

'Maybe you should try.'

'Maybe I will.' She tousled my hair. 'It's a nice thought, characters from stories coming to life. Alice would love it.'

I forced a smile. It wasn't just a thought. It was *real*, and Alice hadn't seemed at all happy about her own characters coming to life.

'Speaking of Alice, has she been home yet?' Mum asked. 'I hope she's still coming to the Summoning with us later.'

'I saw her in town earlier,' I said, sticking a clumsily made hat on Peter Pan's head. 'She said she'll meet us there.'

'Right,' said Mum. 'Well, try not to be too long finishing that Likeness off. I'll make dinner soon; we'll need to eat early if we're going out later.' She left and I heard her footsteps on the stairs as she went down them. Once she was gone, I put the straw Likeness aside and took out the real one from under my bed, where I'd stashed it when I'd heard Mum coming up the stairs. It was a simple figure that I'd cut and sewn from some felt, leaving a small opening at the back so I could stuff it later.

Tabitha poked her head out from under the bed, staring disdainfully at the Likeness's mitten-like hands and feet. 'I can see needlework isn't your strong point,' she said.

I scowled. 'A bit like being polite isn't yours.'

'Touché,' said the cat.

'What does that mean?'

'It means that you're a smarty-pants.'

I couldn't be bothered to ask her to explain in more detail, so I got up, leaving her in my room, and went out to the ladder.

I climbed into the attic. It smelled of paper and ink and Alice. It made me miss her more than ever. I climbed on the bed and looked out of the skylight, across the street. I'd already checked a few times since I'd got home, in case Dolly had followed me, but there was no sign of anyone lurking about.

I got down and dug out an old T-shirt of Alice's from her bottom drawer. It had a hole in the sleeve, but she still wore it to bed sometimes. I threw it down the hatch, then hunted around, looking for anything else I could use. I put Alice's comb and an old notebook in my pocket, then went through the bin. The smell of a blackened banana peel wafted up. Underneath it, I found a grubby plaster smeared with blood, from where Alice had cut her finger making dinner last night. Then I carefully went back down the ladder and returned to my room.

I set everything down beside me and pulled out some golden embroidery silk from the tangle in the boxes, sewing several threads to the Likeness's head. From Alice's comb, I removed some strands of hair and began weaving them through the embroidery thread, knotting them in place.

Next I took Alice's old notebook. I felt like a traitor as I tore out a bunch of pages and scrunched them into tiny balls before poking them inside the gap I'd left in the felt figure.

'What is that?' Tabitha asked.

'My sister's work,' I said quietly.

'Won't she be cross with you?'

I nodded. 'Probably. But this is important and these stories are old. Alice would have typed them up – she'll still have copies.'

'Couldn't you just use newspaper to stuff it?' Tabitha said.

'I could,' I said. 'But, if there really is a chance this could work, then I have to make it as much like Alice as I can. These stand for all the stories that live inside her, waiting to get out.'

I tore, scrunched and stuffed until the felt figure filled

out, until no more paper would go inside. Then I sewed the opening shut. After that, I made a little outfit from Alice's T-shirt and folded a tiny notebook from another torn-out page, which I then sewed to the Likeness's hand. On its other hand, I made a tiny snip with the scissors, then cut out a scrap of the bloodied plaster and stuck it over the cut.

'There,' I whispered. 'Just like the real Alice.'

Tabitha grew tired of watching and settled down to snooze, leaving me to work in silence until all there was left to do was Alice's face. I pulled two blue sequins from a matchbox and sewed them on. 'These can be your eyes.' Finally, I found a tiny, pink, oval bead and sewed that on, too, for a mouth.

It was finished. I set it aside. I had never been very good at making Likenesses, but this was the best I'd made so far. Not that it really looked like Alice, but because of everything I'd used to make it. Her hair, her words, her clothes, her blood. I knew I'd done all I could. It had to work.

It *had* to.

I checked the clock. There was still time before Mum and I would be leaving for the Summoning. Time for me to get reading this story of Alice's for more clues about Gypsy and the other characters – and to check whether Dolly had been one of them. I glanced at Tabitha. She gave a snore, her whiskers trembling.

I unzipped the rucksack and poked through it, pulling out Alice's purse and phone, and the torch and Dad's lucky glasses. My fingers closed round some loose paper. I pulled it out, recognising Alice's writing. A section of the notebook had come away from the rest. It was crumpled and bent, and a thread from where it had been sewn into the notebook dangled like a broken spider leg. I opened the bag wider and looked in. There was no sign of the rest of the notebook. A fluttery feeling started up in my chest.

I reached into the front pocket, finding nothing but the paper bag with the last few rhubarb and custards. I turned the rucksack upside down and shook it, but already I could feel it was empty.

Apart from the few loose pages in my hand, Alice's notebook was gone.

7

Chapter Three

I TURNED THE RUCKSACK OVER, CHECKING FOR tears or holes. There was no damage to it. This couldn't be right. I *never* lost things. Alice was the scatterbrain, not me, and I'd been so careful with the notebook. I'd taken it out only twice, once in the Den and once at the canal. And I *knew* I'd put it back both times.

Someone must have taken it.

Not Dolly. She hadn't come close enough. Gypsy? Could she possibly know about it, too? I hadn't got that feeling from her. And she would have had to get very close to me to steal it, distracting me somehow. I was certain that hadn't happened. I'd have felt it . . .

Then I remembered. The butterflies in my chest fluttered harder.

'That boy!' The one who had bumped into me as I left the square. He'd knocked my bag right off my shoulder.

Tabitha sat up drowsily. 'Hmm? What boy? Who . . . ?'

'The boy who knocked against me earlier. It was him – it had to be. He took . . . something out of my bag.'

She yawned. 'Are you sure? Maybe you dropped it. What was it, money?'

I shook my head. 'A notebook belonging to Alice. It's . . . it's important.'

'She has lots of notebooks. What's so special about that one?'

'It's the story she's working on at the moment,' I said, 'and probably the only copy.'

Tabitha settled down again. 'What's so important about a story? Surely she can just write it again?'

'It's important to Alice.' *And to me*, I added silently. The notebook would contain clues I needed: to work out what the characters of the story wanted – and which of them might be dangerous.

'Even if it's important to your sister, why would anyone else want it?' the cat drawled.

I could think of at least one person: Dolly. But what would that boy want with it? Perhaps he was also linked to Alice's story . . . or maybe there was a simpler explanation.

'It's a small notebook,' I said. 'Perhaps he mistook it for a wallet.' Mum had often warned us about pickpockets when we'd gone into busy cities. One of their tricks was to bump into you or distract you before going through your pockets or bag.

All I had left of the notebook were a few pages. I flicked through them, carefully, like they were treasure. Sixteen pages. Some notes and a chapter or so, hardly anything.

I closed my eyes. 'I feel sick.'

'So do I,' said Tabitha. She gave a little burp and groaned.

'Yes, but that's because you scoffed a whole candyfloss to yourself earlier,' I said.

'Urgh,' she complained. 'Talking about it makes me feel worse.'

I clutched at the pages uselessly. 'I don't know what to do.'

'There's only one thing you can do,' said Tabitha. 'Find the thieving crook and get it back.'

'How?' I said. 'I'll never find him. He'll be long gone!'

'He'll stay as long as the pickings are rich.'

I felt a glimmer of hope. Tonight was going to be one of the busiest nights of the year in Fiddler's Hollow. Perhaps the boy would still be there.

'He's probably ditched the notebook,' I said. 'Why would he keep it if it's money he was after? It could be in a bin getting covered with people's chewed corn on the cobs!' I felt the heat rising in my face at the thought of Alice's work being thrown away like rubbish.

'Fine. It was only a suggestion,' said Tabitha, curling into a ball. Her voice was muffled. 'Sit here being gloomy, if you prefer. See if I care.'

I could already see she didn't.

I pursed my lips and stared out of the window. The street lights were on. Daylight was fading. Mum would be calling me for dinner soon. This was my chance to read what little

I had of Alice's story before the Summoning. And then, I promised myself, I was going to find that boy.

I picked up the loose pages and sat on the bed.

Chapter Three, I read. *The Curator.*

The museum had, like many collections, started out as a single item: one unfinished story and a fierce yearning to know how it would have ended. As Sheridan Ramblebrook surveyed the now huge collection, his eyes rested on the brown exercise book that contained this story, the story where it had all begun. It was dog-eared and the pages were yellowed with age. On the cover there were just a few words: Georgie Squitch, Class 5C, Maths.

He had not opened it and looked inside for a great many years now, for it was held in a glass cabinet. He had no need to look; he knew the unfinished story word for word. He had felt it was his duty, seeing as it was he who had prevented it from ever being finished. He had tried to finish it himself a few times, but had never got further than a couple of pages. Ramblebrook knew he would never do it justice and besides he was no writer.

His guilt became his obsession. He started to wonder about what other unfinished stories there might be out there in the world, and what their reasons for being incomplete were. Whether there might be a person as terrible as he was for preventing a tale from being told. So he started to look for them and his collection grew.

It was surprisingly easy. All he had to do was think about the places he might find them. He befriended writers. He took on a job doing house moves, and even house clearances when people died. There were stories everywhere. Under beds, in drawers, boxed-up in attics. Those he could not take with permission he copied, word for word, photographed, or even stole if he could get away with it. Stories by children, stories by adults, even stories by famous authors. He collected whatever he could lay his hands on, by hook or by crook, not even sure of why he was doing it until one day he looked around his collection and saw how many there were. He realised then that it was time to share them, for what purpose has a story if it's never told?

Ramblebrook liked purpose. He liked having one, and he liked the idea that he was helping all the unfinished stories find theirs as best they could. While it could never right the wrong he had done, it eased his conscience a little. It would be a museum, he decided. The Museum of Unfinished Stories, the only one of its kind. Somewhere all the ideas and magic could be collected and celebrated.

Swept up in his excitement, Ramblebrook never stopped to consider the danger in what he was doing: that stories are a form of magic and some are more powerful than others. Powerful enough to come alive perhaps. And that, for every ten, twenty or fifty stories that deserved to be told, there was perhaps one that should never have been started in the first place. One written by a damaged and wicked mind, invented only as an outlet for evil.

One of these stories had made it into the museum.

Ramblebrook knew he shouldn't have it. He'd betrayed an old friend to get this particular tale. Sweet-talked and lied, and broken promises that he would simply look at it, make a copy and then return it. But, when the story was in his possession, something changed. It became more like the story was possessing him.

His mother had always said that evil breeds evil. She wasn't wrong.

He'd read about the case in the newspapers. Who hadn't? It was everywhere. Murders were always shocking, but when committed by someone who was little more than a child it took things to a whole new level. Especially when the killings had been carefully documented, planned even, in the form of grisly stories. Every detail recorded; every slicing of flesh and description of screaming. Writers, he mused, were often told to 'write what they knew'. This writer had certainly done that.

And when he'd learned that an old friend, now working in an institution for the criminally insane, had access to these stories? Well, he wasn't able to rest. He had to see them. Had to. And, when the friend had agreed, it still wasn't enough. Those crumpled pages, stained with the guilty, inky fingerprints . . . there was something addictive about them. About the malice seeping off the paper; the sheer horror that the person who had imagined these things was actually capable of carrying them out.

He'd given all of these stories back except one. The unfinished one. He couldn't give it back. It was too important;

too wonderfully hideous. He knew as well as anyone that museums needed the macabre. It was what people flocked to see, what they fed off. Museums weren't about 'nice'; they were about truth. This story had truth in spades.

Best of all, there was nothing that could be done to make him give it back. It had cost him his friendship, but that was a small price to pay for such a prize. He could never be accused of anything, never be forced to admit what he had done. One word from him and his former friend would be facing criminal charges.

Ramblebrook allowed himself a small smile. No, the story was quite safe.

No one else wanted it; no one else knew about it. For a time at least.

Except one other person, whom Ramblebrook hadn't stopped to consider. Someone who should have remained locked away from society . . . but didn't.

That someone was the story's writer: the only person in the world who desired it more fiercely than Ramblebrook.

She wanted to finish it, you see.

Here Alice had drawn a line of tiny stars to show a change of scene, then the chapter continued . . .

Dorothy Grimes had been in hospital three times in her life. The first was to visit her dying grandfather. The second was to have her left arm put in plaster after she had broken it jumping from a second-storey window to escape a burning building. And the third was when she was committed to a secure unit for the criminally insane after it was discovered that she had lit the fire that had snuffed out her entire family.

Although, Dorothy thought, as she looked up at the barred windows to her room, it didn't feel like a hospital so much as a prison. She sighed, flexing her fingers slowly. She really should have taken more care when she'd jumped. If she'd broken her right arm, it would have been a far smaller price to pay, but to break her left was just cruel. She glanced over the paper on her desk in disgust. It was ugly and lined, and jagged at the edges from being ripped out of a notebook, and the writing on it – the product of her right hand – looked as if it had been produced by a five-year-old who was still learning.

They'd refused to give her anything to type on. She wasn't even allowed proper ink. All she had were pencils, which she must use carefully so as not to blunt them too much, for they were only sharpened by the nurse at the beginning of each day.

In hindsight, she supposed the story she'd written about stabbing the warden in the neck with a sharp pencil probably hadn't been a good idea, but the thought of a pencil as a murder weapon was too good to resist. She'd made many deaths happen with a pen or pencil, but never in the literal sense. Besides, she'd discovered that there was even a word to describe an ordinary object fashioned into a weapon: a shiv.

Dorothy had always liked words, especially discovering new ones. And, at seventeen years old, she knew more than most girls of her age.

The hatch in the door opened and a face appeared in the gap. She looked up. It was Mr Bates today – a podgy, grey-haired man with a kindly voice. It was wasted on her, though. She knew the kindness was false.

'Morning, Dorothy,' he said.

'Good morning, Bates,' she answered pleasantly.

'Sleep well?'

'No.'

'No?'

'I howled at the moon until wolves came to the windows and howled back,' she said. 'Then they told me stories all night, to try to get me to go with them. But I knew they just wanted to crunch my bones and rip out my throat.'

'Sorry to hear that,' said Mr Bates.

She smiled. They both knew very well that she'd slept right through until morning. The medicine they gave her every night made sure of that.

'Pencils, please,' Bates said crisply, stepping two paces back from the door.

Dorothy picked them up and put them through the hatch, placing them in a small basket on the other side. She saw a slight grimace cross Bates's face as he glimpsed her hands before he managed to look impassive again.

'Now three steps back, please.'

She did so.

He collected the pencils, then sighed. 'Where's the other one?'

'What do you mean? They're all there, all three of them.'

'No, there are two. This one and the two halves of the pencil you snapped.'

She produced the third pencil from her sleeve and passed it through the hatch obediently.

'Nice try.'

'Thank you.'

He picked up the last pencil and took all three of them to a locker nearby, stashing them safely inside before returning to the door.

'Hands, please.'

Again she obeyed, allowing him to cuff her. Only then did he finally unlock the door and lead her away down a white corridor.

'I hate the way everything is so white here,' she said. 'It's annoying.'

'It's not supposed to be annoying, Dorothy,' Mr Bates replied. 'It's white so it looks all fresh and clean, and to keep our guests calm.'

'It doesn't make me calm.' Her fingers twitched. 'It just makes me think of blank paper that's waiting to be written on.'

'What colour would you find calming, Dorothy?' he asked, steering her round a corner. 'A nice pale blue perhaps?'

'Red,' she said dreamily. 'I'd like all the walls to be red.'

He didn't ask why. They walked the rest of the way in silence, soon arriving at a door. After knocking, Mr Bates escorted her inside and she was seated, her feet strapped to the chair legs.

A red-headed lady smiled at her from across a desk. 'Hello, Dorothy.'

'Hello, Dr Rosemary.'

'How are you?'

She chewed her nail, wincing as she bit too hard and tore it, making it bleed. 'I don't like the walls. I want to paint them.'

'How would you like them to look?'

'Red. With words. Or red words.'

Dr Rosemary looked at some papers in front of her. 'I'd like to talk to you about your stories if I may.'

Dorothy giggled, tried to look serious, then giggled again. 'You may.'

'The one called The Paper House. When did you write that?'

'A while ago.'

'Can you remember when?'

She shrugged. 'Last year. On my birthday, I think. But I rewrote it once or twice because it wasn't right.'

'What didn't you like about it?'

'It was just some small details. Like how to keep the fire burning, and how the girl who lit it would escape.'

Dr Rosemary was quiet for a moment. 'The story bears

a lot of similarity to the fire that you started, Dorothy. The paper scrunched up around the rooms, the window in the bedroom being left unlocked. Was it something you'd been thinking about for a long time?'

'Only since I wrote the story.'

'And then you decided you liked the story so much you wanted it to be real?'

Dorothy grinned. 'Maybe.'

'I see. I've been looking through some of your other stories. They were very interesting, too. Especially after speaking to your teachers and classmates. There seem to be other coincidences in the stories that tie in with things that happened at your school and at home. Accidents, people getting hurt, or falling sick. Tell me about these.'

'They were for practise.' Dorothy fidgeted. 'When do I get my stories back?'

'We need to keep them for a while yet. Can you tell me more about what you mean by "practise"?'

'I thought doctors were supposed to be clever?' Dorothy sneered. 'Practise! You know, to learn something and get better at it?'

'So, really, all these earlier stories . . .' Dr Rosemary leafed through some papers. 'Let's see, Poisoned Apples, Pride Before a Fall and Teacher's Pet for example. These were written before the, uh, incidents at school?'

Dorothy drummed her fingers on the arms of the chair. There was a pen on the desk in front of her, but it was out of reach. She wanted it very much.

'Yes. Except for *Pride Before a Fall. Can I* hold that pen?'

'I'm afraid not, Dorothy. So you wrote that one after you pushed Jessica Pride down the stairs?'

'Who says it was me who pushed her?'

Dr Rosemary ignored the comment.

'And the other two stories were written before?'

'Correct.'

'Would you say you preferred writing the stories before or after these things happened?' the doctor asked.

'It depends.'

'On what?'

'Whether a story is for planning or just as a keepsake. You know, to remember.'

'Like a sort of . . . trophy?'

Dorothy pulled against the cuffs. The metal bit into her wrists. 'I want to go back now. These are hurting.'

'They won't hurt if you sit still and don't pull against them. Would you say your stories are trophies?' the doctor repeated.

'I don't know. Maybe, if that's what you want to call them.' Dorothy rolled the word around on her tongue, liking the sound of it. 'Yes, trophies. When do I get them back? I want them.'

'Soon. You can have them soon.'

'Are you sure they're being looked after?' Dorothy asked. Was it her imagination, or did Dr Rosemary look uncomfortable?

'Of course.'

'Because there's one I need to finish,' she complained. 'They took it before it was ready.'

She wasn't imagining it. The doctor's face was reddening.

'Perhaps we could talk about that,' she said. 'I think, going forward, that if we could steer your stories in a different direction, it would greatly improve your chances of recovery.'

'A different direction? You mean you want to tell me what to write?'

'Not tell you, no. But there are some exercises we could try that—'

'I want to finish that one.'

'I don't think that would be helpful to anyone.'

'It would be helpful to me.'

'Well, I don't think it would be helpful for the people that die in that story. Unless you'd be prepared to change the names at least? It's not very nice to use the names of living people. People that know you.'

'Oh, you've read it then? What did you think?'

'I've read everything you've written, Dorothy. Including the story about how you escape from this hospital.' The doctor shuffled her papers. 'I think we should try the exercises I mentioned in our next session. You clearly have a great imagination—'

'I'm not writing what you or anyone else tells me to write. They're my stories.'

Were the cuffs getting tighter? Why were they hurting so much?

106

'Calm down, please. Would you be prepared to give it a go?'

'No. I want that story. Right now!'

The doctor sighed and reached into the file, looking thoughtful. She placed a handful of pages on the desk and spread them out. 'I'll make a deal with you. You can have the story. We'll keep the beginning, but, to continue it, we'll try the exercises. Does that sound fair?'

Dorothy peered at the pages. 'What's that? That's not my story. It's typed.'

'They had to be typed for our files.'

'I want the original.'

'I'm afraid that's not possible—'

'GIVE ME MY STORY!' She threw herself back in the chair, rocking it dangerously, but before it could tip it was caught by burly arms behind her. 'I want my story! I'll write new ones, I swear, and you'll die in all of them—'

Dr Rosemary gave a nod to the burly arms. 'Take her back and give her something to calm her down.'

'Give me a pen!' Dorothy screeched, struggling against her captor. 'Writing about your blood will calm me down! Give me a pen, I said! I'll rip your throat out with my teeth!'

Dr Rosemary stayed seated as Dorothy was dragged from the room, and she remained that way until her screams had faded away down the corridor. Only then did she look down and see her hands pressed so hard against the surface of the desk that her fingertips were white.

She released a long breath and put the papers in a neat pile before sorting through them again. Then she closed the folder, picked up the telephone and dialled a number.

It was answered almost immediately.

'It's me,' she said. 'I've just seen Dorothy Grimes.' She paused. 'No, it ended badly, as usual.' Another pause. 'I'm trying. There may be a chance she'll co-operate, but only if we can continue with a certain story she began before her incarceration. Yes. Yes, that's the one. I know I have it, but it's from the transcript. She's demanding the original.' Frustration crept into her voice. 'Well then, you'd better find it, or else come up with a jolly good forgery! What? I don't see how it could have been mislaid for this long.' She massaged the bridge of her nose. 'It should have been guarded properly! You know how high profile this case is, how many people are sniffing around after those stories. They're not to be seen by the public, whether they're unfinished or not.' She held the phone away from her ear slightly as the voice at the other end rose.

'I think you know more than you're saying. And, if you value our friendship, you'll make sure that story finds its way back here, or it'll be my head on the chopping block!'

She slammed the phone down, breathing hard. She shoved the folder into the cabinet, glad to have it out of sight.

Heads on chopping blocks? That wasn't like her. She shuddered. There was something about Dorothy Grimes that got under her skin, infected everything. Like ink that had seeped into the doctor's veins, slowly poisoning her.

The chapter ended there. I put the pages down, my skin crawling. If Gypsy was here, and Tabitha, then Ramblebrook and Dorothy Grimes could be, too. A man obsessed with unfinished stories and a bloodthirsty girl who had killed, and wanted to keep on killing.

I skimmed the chapter again. From what I'd read before, about Ramblebrook, and the evil story that had made it into the museum, I knew it had to be this one of Dorothy's. If she *was* here, then her aim must be to get her story back.

What lengths would she go to, and how far was Ramblebrook prepared to go to keep it?

Suddenly, I was beginning to see how much trouble Alice's story had unleashed; how much danger she could be in if the characters of the story got to her.

And how much danger it had put me in, too.

8

Melody

IF TOWN HAD BEEN BUSY IN THE AFTERNOON, IT was rammed on Saturday evening. The air was cold, but thick with smokiness and chestnuts and roasting corn. Mum and I clutched warm, fragrant, spiced apple juice, our fingers sticky from accidental spills as people bumped into us.

'Stay close,' Mum kept saying, glancing back at me as I followed her through the crowd. I was busy thinking about Alice's story and looking into the face of every passing stranger, expecting to see Ramblebrook or Dorothy Grimes, which was stupid as I had no idea what they looked like. If Alice had described them, then it was lost with whatever character notes she had, or perhaps in an earlier part of the story. Sometimes she barely mentioned a character's appearance at all. When I asked her why she did this, she said it was for two reasons. Sometimes she preferred to let the reader build up their own picture. Other times she never really even knew herself, seeing only a vague image like in a dream.

Despite this, I felt sure I'd recognise Ramblebrook. I'd imagined a weasel of a man with a long nose and sweaty hands that dampened the pages of the stories he had collected and stolen. Dorothy was harder to picture. In my mind, I couldn't see much more than a tangle of greasy hair and mad eyes staring out from behind it, but that was enough. I didn't want to imagine the rest.

We moved closer to the centre of the square. Behind a safety barrier, the huge bonfire towered above people's heads, a mountain of dry wood waiting to be lit. This wouldn't happen until eight o'clock and, until then, people were queuing up to place their Likenesses on the bonfire. Through gaps in the crowd I caught glimpses of the dolls already in place and there were hundreds: some the size of a regular doll and others not much more than finger puppets.

When I finally reached the front of the queue, Mum waited at the barrier while I slipped through. I strayed further round than I needed to, to be sure I was out of Mum's sight. Once I'd gone far enough, I took the two little figures out of my bag: the decoy Peter Pan, which I threw on carelessly, and then the real one, the one of Alice. I cleared a few twigs aside, making a little hollow, and pushed the Likeness inside, before arranging the twigs back in place.

I glanced back to where Mum was waiting, feeling only

slightly guilty for what I was about to do. I felt a surge of adrenalin as I slipped through the hordes of people and further from her, in the opposite direction. Gradually, the crowd thinned out and it became easier to move. Within a couple of minutes, I stood clear. There was little chance of Mum finding me unless I wanted to be found. I just hoped she wouldn't worry too much – she knew that I could find my way round the town and wouldn't get properly lost. Besides, ever since I could remember, we'd had a meeting point if we became separated: the clock tower in front of the town hall.

I scuttled into Cutpurse Way, in the direction of the bookshop, praying Gypsy was still there as she'd said she would be.

Was she still looking for the story, or had she given up? Why was she looking for it in the first place? And who had told her about it? So many questions. The more I thought about it, the more I realised that one question often wasn't enough. Questions led to *more* questions. I was starting to get worried. If the Summoning *did* work, I didn't think one question would be nearly enough to find Alice.

Chapters had three floors and was full of little nooks and crannies which were perfect for accidentally-on-purpose getting lost in when you wanted an extra few minutes to browse. Not so perfect when you were the one who was looking for someone. After searching the uppermost floor with all the second-hand books and finding no sign of Gypsy, I frantically hunted round the bottom two floors with no more luck. She wasn't there.

My face grew hot. I felt let down and stupid. Mum had always warned me against trusting gypsies after her own experience with Alice's dad. It was starting to look as though she'd been right.

But she promised, a little voice whispered in my head. This Gypsy had to be different, didn't she? She was Alice's after all. The way Alice would want gypsies to be: wise travellers with just a bit of magic about them. Even though Gypsy had promised she'd be there and wasn't.

So where was she? There was one other place I could look – her boat. Could I make it there and back again in time for the Summoning? If I ran as fast as I could, maybe there was time. It wouldn't take a minute to see if she was there. Getting her to help me was a different matter. I couldn't make her do anything if she didn't want to.

Unless I gave her something she wanted in return.

I started to run, my feet pounding over the cobbles. Would it really be so bad to share the story – or what I had left of it – with Gypsy? There was no mention of her within those few pages, and it would give her a reason to trust me. To stay close to me. She didn't need to know she was part of it, not yet.

But how did she even know about it at all?

I needed to find that out. There were a lot of things I needed to find out and, the more I thought about it all, the bigger the headache it was giving me.

I ducked into a nearby alleyway, one I noticed every time we passed it, because of its name: Mad Alice Lane. It was definitely an alleyway and not a lane, but it cut through to more shops on the other side. Every time I'd passed it with Alice, she did something kooky, whether it was quoting lines from *Through the Looking-Glass* or cackling like a demon. Then she would shout, 'I'm Alice and I'm mad!' so that it would echo off the walls.

My throat ached suddenly. *Alice, where are you?*

I came to the other end of the alley. It was busy here, too, with people crowding round someone playing a flute. I went to move past, then stopped. The hairs on the back of my neck stood on end as the melody caught my attention.

I knew that tune. It was Alice's tune, the one she'd been humming all day yesterday, like it was stuck in her head.

I moved towards the sound. It was more tuneful than Alice's humming had been, with little bits added in here and there, but it was definitely the same melody. I still couldn't see the player, but people were throwing coins and I could hear soft clinks as they landed on cloth.

I followed the sound, squeezing past people, treading on toes, but no one seemed to take much notice as I wove my way to the front.

When I saw who was playing the flute, my fingers curled into the palms of my hands, making fists in my coat pockets. It was *him*. The boy who'd bumped into me earlier. The one who had stolen Alice's story.

I looked at him more closely. I could see now that he reminded me of someone: a boy Alice had liked for a long time, but whose name I couldn't remember. He had the same tanned skin and shiny hair, cut short at the sides, but with a long fringe that fell across his eyes. He was not that boy, but he *was* playing Alice's melody.

I waited as he drew out the final few notes of the tune, then bowed. There was a gaping silence. Then, slowly, as though they were dazed, people began to clap. I didn't join in. There was something a little eerie about their expressions, something a little too glassy about their eyes that I didn't like, and a feeling about the whole thing that bothered me.

I was on the verge of working it out when I noticed a figure a short distance away who, like me, was motionless. She stood with her arms folded, watching the musician through narrowed eyes.

I'd found Gypsy Spindle after all.

9
Piper

WHEN IT BECAME CLEAR THAT THE BOY didn't intend to play anything more, people began drifting away. All except Gypsy and me. We watched as he slid the flute into a slim leather case, then knelt and began scooping the money up. He had the same expression on his face that I'd noticed before: a slight smirk that twisted his lips. I could feel my temper rising and, before I knew what I was doing, I had stepped forward and brought my foot down on a cluster of coins just as the boy was reaching for them.

'Hey,' I said. 'I want to talk to you.'

He looked up, annoyed.

''Scuse you.' He waved his hand as if to shoo me away. 'That's mine.'

I didn't move. 'It's annoying, isn't it?' I said loudly. 'When someone takes something that doesn't belong to them.' I held out my hand expectantly.

116

He shook his head, his silky hair sweeping into his eyes. He brushed it away and stared back at me. I searched his face for any sign that he recognised me, but there was none. His eyes were dark brown, like bitter chocolate.

'Sorry. No idea what you're on about.' He lowered his gaze and moved to a different patch of coins. 'I earned this money fair and square.'

'I don't care about your money. I'm talking about the notebook you stole from me earlier!'

There was the slightest of pauses before he shrugged. 'Still no clue what you're on about. You got the wrong—'

'I *know* it was you.' I crouched in front of him. 'You bumped into me this afternoon, but it wasn't an accident. You stole a notebook from my rucksack and I want it back. Right now.'

The boy's chin jutted out defiantly. 'Never stole nothing.' He motioned to the money on the ground. 'No need to – I make my own money.'

Gypsy kicked a coin from where she stood. It skittered towards him, then rolled in neat little circles at his feet. The boy spun round, noticing her for the first time. His eyebrows shot up in surprise.

'Well, well. The one and only Gypsy Spindle.' He got to his feet. 'Last person I was expecting to see here.'

'You two know each other?' I asked, unable to help myself. I realised then that this had to be the street performer mentioned in Alice's character notes. I wished again that I'd paid more attention to those names, for once

117

again I couldn't recall it. I glanced from the boy to Gypsy, fearful now as well as angry. Had he read it? Did he know?

Gypsy moved closer. She seemed to look even more like Alice than I remembered. She nodded and scowled.

'Now, now,' said the boy. 'No need for that.'

Gypsy wrote something in her notebook but the boy made no attempt to look at it. Annoyed, I read it aloud to him.

'Piper, whatever you took just give it back, will you?'

'What makes you think I took anything?'

Gypsy folded her arms, staring at him.

Piper threw his belongings over his shoulder. 'Fine.' He glanced at me. 'I haven't got it any more. I got rid of it, all right?'

There was something about the way he said it that made me believe him – but that still didn't explain why he'd taken it. Was he a thief and by unlucky chance I'd been picked as a victim? Or did he know what the notebook contained?

'No. *Not* all right.' Hot fury bubbled up inside me. I marched up to him and jabbed him in the chest. He stepped back, shocked, but not quite as shocked as I was. I'd always been meek; at school I was usually the one who tried to break up the fights. I knew I shouldn't be doing this. Piper was older than me, and bigger, and he clearly didn't like being poked. But I was too angry to care, and all I could think of was that I had to do *something*.

'That notebook belongs to my sister and I need it,' I said. 'She's missing and I think it might have a clue about where she is. So, wherever you dumped it, you can just take me there RIGHT NOW!'

'Quite sparky for a littlun, ain't you?' Piper stared at me through his long fringe and I thought I saw a grudging respect there. 'What makes you think I dumped it?'

'Because . . . you probably thought it was a purse or wallet,' I blustered. 'And once you realised it was worthless—'

'Who said it was worthless?' Piper asked. 'I never said that. I was paid good money to nick that notebook.'

'*What?*' I gasped. 'Someone . . . someone *paid* you to steal it? Who?'

He shrugged. 'The only question I was interested in was the price, and the price was right.'

'You . . . you *idiot!*' I spluttered. An icy dread took hold of me. 'You don't realise what you've done!'

A trace of guilt crept into his eyes and for a moment it seemed he was about to say something, offer an apology perhaps, but then Gypsy held up something for us to read.

I'm sure your sister will turn up. The notebook can't be the only clue.

'You don't understand . . .' I trailed off, still too angry with Piper, and myself for being the one to let the notebook go, to think clearly. I couldn't risk blowing it; I needed Gypsy's help, but one wrong word would ruin everything.

'Alice is a writer,' I said finally. 'She often bases her stories on things that have happened to her, or are important to her. So I figured that if there's somewhere secret she could have gone, or perhaps someone she could be with, it might be mentioned in the notebook.'

Gypsy nodded. *Makes sense.*

'There's more.' I felt short of breath, like I'd been running very, very fast.

Gypsy indicated that she was listening. Out of the corner of my eye, I noticed that Piper was, too.

'The notebook was her latest story,' I said. 'The one she was working on when she went missing. But it's not just any story, it's a novel. Her *first* novel. Months and months of work.'

Gypsy nodded. *I understand. Of course you'd want to get it back.*

'That's just it, though,' I said. 'You don't understand. There's something else going on here, something crazy . . . or magical.'

Gypsy smiled. *Lucky for you I believe in magic.*

'Alice's novel is called *The Museum of Unfinished Stories*,' I said quietly.

Her smile faded. I had her attention now.

How did you know that's the title of the book I'm looking for?

'I saw it written down earlier,' I admitted. 'In the bookshop. I didn't say anything then, because it seemed too odd. I wasn't sure you'd believe me.' I lowered my eyes, uncomfortable with this half-truth.

Why should I believe you now? Gypsy wrote, her eyes untrusting. *It seems convenient that you want my help, and you suddenly say you know about the book I've been searching for.*

'That's why I didn't tell you straight away,' I said. 'Something weird is going on and that notebook is part of it. So, if you want it as much as I do, then you'll help me find it!'

I do want it. Very much. So I suppose I have no choice but to trust you. She sighed. *It's not like I'm getting anywhere by asking in bookshops: no one's ever heard of it. It makes sense that it hasn't even been published yet.*

'So you believe me?' I asked.

Gypsy chewed her lip in the same way Alice did when she was trying to make up her mind about something, then nodded.

Piper muttered something under his breath. I glanced at him. He was rolling a pebble under his boot, staring at the ground.

'What did you say?' I asked.

'I said it *is* the truth,' he repeated. 'I had a look through the notebook before I . . . before I passed it on.'

'How much did you see?' My voice was high-pitched, scratchy with fear. What if he'd read it? What if he *knew*?

Piper looked uncomfortable. 'At the front it had the title. One of the words was "museum".' He kicked the pebble into the gutter.

'*One* of the words?' I asked, confused.

'It was the only word I recognised.'

There was a moment of silence in which I understood a second before he lost his temper.

'Because the title was in capitals!' he snarled. 'The rest of it was in joined-up writing, so I didn't . . . couldn't . . .'

'Oh,' I said softly. 'You *couldn't* read it.'

'So?' he snapped. 'You think that makes me stupid?'

'No.' I didn't think it, either. It just made *me* incredibly lucky.

If Piper couldn't read, he wouldn't have seen what – or who – the story was about. The secret was safe, for now.

Piper rubbed his nose and sniffed. 'It was pages and pages. Little drawings and stuff. Must've been months of work, just like you said.'

I couldn't help feel a bit sorry for him. He'd admitted stealing the notebook without putting up much of a fight, but confessing that he couldn't read must have been harder for him. Despite this, I still felt cross. If it weren't for him, I'd still have the notebook. For a second time, I thought it seemed like he was about to say something, but the clock tower chimed the hour just then, and an expectant silence fell over the town.

'I've got to go,' I said. 'My mum is looking for me; she'll be worried.'

I stared into Gypsy's clear green eyes. She was still watching Piper, deep in thought. There was no pity on her face, only coldness.

'Are you still going to help me?' I asked. 'You said you would.' I paused. 'Why weren't you at the bookshop?'

I only left to get a drink. I was just about to go back when I saw him. She jerked her head towards Piper, then sighed.

122

I'll help. But are you sure your mother is going to believe this? Me pretending to be Alice?

'Why wouldn't she?' I said.

Aren't you forgetting something? she wrote. *My voice. Unless Alice can't speak, either.*

'Let me do the talking,' I said. 'Unless you have to. If you do, pretend you're doing research for a story, about someone who can't speak.' I looked her up and down. 'We need to make you look a bit more like Alice.'

How?

'Tie your hair back and take those little plaits out,' I said. 'And take off your jewellery.' She did, combing the tiny plaits out with her fingers and sweeping her hair back. I gasped as her neck came into view. There, just below her ear, was a small tattoo of a scorpion with its tail curved over its back. I stared at it, stricken. I'd completely forgotten about that.

'Wait, no, put your hair down again, but mess it up a bit. Mum will go mad if she sees that on your neck.'

Gypsy rolled her eyes, but did as I'd said.

'That's better.' I studied her. 'We can't do much about the clothes.'

Gypsy frowned. *What's wrong with my clothes?*

'They're just ... not what Alice would wear,' I said. *Though they were clearly what she'd* want *to wear if she were brave enough.* 'Let's go. We can talk about the rest on the way. You, too,' I called to Piper, who'd started to slink away.

He turned, cocky again. 'I'm not sure Gypsy wants me around.'

The look on her face suggested she agreed, but in her notebook she wrote:

We're not going anywhere without him. He's coming, too.

I repeated the message to him.

Piper grinned. Some of his teeth were a little crooked, but it was a charming grin nonetheless, although wasted on Gypsy.

For a long moment, they stared at each other and, though no words were exchanged, an unspoken message passed between them. I could sense it. Gypsy's was a cold loathing and something else . . . hurt? What had he done to her? Piper's face was harder to read past his ever-present smirk. But there was more warmth in his eyes.

'Aw, I never knew you felt that way about me,' he said at last.

Gypsy stabbed at her notepad. Her writing had become jagged and ugly.

'She says she doesn't,' I said. 'That's underlined. She says you know more than you're telling us, and that she's not letting you out of her sight.'

'Oh, does she?' Piper's grin was gone. 'And what makes you think I take orders from you, Gypsy Spindle?'

I waited for Gypsy to finish. My eyes strained in the gloom of the evening to make out the words. Hatred seeped off the page.

'Because of what you took,' I began.

The blush that had coloured Piper's cheeks only moments earlier drained away, leaving him grey.

'You have a debt to repay and it starts here.'

He lowered his eyes and nodded. Then, like a dog that had been kicked, he skulked after us.

My eyes darted from Piper to Gypsy and back again, trying to figure out what was going on. What could Piper have taken? It must have been something huge if Gypsy had such a hold over him. Had she witnessed whatever he'd stolen and was threatening to rat on him?

None of us spoke. We passed through Mad Alice Lane and went towards the square. I was aware of Piper's presence at my back, the hiss of his breath over the top of my head. Having him so close made me want to pat my pockets, but I stopped myself. There was nothing in them worth stealing.

'It's started,' I said, pointing to the sky. Thick smoke drifted in the air above. We headed for the clock tower, skirting round the edge of the crowd as far as possible until there was no choice but to break into the thick of it.

'Stay together,' I told them.

I slipped my hand into Gypsy's. It was only slightly bigger than mine, and cold and dry to the touch. She didn't seem to mind.

I spotted Mum before she saw us, waving to get her attention. We pushed the rest of the way through to her, and I was glad to see she looked more relieved than annoyed, which meant less of a telling-off. There were a few cross words and questions, but I quickly put an end to them with the fib I'd thought up.

'I was almost at the clock tower when I saw Alice,' I said, realising I was speaking a little too quickly, the way I always did when I told a lie.

'I was wondering when you were going to show up, young lady,' Mum said to Gypsy. 'Next time you decide to disappear all day, leave a note, will you?'

Gypsy nodded. I held my breath, waiting for something to go wrong, for Mum to notice her eyes or something else we'd overlooked, but it was too dark and smoky for that. Luck was on our side and, besides, there was no reason for Mum to think she was seeing anyone other than her daughter.

'Is that a new jacket?' Mum asked.

Gypsy nodded.

'It suits you.' Mum nodded approvingly, then noticed Piper lurking behind me. 'Alice, who's your friend? I don't think we've met.'

I held my breath as Gypsy flipped open her pad and began to write. I peered over her shoulder, with quick glances at Mum. She was distracted by the smoking pyre in the town centre, but kept sneaking looks at the boy behind me.

His name is Piper, Gypsy had written. *I met him at the library. He's helping me with the story I'm working on.*

'That's nice, dear. Why are you writing things down instead of talking? Have you got a sore throat? It is quite smoky, I must say.'

Gypsy shook her head and wrote something else.

It's for research. I'm writing about a character who can't speak.

Mum rolled her eyes, but her smile was fond, if a little sad. She was used to Alice doing odd things to get 'in character' as she called it, but I guessed she must be reminded of Alice's father. 'You do the daftest things for your stories.'

Her voice was muffled, lost in a crackle of dry wood rising up around us. A faint orange glow lit up the faces of people in front, growing stronger until the flames were visible and the crackling of the fire became a roar. Likenesses blackened and charred like tiny, wingless birds tangled in a giant nest. I thought of the Alice Likeness, tucked inside the twigs like an egg waiting to hatch. Had she burned yet, or was she still smouldering?

Sparks flew through the air like tiny sprites, glowing and fizzing, and I felt as if some had gone into my tummy and were fizzing there, too. One by one, the lamps lighting the square blinked out. The town glowed amber. This was the signal. It was time to say the words: the words spoken on this night every year. I knew them by heart.

'When straw and cloth burn to ash
And the smoke reaches the ends of the earth to find them
They will be Summoned.
For one night
No more, no less
To answer a single question
No more, no less.'

I thought of Alice and wondered if it could happen. If she *could* be Summoned. If the magic was real. What was the one question that would unlock the mystery of where she was?

The heat of the rising flames warmed my cheeks. Something hissed within the bonfire and twisted free, shooting up into the air in a shower of silver sparks. They streaked through the smoke, glittering like sequins, then rained down over the flames. Some of them drifted over the heads of the people in front, fanned towards me by the breeze, and, as they got closer, I saw they were white-hot flecks of ash. For a split second, they seemed to be letters tumbling through the air like broken words. I blinked and they were ash again, fading as the heat left them. I thought of the pages I'd stuffed in the Alice Likeness.

A murmur went through the crowd, of excitement and confusion. Had others seen it, too? It was going to work. At that moment, I felt absolutely certain that Alice would come to us, because I knew that some magic *is* real.

I only had to look at Gypsy and Piper for proof of that.

10
Mistaken Identity

T HE LAMPS ABOVE OUR HEADS FLICKERED BACK
on. A few people began to drift away, but many
stayed, eager to make the most of the atmosphere
and the shops being open later than usual.

Mum went off to buy us paper cones of sweet roasted
nuts. We stood in silence, not quite sure what to do next.
Piper would clearly rather have been anywhere else and
looked like a snared fox that was thinking about chewing
off its own leg in order to escape, but whatever power it was
that Gypsy held over him kept him there.

Once he took his flute out and brought it to his lips,
but Gypsy swiped it away from his mouth and scribbled
something down, holding it out for me to read.

'She said put your flute away,' I said slowly. 'And don't
try any of your tricks with us, or she'll snap it under her
boot.'

Piper put the flute away sulkily. I watched him,

remembering the eerie faces of the people who had been throwing coins to him earlier. Had he been using the music to cast some kind of spell? Charming their money from them? What was he trying to do now – escape?

When Mum returned, she handed out the treats, then glanced at Gypsy. 'I have to go now, my darlings. My car to the airport will be picking me up soon. But you two stay out and enjoy the evening. Not too late, though.'

Gypsy nodded.

Mum eyed Piper. I could tell she didn't much like the look of him. 'No guests tonight, either.'

I looked over Gypsy's shoulder as she wrote something.

Don't worry, I'll take care of everything.

Mum kissed the both of us, then shrugged her handbag further up her shoulder and left. We watched her go in silence. Gypsy held her fingers to her cheek where Mum had kissed her, like she had forgotten what a kiss felt like.

'Now what?' I asked.

Gypsy shook her head slightly, as if shaking a cobweb or a memory away.

We find somewhere quiet to sit and have a drink, she wrote. *Piper's paying. And then he's going to tell us everything he knows about that story and who he stole it for.*

We found a stall and each got a frothy hot chocolate with cream and marshmallows, then sat on some stone steps nearby. They were cold and damp and within seconds my bottom was freezing. I shivered, hoping we wouldn't be long.

130

If the Summoning had worked, we needed to be home in time for midnight; that's when the Summoned were supposed to appear. I wanted to be in Alice's room, around her things, if she did come. I needed to plan what to say. I sipped the hot chocolate, too anxious to enjoy it, but glad of its warmth in my hands.

Luckily, Gypsy wasn't planning on wasting any time. She settled next to me, indicating that I should read out the questions she'd written.

'Who told you to steal the notebook?' I asked.

Piper stared at me, a slight sneer about his mouth, then he looked away. He'd refused to sit down, instead leaning against a wooden door set back in the wall.

'A woman,' he said finally. 'Well, a girl, I s'pose.'

I frowned. Gypsy made another note.

'Which is it?' I read. 'A girl or a woman?'

'A girl,' said Piper. 'About Gypsy's age, maybe a bit older. She was small, thin.' He bumped his shoulder into the door like he wanted it to open and reveal an escape route. 'I . . . I didn't like her. Proper creepy, she was.'

'Describe her.'

Piper drained his paper cup, then crushed it in his fist and dropped it. Gypsy shot him a loathsome look, but it was wasted. When he spoke, his breath misted the air.

'I just did.'

Try harder.

He shrugged. 'Sort of pretty if you looked at her quick. In a plastic kind of way.' He paused, glancing in Gypsy's direction. 'Not . . . not natural. But when she spoke to me that's when I saw her properly and she just looked . . . weird. Like a doll that had been put together wrong. Her clothes were too big, like they belonged to someone else.'

I waited tensely for him to go on, a feeling of dread spreading in the pit of my stomach. Gypsy sighed in a way that suggested she was finding none of this very helpful. *What else?* She wrote. *Hairstyle, scars?*

I repeated this aloud to Piper.

'Black hair, too neat like a wig. Bright red lipstick.'

Dolly. The hot chocolate curdled in my stomach. I put the cup down, feeling sick. She'd known there was no way I'd give her the notebook – or that she'd even get near me again after I'd run – so she'd sent Piper instead.

Gypsy made a note.

'And her eyes were like blue glass.' He picked at a flake of paint on the door. 'I didn't see her blink once. But it was her hands that really got to me.'

I read out Gypsy's next question, my voice hoarse. 'What about them?'

At this, Piper shuddered. 'She had gloves on at first, but she took them off when she paid me. Her hands were just . . . *black*. Rotten with oil, or dirt or something. And her nails were bitten, ripped off right down as far as they could go, all bloody and scabbed round the edges.' He grimaced. 'But it was good money, or I'd have told her to forget it.' He looked at me, then Gypsy. Both of us were glaring. 'Knew it was a bad idea,' he muttered.

Boohoo, Gypsy wrote, which I didn't read out. *Where did you meet her and what did she say?*

Piper folded his arms. 'I'd pitched up in the square for a while, over there.' He nodded to the other side of the roaring bonfire. 'She asked me how much money I'd made.' He allowed himself a small smirk. 'I thought about telling her to keep her nose out, but I'd had a good afternoon, so I told her. Added on a bit extra for good measure, like. She said she'd double it if I collected something for her.'

An angry noise escaped my lips, something between a bark and a hiccup. '*Collect?*'

'Yeah.' The corners of his mouth turned down. 'I knew it wouldn't be nothing good, not for that amount of money, but it was easier than I thought it'd be.'

'What *were* you expecting?' I asked, curious.

'From the state of her hands, I thought she'd been trying to dig something up. Something buried maybe. So, when she said what she wanted, it didn't seem a big deal. Easy just to take something from a kid.'

'Did she describe me to you?' I asked.

Piper shook his head. 'Nah. She just pointed. You were walking through the town square right at that moment.'

The sensation I had then was as though a large spider had crawled over the back of my neck. So, even when I thought I'd escaped Dolly earlier, I'd been wrong. She'd been watching me from a distance. But how did she even know who I was? Had she been watching before today, too?

'She came up to me earlier,' I said quietly. 'She was trying to get me to give the notebook to her – she told me her name was Dolly and that she was a friend of Alice's. I didn't believe her.'

What would she want with the notebook, though? Gypsy wrote.

Piper shrugged. 'Seems like there's a lot of people who want it. Gypsy, you and this Dolly. And, if you lot want it, then there's bound to be more who are looking for it, too.'

I didn't like the idea of that at all.

Gypsy flapped the notepad, drawing everyone's attention back.

What about the notebook? What did it look like? How big was it?

'Pretty small,' said Piper. 'But thick, and well made, not cheap. Stitched together, not glued, but so well used the binding was falling apart. Some pages were missing.'

I kept my eyes on Piper, not daring to look at Gypsy. I couldn't let her know I had the missing pages. They were all I had. I didn't want to risk losing them, too.

How many were missing? My voice croaked as I read.

Piper fidgeted, looking uncomfortable. I wondered, as he couldn't read, if maybe he was unable to count, either. 'I dunno.' He held a thumb and forefinger a tiny distance apart.

Gypsy seemed to be doing a small sum in her head. She scribbled something, then tapped the page.

Probably only sixteen pages.

'What makes you think that?' I asked. Her accurate guess unnerved me.

Gypsy wrote impatiently. *It's to do with how books are made. My father worked with someone who repaired books. A bookbinder. Sometimes I'd talk to her and she'd tell me about her work. That's how I know. But it's just a guess.*

'Gypsy?' Piper's voice was low. He was half hidden in the shadow of the doorway. 'I'm ... sorry, all right? If I'd known you were looking for that story, I'd never have given it away.'

Gypsy stared at him, her expression unreadable. Perhaps, like me, she was wondering if he was genuinely sorry, or just trying to make things easier on himself.

'You didn't give it away,' I said huffily. 'You sold it! And don't ever tell me how much you were paid, because it'll never, ever be enough!'

Piper shrank back further into the shadows as if they could shield him, but it just made me angrier.

'Anyway, why are you saying sorry to Gypsy? *I* was the one you stole from. Me! That notebook belongs to my sister, who's missing. And that story is more important than you can possibly know!' I broke off as Gypsy took my hand. It was trembling with anger.

'I can make it up to you.' Piper's voice was low, unexpected. There was no trace of arrogance now. If anything, he sounded a little afraid.

'How?' I muttered. 'Not that you can make things much worse.'

Piper slid down the door and rested on his haunches.

'I think Gypsy was right. There weren't that many pages missing when I took it. But before ... before I handed it over ... I pulled out another section.'

'*What?*'

Gypsy sat bolt upright. She began writing frantically.

You'd better not be lying.

'I'm not,' he said. 'I swear.'

'Where is it?' I asked. 'Show us.'

'I ain't got it on me. I knew she'd be suspicious if some of it was missing and ask me to turn out my stuff, so I stashed it.'

Where? Gypsy scrawled.

He swallowed. 'Somewhere close. It's safe.'

'Why did you take it?' I asked.

'Dunno. I hadn't meant to. I only thought of it when I saw part of the book was already missing. I thought if some pages were gone it wouldn't hurt to take a few more.' He stopped, clearly reluctant to finish.

'Go on,' I pressed.

'I could tell how bad she wanted it,' he continued. 'It made me wonder who else might want it, too.' His hair flopped over his eyes, but he left it there. 'I figured it wouldn't hurt to keep some of it as a sort of ... leverage.'

Gypsy looked as if someone had dangled a dead rat under her nose.

'Yeah, yeah,' Piper said, his mouth set in a sulky, vicious line. 'I know what you think of me. But at least I told you. I could've kept quiet.'

Gypsy clambered to her feet.

136

'Where are you going?' Piper asked.

Take us to wherever you stashed the pages, she wrote. *I want to see them.*

'Now?'

Why wait?

'Perhaps we *should* wait,' I said quickly, trying to keep the worry out of my voice. If the pages Piper had taken mentioned Gypsy, or him, it could be disastrous. I also had another reason for wanting to delay it. 'We still don't know anything about Dolly. She was watching me before. What if she's watching us now?'

Piper's dark eyes darted about. 'He's right. We should wait till tomorrow; it'd be easier for us to be followed and not realise it tonight when it's dark. We could be leading her straight to it.'

Gypsy huffed out an impatient breath, then nodded reluctantly.

'So now what?' Piper asked.

'I need to get home,' I said. 'There's not much else we can do tonight.'

Except wait for Alice to be Summoned, I thought, but kept this to myself in case Gypsy asked to listen in. But, as it turned out, Gypsy had another request.

Perhaps there are other clues in Alice's work somewhere, she wrote. *Even if it's not the story itself, there could be notes, pictures, or something. I should come with you.*

'What about me?' Piper enquired. 'Take it I can go now?'

He was rewarded with a withering look from Gypsy.

137

You're coming with us, she wrote.

'*Him?* At my house?' I said doubtfully.

He's more slippery than a slug in a bowl of jelly. And until we have those missing pages I don't want him out of my sight.

'All right.' I shot him a warning look. 'But if anything goes missing, even a crumb, I'll know who to blame.'

We got up and moved through the town. Only a few people remained now and most of the streets were empty. Litter was strewn across the cobbles and we followed it like a trail until we reached the corner of Cuckoo Lane. I stared past the shop, now closed, to our house a short way down. It would be empty now, apart from Twitch . . . and Tabitha, if she was still where I'd left her asleep earlier. No Alice, no Mum and no Dad. I thought back to this morning when I'd seen Gypsy for the first time.

'What were you doing here today?' I asked her. 'You looked like you were staring at our house.'

Gypsy slowed a little as she wrote her response. I slowed with her.

It seemed familiar. The house and the street. It looks a lot like the one I grew up in.

'Thought your ma said she was going away?' Piper interrupted.

'She is.' I gazed at the house and stopped walking. It should have been in darkness, but it wasn't. A light was on in the attic.

'Alice's room,' I whispered. 'Someone's there . . . maybe she's back!'

My legs felt stringy and clumsy as I raced to the front door, my feet slapping loudly on the path and then the hallway tiles. Was Alice really home? What would happen if she came face to face with two of her characters?

A draught whistled through my hair as I flew up the stairs and thumped up the ladder to the attic. Behind me, I heard two sets of footsteps on the stairs: the real sounds of imaginary people.

'Alice?' I called. 'Alice, are you up here?'

I crawled into the attic. When I saw Alice's room, a small cry escaped my throat.

It was empty, but someone had been in there all right.

Alice's desk was swept clear. Her inspiration wall was plucked bare, notes and photos drifting about the room like loose feathers. Notebooks were strewn all over the floor, some open like fallen birds. Her beautiful old typewriter lay on its side next to her little tea tray. A used tea bag was split open on the floor. I stared at the smeared tea leaves, wishing I could read whatever answers they may have held, but finding only more questions.

I stared at the wreckage, aware of low voices on the landing below, and a dull, repetitive thumping noise, but they all seemed so far away.

I shrieked as something moved in the corner of my vision, a dark shape slinking out from under Alice's bed. A black cat stared up at me, quivering and wide-eyed.

I scooped it up in my arms, burying my face in its fur.

139

'Twitch!' My voice was muffled. 'Thank goodness you're all right!'

'No, not Twitch, I'm afraid,' said Tabitha from the depths of my hug. 'She's gone.'

'No wonder,' I said hoarsely, still clinging to Tabitha. 'She must have been terrified. She ran away once before when there was a bad storm.'

'Who are you talking to?' Piper called, but I was too upset to answer him.

'No,' said Tabitha, wriggling out of my grasp. She landed delicately on all fours, then sat and curled her tail round her feet. 'She didn't run away . . . she was taken.'

'But . . . why?'

Tabitha's golden eyes were solemn. 'I thought that was obvious. I believe she was mistaken for me.'

11

Alice in the Looking Glass

'SO WHOEVER TOOK TWITCH ... THEY REALLY wanted you?' I asked. 'Why?'

'I have no idea,' Tabitha answered. She licked her paw and smoothed it over her ear, like a lady fussing with her hair.

'Did you see who it was?'

'Not from where I was hiding, no,' the cat replied. 'I was asleep, but all the crashing and thumping woke me.' She glanced about at the mess. 'Whatever it was they were looking for, I don't think they found it.'

I stared at the wreckage of Alice's room and had a pretty good idea of what they'd been searching for. 'If they were looking for something in this room, why would they want you?'

'How should I know?' Tabitha said haughtily. 'Why *wouldn't* they want me? That's a better question. Talking cats are quite out of the ordinary here apparently.' She sighed. 'I really should stop speaking to strangers; it's a bad habit.'

I gave her a cold look. 'Yes. A habit that's probably got Twitch catnapped. Didn't it cross your mind to tell them they were taking the wrong cat?'

'And get *myself* catnapped? I think not. They'll realise their mistake soon enough and let her go, I would imagine. No harm done.'

'That's the problem,' I said. 'You *think*, but you don't know. How can we be sure Twitch is safe? What were you doing up here anyway?'

The cat blinked insolently. 'Napping, like I said.'

'You can't just come and go as you please,' I said. 'It's bad manners.'

'Speaking of manners,' said Tabitha, 'I could murder a cup of tea.'

Once again, I felt the cat was being deliberately awkward and I decided I didn't trust her. Not one bit.

'Fine. Don't touch anything. We should check the rest of the house.'

We climbed down the ladder. Piper and Gypsy were already downstairs, for we could hear their footsteps wandering from room to room. A quick glance in the bedrooms told us they hadn't been interfered with, and before we even began down the stairs I had the feeling it was only Alice's room that had been ransacked. The rest of the house was untouched.

In the living room, a light was flashing on the phone. Someone had left a message. *Alice?* I grabbed it and pressed the button, holding my breath, but it wasn't Alice's voice I heard. It was Dad's. As always, he kept things short, telling a couple of silly jokes, and said he was coming home in two weeks. I clung to the receiver, wishing he were here now. I played the message twice, just to hear his voice. Then I hung up, feeling even more alone.

Piper and Gypsy were in the kitchen. There we found the cause of the thumping noise I'd noticed up in the attic, as well as the draught I'd felt when we'd first entered the house. The back door was open, flapping like a useless wing. The lock had been broken.

'We heard it banging from upstairs,' Piper said. 'That's why we came down. We didn't touch it in case you want to call the police.'

I shook my head dully. 'No point. I don't think anything's been taken.' Apart from the cat, but I couldn't exactly report that, not with Tabitha as the only witness. People stole pedigrees, not smelly old moggies with bad teeth.

'Can you fix the door?' I asked Piper.

'Me?' He looked doubtful. 'Dunno. I'm more of a breaker than a maker.'

Gypsy came over and inspected the lock. *I think I can fix it. Do you have any tools?*

I fetched the toolbox from the cupboard under the stairs. Piper looked relieved as she set to work. He pulled out a chair and sat down at the table.

'Who were you talking to upstairs?' he asked. 'Is your sister back?'

'No,' I said. 'Alice definitely isn't back.'

'So who . . . oh, hello.'

Tabitha had jumped on to the table and sat in front of him, looking at the teapot expectantly. Piper lifted his hand and ran it along the cat's tail.

'And what's your name, puss?' he murmured.

'Tabitha,' she replied, flicking her tail. 'Who are you?'

'Whoa!' Piper jumped up from his chair, scraping it along the kitchen floor. 'How did that . . . I mean, what—?'

'Whoops,' said the cat. 'See what I mean?'

'For goodness' sake,' I snapped. 'You can't keep quiet for five minutes, can you?'

'I can't help it, I'm thirsty,' Tabitha complained. 'And I've had a shock. It's hard to concentrate when I'm parched.'

'I'm making your tea now.' I filled up the kettle and threw a handful of tea bags into the pot.

'Lovely,' said the cat. 'Milk and two sugars. Sweet tea is good for shock.'

'It d-drinks tea?' said Piper. 'What kind of a cat drinks *tea*?'

'The kind that talks,' I said sarcastically. 'You've never met a cat that talks before?'

'Not since I was a kid,' said Piper. 'I thought they'd all been rounded up and killed.'

It was my turn to stare.

'You've seen cats that talk before?' I asked, unsure if he was fooling me.

'You haven't?'

'No.'

He shrugged, taking his seat again. 'Like I said, I haven't seen any for years.'

Gypsy drew closer to the table, nibbling her lip. Seeing her now, in our house, it was hard to believe she wasn't Alice.

Piper nodded to Tabitha. 'When was the last time you saw a mischief?'

'A mischief?' I asked.

'That's what they're called,' said Piper. 'Cos they usually lead to trouble.'

Gypsy shrugged. *Not since I was a little girl.*

'I'm not mischievous,' said the cat. 'I just want a quiet life with lots of naps and the odd cup of tea.'

You shouldn't keep these cats, Gypsy wrote. *You can get into a lot of trouble where I'm from if you're found harbouring them.*

'It's not my cat,' I said, setting a cup of tea in front of Tabitha. 'It just arrived out of . . .' I caught myself in time. 'Out of nowhere.'

'Must still be a few out there then,' Piper said. 'Even if people don't realise it. Making out they're ordinary cats.' His mouth twisted as he observed Tabitha lapping daintily from her teacup. 'Ones that are better at it, too.'

'You said you can get into trouble for having them where you come from,' I said. I slid into a chair next to where Gypsy stood. 'Where is that?'

Gypsy set her notebook on the table and sat down. *Everywhere and nowhere,* she wrote. *I go where the waters take me. But I grew up in a town called Twisted Wood, and the house I lived in was like this.* She looked round the kitchen. *A lot like this.*

'What brought you to Fiddler's Hollow?' I asked.

I don't know. I must have taken a wrong turn somewhere. This town isn't on any of my maps; that's why I moored and got out to ask directions. She frowned. *It's like this place doesn't exist.*

I stared at the woodgrain in the table surface, imagining that the lines were roads leading to faraway places: places that were only real in Alice's imagination. How soon before Gypsy figured out that it was her map that didn't exist, not Fiddler's Hollow?

'How about you, Piper?' I asked.

'I didn't mean to come here, either.' His dark eyebrows knotted together. 'I was hitch-hiking. Didn't really care where I was going as long as it was south. This is where I ended up.' He glanced at Gypsy. 'On exactly the same day as you.'

Gypsy looked at each of us in turn, seeming to shrink in her chair. She thought for a moment, then started to write.

Something weird is going on here. The last time I saw Piper was six years ago, and now he turns up on the same day as I do in a town that doesn't exist, as well as a mischief. The story I've been searching for turns out to be unfinished, and written by your sister, who happens to look exactly like me. Not only that, but someone else wants this story, too. Badly. She looked at me, hard. *Are you sure there's nothing else you should have told me?*

146

I forced myself to look at her, certain she knew I was squirming. 'Odd things have been happening ever since Alice went missing. I don't know what's happening, either, or why.'

A gust of wind shook the back door, rattling us all.

Gypsy stood up and went over to it, examining the broken lock. She took a screwdriver from the toolbox and began to work on it. Splinters of wood around the lock came away like loose teeth.

'I don't want to stay here tonight,' I said, before I could stop myself. 'It doesn't feel safe any more.'

The cat looked up from her tea and hiccuped. 'I doubt she'll be back any time soon.'

I whipped round to face her. '*She?*'

'Didn't I mention that it was a girl who took your cat?'

'You said you didn't see who it was.'

'I didn't,' Tabitha confirmed. 'Not the face anyway. I only saw her shoes – right fancy, they were. Pointed with little red bows.'

Piper's hands flattened against the tabletop. 'That's her. The one who's got the notebook.'

I nodded, shivering at the thought of those cold, blue eyes searching through our home, Alice's things. 'Dolly.'

Another horrible thought struck me. 'Tabitha,' I said urgently. 'My mum . . . she came back to get her bags earlier. She wasn't here, was she? She didn't get in the way . . . or get hurt?'

'No,' said Tabitha. 'I heard her leaving. She's quite safe.'

'So it can't have been long before we got back.' My knees felt shaky. I was glad I was sitting down.

'It wasn't,' Tabitha confirmed. She began to wash her whiskers, more relaxed now she'd had her tea.

'I don't want to stay here,' I repeated. 'But there's nowhere else we can go.' I stared round the kitchen. Everything was there just like it normally was: the toaster, the drippy tap, the clock ticking closer to midnight. Ordinary, homely things. Only tonight they felt different. Unfamiliar. It felt as if everything in the house had eyes and was watching us like unseen, lurking spiders.

We sat wordlessly, only the ticking clock breaking the silence. Gypsy pushed her notebook towards me.

You can stay with me tonight.

I didn't need telling twice. 'I'll go and pack some things,' I said.

'Excuse me,' the cat interrupted. She was staring into her teacup.

'You'll have to wait, Tabitha,' I said crossly. 'I don't have time to make you tea all night.'

'That's *not* what I was going to say actually,' Tabitha sniffed. 'I was trying to tell you that there's a girl in my teacup.' She peered closer. 'Are you sure that was ordinary tea?'

Piper leaned over the cup and gave a low whistle.

I leaped out of my seat, grabbing the cup. The tea dregs sloshed up the sides, then stilled at the bottom. Already I could see a face forming there, reflected back at us.

148

I gasped. '*Alice?*'

Chairs scraped and tools clattered to the floor as four heads – one of them furry – crowded round the teacup.

'Get back, it's too dark to see with all of us leaning over!' Piper complained.

'You get back!' I elbowed him, panicking. I'd forgotten all about the Summoning, but it had worked, even if it was in a way I hadn't expected it to. Alice was here and I hadn't even thought about what to say to her. One question . . . just one . . . and she'd be gone. I couldn't bear it. Perhaps the cat had been right – perhaps I *could* keep her talking longer, without asking questions, if I was clever enough.

'That's your sister?' Piper said incredulously. 'Why's she in a teacup?'

'I do hope that doesn't upset my tummy,' said Tabitha. 'This is most absurd.'

'Everyone just shut up!' I roared, slapping my hand on the table, then wishing I hadn't. Alice's face rippled, then stilled again. The kitchen was silent. 'I need to think. The rules of the Summoning say that you can only ask one question. But one question won't be enough. I can't just ask her where she is, if she's safe, or why all this is happening. Or how we get her back. I need to know *all* these things, not just one.'

'So you decided to take my advice,' said Tabitha. 'Maybe you are more sensible than I gave you credit for.'

'I wouldn't take advice from a mischief,' said Piper.

'I wouldn't offer any to a thief,' she shot back.

'Quiet!' I said, exasperated. I leaned over the cup. 'Alice? I hope you can hear me.'

Alice's lips moved, but only bubbles came out.

My heart sank. 'Maybe it doesn't work if you don't ask a question.'

'Or maybe it doesn't work if you can't talk underwater,' Tabitha said sarcastically.

I sat back and looked at the cat questioningly. Her tail flicked towards the window, like a finger pointing. I got up from the table. The curtains were still open, the other side of the glass dark as ink. The kitchen and everyone in it were reflected back at me clearly . . . but aside from the cat there were four figures, not three.

Alice stood next to me in the glass, her mouth still moving silently. I could see her more clearly now. Her face was solemn, and there was a dark mark on her forehead and another on her cheek. They looked like bruises. Had someone hurt her?

'I can't hear you!' I said helplessly.

The Alice reflection pointed up. I resisted the urge to ask her what she meant, for it would still count as a question.

'I don't understand,' I told her.

Alice's lips moved again, mouthing a word. *Mirror.*

'She wants me to go to a mirror,' I said. 'Just me. The rest of you wait here. There's one upstairs.'

I turned, passing the sink. Shallow pools of water had collected in a few cups and dishes that were waiting to

150

be washed. Several watery Alices stared back from them, bubbling softly every time she tried to speak.

I ran through the house and up the stairs. Alice's face gazed back from the glass of every framed photo and every picture, reflected like a ghost that wouldn't give up haunting us.

I reached Mum and Dad's room, flicking on the light and skidding to a halt in front of the large, free-standing mirror reflecting the room behind me: the hastily made bed, the dressing table, the nightdress hanging from the back of the door.

All that was missing was me ... and Alice.

'Where are our reflections?' I whispered. I lifted my hand and waved it in front of the glass, seeing no evidence of it mirrored there. 'Alice,' I said. 'If you're there, show yourself.'

In the doorway reflected behind me, a figure stepped into the room, coming closer to the mirror from within. She moved right up to the glass, her fair hair loose over her shoulders. She wore an old T-shirt that I'd seen many times before. There was a hole in the sleeve. I realised with a jolt that it was the same T-shirt I'd used to make the clothes on the Likeness.

Alice lifted one of her hands to the glass and rested it there. Her mouth moved, and I knew the shape of my name on her lips so well that it was a second before I realised that I hadn't actually heard the word out loud.

'I still can't hear you,' I said.

Alice took her hand from the glass, then placed it back in the same position, indicating that I should do the same. Slowly, I lifted my hand and held it up to hers, a mirror image. The glass rippled where our fingers met, before lying flat. Then, like I'd come up to the surface after swimming underwater, I heard her.

'Can you hear me now?' Alice asked. There was a slight echo to her voice, as if she were in a large, open space.

'Yes!' I pressed my fingers harder against the glass, as if I could somehow grab her and pull her into the room with me, but the glass stayed flat. A familiar smell filled the room, a smell that I associated with Alice. Not her perfume, or her shampoo . . . something else. A musty, papery kind of smell.

Books.

Questions crowded into my mind. It was all I could do not to blurt them out. I had to think of ways to ask them without actually asking, ways to get Alice to tell me what I needed to know.

'You know how this works,' Alice said softly. 'You only get one question. Choose it well.'

I nodded, determined to play the game. To bend the rules. 'You have marks on your face,' I said at last. 'They look like bruises.'

'On my face?' Alice lifted her other hand, the one that wasn't against mine, to her face. 'I don't remember getting any bruises.'

'On your cheek and forehead.'

She frowned. 'I can't feel anything.'

'I don't know who you're with,' I continued. 'Or where you are.'

'There's no one else here,' Alice answered. 'I don't know where I am, either, but I'm all alone here. There are no people, only words.'

Only words? What did that mean? My eyes stung, hot with tears. But it was working. I was getting answers without asking questions. 'I miss you. I wish you were back here.'

'I don't know how to get back. I'm trapped! You're the only one who can help me now.'

'Tell me what to do,' I said, then flinched as something ran across Alice's forehead. Something small and dark like a bug, but when I looked closer I saw it was a word. *Twist*, it said, in Alice's curly handwriting. I blinked, unsure of what I was seeing, until it wriggled out of view. A few seconds later another word appeared on her cheek. This one was *trapped*. It vanished into her hair.

'I'm in trouble, big trouble,' said Alice. 'I didn't know where the story was going. I lost control of it. So I tried to get it back, but it went wrong . . .'

How? I wanted to shout. *What have you done? How do we put it right?* Instead, I waited, saying nothing and praying she would continue.

'They'd already started coming for me.' Her voice had dropped, only a little above a whisper. 'I knew it was only a matter of time before they all got out of the story, but

I thought maybe if *I* were the one to bring them here, I could still control them somehow. And then I changed my mind . . . or tried to. I was too afraid after what happened last time . . .

Last time? Of course. Last summer. The other story that Alice had destroyed.

'The Hangman,' I remembered. A shiver crept over my skin, like pins were being jabbed all over me.

Alice nodded. 'And others. They wanted their ending and I couldn't give it to them.'

'And now it's happening again. Gypsy, and Piper, and the cat – they're all here.'

Alice nodded solemnly. 'It won't just be them. There are others, ones you need to watch out for. They're dangerous, and crazy . . . and they won't want the ending I had in store for them – they'll want to change it.' Her eyes were wide, fearful. 'Ramblebrook and Dolly Weaver, but there's something you need— '

'Dolly Weaver!' I blurted out. So she *was* one of Alice's characters. 'I haven't met Ramblebrook yet,' I told her hurriedly. 'And I don't think Gypsy, or Piper, or the cat know that . . . know what they really are. But they know about the notebook. Gypsy's searching for it – and so is Dolly.'

'I know and that's why they mustn't get it!' Alice's voice was panicked. 'Put it somewhere safe, somewhere only you know about. And Midge, I have to tell you something about Dolly—'

'It's too late,' I interrupted. 'I'm sorry. It was stolen, except for a few pages. The rest was taken by Dolly, and she's even been here in the house tonight, looking for the loose pages.'

Alice closed her eyes. 'I was afraid you'd say that. I thought we might still have time, but it's all happened so quickly.' She opened her eyes. 'All this is my fault.' She shook her head miserably.

'Then tell me how to fix it!' I pleaded. 'There must be a way.'

'Get the notebook back,' Alice instructed. 'Hide it. Then you have to find my father. Ask him about the curse . . . and how to break it.'

Her father?

'That's where this all began,' Alice continued. 'And where it has to end.'

'How do I find him?' I said. 'You barely found him yourself—' I clapped my hand over my mouth, realising my mistake. I'd done it. I'd unthinkingly asked a question. 'I'm sorry,' I groaned. 'I didn't mean to – it just popped out!'

Alice looked at me, her face a mixture of pride and sadness. 'Don't be sorry, little brother. You've done so well and been so clever. But now I can only answer this, then I have to go.

'There's a box under Mum's bed. She thinks no one knows about it, but I do. She keeps things in there, things from the past. Look inside it and it'll tell you how to find him.' Another word scuttled across her face and she flicked at it. It landed on the mirror, back to front, then flipped itself over like a little caterpillar. *Hearth*, it read. It skittered away in the mirror's reflection. I turned, unable to help myself, scanning the floor for it, but there was no sign. When I turned back to the mirror, I was just in time to see it vanish under the bed. What were all these words surrounding her? A thought hit me: if Gypsy, Piper, Dolly and the cat were here, then could Alice be . . . *there*? In the story they had left?

The room behind Alice in the reflection began to darken, like the light was failing. Above my head, the light bulb flickered. My hand was still pressed against the glass to Alice's. I was aware that it was getting warmer, uncomfortably warm. The darkness in the mirror got thicker, like smoke, and words were floating through the air like ash.

'Alice,' I begged. 'Don't go yet!'

She shook her head, as helpless as I was, and I saw that she was speaking, but I was unable to hear her any more. I thought I could make out the word 'Dolly' on her lips but whatever she was trying to say was now lost, as she was. Stricken, I realised I'd interrupted Alice twice when she'd been trying to tell me something, in my desperation to get my own words out. Now it was too late.

Her eyes and hair were wild. She was barely a shadow now. The heat from the glass was too much to stand. I pulled my hand away and there was a resounding crack as Mum's mirror shattered. I scrambled back, afraid the glass would fall, but it stayed where it was, blackened around the edges and reflecting my shocked face back at me.

Alice was gone.

I'd messed it up. If only I'd stayed smart, if only I hadn't forgotten myself and blurted out that question. If only.

I stared at the cracked mirror, my heart drumming like thundering hooves. What were all those words that had wriggled over Alice in her glassy prison?

Trapped . . . Hearth . . . Twist?

Hearth . . . ?

I turned and ran downstairs into the living room, crouching down in front of the fireplace. I knew what I was looking for now. I'd remembered.

The grate still had the remains of the fire from last night. No one had swept it out. I shifted the coal bucket out a little, streaking ash across the hearth. A balled-up piece of paper rolled out from where it had been lodged out of sight.

Alice had been aiming for the fire, but she'd missed.

I picked up the piece of paper and smoothed it out, then began to read.

12
Writer's Block

A T AROUND THE SAME TIME AS GYPSY SPINDLE
*was puzzling over her map, and Piper was hitching
his third ride of the morning, a girl who looked very
much like Gypsy was sitting warm in front of a fire at home in
Fiddler's Hollow.*

*The girl's name was Alice and, like Gypsy, she was sixteen
years old. She also happened to be – again like Gypsy – a
writer. She had a notebook open on her lap and a pen in her
hand, but she had not turned the page all evening, nor managed
to write a sentence without crossing it out.*

*She was writing a story, but she knew now that the story
was getting the better of her. It was not just any story, like the
ones she had written many times before to amuse her younger
brother. It was a novel, and her most ambitious work to date,
but, despite beginning well and being over three-quarters
written, she now found herself stuck.*

She stared at the page, rereading the same sentences. She'd read them so many times that they no longer held any meaning, like a threat repeated, but never carried out. Yet Alice was aware of a real threat, should she not continue with the tale. She had been stuck like this before. It had not ended well for her or that story, for she had been forced to destroy it, and she felt that things might be going the same way now.

She didn't want to destroy this. She couldn't. She was too close and had worked too hard on it to give up. There had to be a way. She had to find an ending before the characters chose it for themselves.

Long ago, Alice's father had told her that, if she wanted to be a writer, every story must have an ending. Even if it wasn't very good, or if it was silly. He'd made her promise, and she always thought it was simply advice. It wasn't until sometime later that he told her the reason why, and after she'd had a glimpse of what could happen if she disobeyed.

The first time she defied this advice was when she was twelve years old. The story she'd been working on had dried up and become stale, and she was feeling particularly bitter about her father not being around. She left the story unfinished and began another, but soon became plagued by dreams in which the characters in the abandoned tale were bothering her. Night after night they came, demanding answers, demanding endings, until finally Alice could bear it no longer and forced herself to finish the story. With that, the dreams stopped, and she told herself she wouldn't leave a story unfinished again.

She kept to this for three years until she decided to try her hand at a slightly longer yarn, eventually writing her characters into problems she could find no solution to. After several days of being unable to move the story on, the dreams began again. This time, however, with the improvement in her writing skills, they were far more vivid.

At first, she welcomed them, for it was a strange and wonderful thing to be able to speak to the characters she had created and imagined for so long. But in every story there has to be a villain, and the problem with monsters is that those of our own making are the most terrifying of all.

Alice began to sit up at night, drinking coffee to stay awake, hunched over her notebooks and willing the words to come. They wouldn't.

Soon after that, the characters came instead and not just in her dreams.

They started off as shadows, quick movements glimpsed out of the corner of her eye. Then came reflections in shop windows, the footsteps behind her on an empty street, the figure sitting outside the house.

The doorbell ringing in the middle of the night.

She burned the story soon after. Every page, every last note, exorcising them like ghosts. She didn't miss them. She became well again. She wrote other stories. She remembered it as an illness, a fever, the product of an overworked mind.

The following year she felt strong enough to try again. A new novel, new characters. She told no one what she was doing; it was to be a surprise. She wrote and she wrote. Five thousand words became ten thousand. Ten thousand became twenty.

The blank pages in her notebook lost their crispness, becoming fat and full like a feather pillow.

Then one day the words stopped coming.

There were days Alice didn't write at all, and days she did only to delete more than she'd written. When the dreams began, she told herself it was fear, nothing more. But then the shadow movements started, and she knew that it wouldn't be long before the characters came for her. Soon one did; the worst one of all.

She knew the others would follow, one by one, stepping out of the pages and beyond her control. And what then? Where did she fit in, and what role would she play, if the story were no longer hers? That night, as she watched the flames dancing in the grate, a glimmer of an idea took hold. An idea for a truly wonderful twist . . .

Alice had always enjoyed a twist in the tale.

Perhaps there was a way she could still be the one in control of it all. If they were coming anyway, what harm could there be in Alice speeding things up? In actually writing them out of the story herself? At least this way she would be ready for them, and it might give her some idea of how much power she still had over them.

Alice chewed the end of her pen, thinking deeply. Then she began to write.

Gypsy's and Piper's paths had not crossed for six years, but fate was about to play a part.

It was a wet and windy morning when Gypsy's fortunes

appeared to change. She woke shivering and dressed quickly, then shook the last few porridge oats into a pan on the stove with some milk to warm. She'd have to stop off somewhere today. Supplies were low. While she ate, she had a quick look at her map. The nearest town was three miles south. She could be there by mid-morning.

When breakfast was finished, she washed up, then went out on deck. The rain had stopped, but the air was still damp and stung her cheeks. It didn't help her already low mood. She was still hungry and exhausted. Her plan wasn't working. The search for her mother was running out of clues.

She'd always imagined that looking hard enough for something meant it would eventually have to be found. She now realised that perhaps this didn't apply to people who wanted to stay hidden. She had to find another way to undo the curse.

The trouble was she was broke and all out of ideas. Plus, her papa must be wondering where she was by now. She sighed, pulling a dead plant from a flowerpot on the roof and throwing it into the canal. Perhaps it was time to go home. She clambered down inside the cabin again, then noticed that her little notepad, the one she carried everywhere with her, was on the table.

It was open.

A pencil lay beside it, its lead resting on the creamy white paper like a pointing fingertip. She didn't remember leaving it open. Something had been written on the page in a hurry, in writing similar to but not exactly like her own:

The answer you are searching for is close.

It is in a tale called The Museum of Unfinished Stories.

Gypsy snatched up the notepad and held it to her chest, eyes darting round the cabin. It hadn't been there when she was having breakfast, she was sure of that. But there was nowhere to hide, and only one way in and out; the rear entry to the cabin was locked. Surely someone hadn't been able to sneak down here in the brief moments she'd been out on deck?

She ran outside again, searching the muddy banks and towpaths for any signs of movement. There were none except for a few wild swans and moorhens. There weren't even any other boats in sight. She was alone on the water.

Unsettled, Gypsy unhooked the mooring and moved off, steering the boat through the waterways. The swaying motion helped to calm her racing mind. She was so lost in her thoughts that it was a while before she noticed the path she was taking did not resemble the one on her map. The first she knew of it was a crooked signpost saying BLACK WATER – 1.5 MILES.

She looked at her map again. There was no Black Water marked on it anywhere near and she couldn't recall having seen any sign of a town for some time. Strange. Ahead of her, the next place to be signposted was Fiddler's Hollow. That was nowhere on her map, either. She wondered if the

163

map was out of date. It was possible. It was old and had been on the boat ever since she could remember. Her papa wasn't one for replacing things unless they were broken or lost.

If only all lost things could be replaced.

Ahead, through the trees that lined the canal, the sun broke through the clouds and glittered on the murky green water. Gypsy lifted her face to it. She wouldn't be going home just yet.

She had a story to search for.

Seven miles away, Piper clambered into the cab of an oil tanker and pulled the door shut, his teeth chattering. It had been a filthy morning and his clothes were soaked through. He hadn't had much luck getting people to stop on this stretch of road, but a lay-by in which a few truck drivers were taking their breaks had changed his luck.

The driver, a ruddy-faced man, climbed in on the other side. He'd been stretching his legs when Piper had approached him to ask for a ride. He handed Piper a plastic cup that he filled from a flask. 'Get this down you, lad.'

Piper nodded his thanks, but held on to the cup, warming his hands and waiting. The driver took out another cup and filled it, then drank some himself. Only then did Piper relax; you could never be too trusting. The tea was weak and sweeter than he liked, but he was grateful for it and accepted a refill when the first cup was quickly drained.

'Have you come far?' the driver asked.

'About twenty miles,' Piper lied. It was more like six, but he didn't care to tell strangers his business.

'Got far to go?'

Piper sighed. Why did he always manage to get the chatterboxes? The ones who wouldn't shut up, who wanted to hear your life story and to tell you theirs?

'Sorry,' the driver continued. 'Don't mean to be nosy. It just gets boring on the road. Nice to have a bit of company, that's all. No problem if you don't want to chat.' He checked his mirrors and pulled out of the lay-by, rumbling along the road.

'No, it's all right,' Piper muttered, feeling a bit rotten now. The man had been kind after all. 'I'm just not much of a talker.' He pushed his dripping hair out of his eyes. 'I'm visiting my cousin in Puddletown.' Another lie: he had no cousins.

'Can't say I've heard of it,' the driver replied. 'And I know pretty much every town there is around these parts.'

Piper shrugged. He'd heard of Puddletown and liked the name, but the truth was that he didn't care where he ended up. He was feeling reckless, although he couldn't really explain why. He leaned his head back and feigned sleep, hoping the man would take the hint.

He didn't.

'You travel light.'

Piper opened his eyes and glanced at his bag on the seat next to him where he'd thrown it. It was clear it didn't hold much and, compared to his well-kept flute case, the bag was tatty like the rest of him.

'You play?' The driver asked, touching the flute case. His voice was still friendly, but there was a slight edge to it that Piper picked up on immediately.

He thinks I nicked it.

'Yeah,' he replied, then looked out of the window, deliberately evasive.

'Go on then, give us a tune.'

Piper continued to stare out of the window as if he hadn't heard. He could refuse, but as usual vanity won out. There were enough people in the world who thought he was a good-for-nothing toerag. He needed to remind himself at times that there was something he was good at.

He took out the flute, bringing it to his lips. It was cool in his fingertips. He thought for a moment before settling on a well-known composition – not one of his own, even though the temptation was great. One of his own tunes could prove too dangerous to someone who was driving and, besides, there was nothing Piper wanted from the man anyway, apart from the transportation he'd already offered.

'You're good!' the driver told him and Piper could hear the disbelief in his voice. He finished that tune and began another. It was keeping the driver quiet, keeping Piper from answering questions, and that was fine by him.

He broke off mid-note as a sign whizzed past. 'What did that say?'

'Fiddler's Hollow, two miles.'

Piper frowned. It was true that he didn't mind where he ended up, but he'd planned to go somewhere that he'd heard of and knew he definitely wouldn't be recognised.

'There's no such place as Fiddler's Hollow. I've never heard of it.' He pressed his nose to the window. Had they gone off track, down some unmarked country lane?

The driver chuckled. 'I drive this route week in, week out. I can promise you there is such a place.'

Piper stared at him, trying to work out if they'd met before . . . if perhaps he had crossed him in the past, but there was nothing about the man's face that he recognised. He wasn't about to take any chances, though.

'Let me out,' he said.

'Eh? I can't stop here; you'll have to wait—'

'Stop, right now.' Piper shoved his flute back in its case and grabbed his bag. He tried the door handle, but it wouldn't budge.

'What do you think you're doing?' the driver demanded. 'It's a safety lock; the door won't open while we're moving!'

'Let me out!' Piper yelled.

The driver swore, all good humour gone, and swerved dangerously to the side of the road. The tanker jerked to a stop and there was a click as the safety lock unlatched. 'Go on then.' He glared at Piper. 'That's the last time I do one of your lot a good turn.'

Piper didn't answer. He scrambled out of the cab, landing light as a cat. The truck growled away from him, spraying gravel into his face. He was alone on a country lane, breathing raggedly.

He caught his breath and set off, making no attempt to thumb another ride. He had no idea where he was going, or where he'd sleep, but walking would keep him warm. It had stopped raining at least and, oddly, the ground underfoot was dry, like this place had missed the earlier downpour entirely.

He had walked about a mile when he saw a signpost and the outskirts of a town up ahead. Soon he was close enough to read what it said.

If only he could read.

He stomped on, passing a pub and a church. Both were closed. It was still early. He crossed the town square, empty except for some sort of huge bonfire waiting to be lit. On the other side was a bakery and it was open. He went in and the scent of fresh bread around him was like a warm hug.

'What town's this?' he asked the sleepy-eyed girl behind the counter.

'Fiddler's Hollow,' she replied.

So the driver hadn't lied. Piper frowned. 'Is this anywhere near Puddletown? I think I'm a bit lost.'

'Can't say I've heard of it,' she said.

He closed his eyes in annoyance. Did no one know their way around in these parts? 'How much are the bread rolls?' he asked abruptly.

'Thirty pence, or four for a pound.'

168

He stared at her, confused. 'Eh?'

She repeated herself, then pointed to the price list, which he ignored.

'How many do you want?'

'Er . . .' He rummaged in his pockets, scraping out the few coins there.

The girl looked at him kindly. 'What have you got? If it's a bit short, I can let you off. You look hungry.'

'I am.' Shamefaced, he held up his hand, showing her what he had.

She peered at the money. 'What currency is that? It's foreign, ain't it? I can't take it.'

He blinked. 'Foreign?'

She shook her head. 'You really are lost, aren't you?' She glanced over her shoulder, then pushed a paper bag at him. 'Here. Take it, quickly, before the boss sees.'

He took the bag, the bread inside warming his numbed fingers. 'You mean . . . I can't spend this money here?'

She shook her head again. 'You'd better hop it, or we'll both be in trouble.'

He muttered his thanks and stepped out on to the street, trying to make sense of it all as he wolfed down the hot bread. The knowledge that his money was useless here was confusing him, though he wasn't too worried about having none. He could easily get money, whatever it was they used here.

He just had to figure out where 'here' actually was. And that was what worried him.

There Alice stopped. She had done what she could – all she could. At least this way, Gypsy and Piper stood a chance of finding each other before they found her. As for what happened next, she didn't know. Perhaps her bringing them here, meeting them, would change that.

Alice put down her pen.

13

Gingerbread Cottages

WHEN I FINISHED READING, I TUCKED THE crumpled paper in my pocket and sat in silence. In the kitchen, I could hear Piper and Tabitha talking in low voices, and the occasional clink as Gypsy fixed the lock.

So this was what Alice had been writing last night, before she disappeared. I remembered her panicked words . . .

. . . I thought maybe if I was the one to bring them here, I could still control them somehow. And then I changed my mind . . . or tried to.

Alice had made it happen, but she hadn't meant it to. It was just her mind's way of wandering, trying to figure out solutions to the story's problems. Instead, when she'd thrown the page at the fire and missed, she'd created a bigger one, not only by leaving the story unfinished but by taking it in a new direction. The crumpled page in my pocket was just another piece of a puzzle that only seemed to be growing, and there was still more I had to figure out. I crept upstairs into my parents' room again, poking about under the bed. It was a couple of minutes before I found what I was looking for, hidden under odd socks and dust balls.

A small wooden box, just like Alice had described.

Somewhere within it was the answer to finding her father. I took it downstairs, its contents rattling as though trying to escape. I wasn't sure I could keep doing this alone, or how much longer I could hide the truth from Gypsy and Piper. As soon as Piper took us to the other part of the story that he'd stolen, Gypsy would want to read it – and if it mentioned either of them the game would be up.

I pushed the thought away and skulked into the kitchen like a dog that had stolen a biscuit.

Piper looked up. 'Did it work? Did you speak to Alice?'

I nodded. My mouth was dry all of a sudden.

'Where is she?'

'I'm not sure.' I looked down at my hands. There were specks of black dust on them. I thought of the smudges on Alice's face. Not bruises after all. Coal dust.

Gypsy put down the screwdriver she was holding and came towards me, jotting words down.

What did she tell you? Do you know how to find her, or what's going on?

I shook my head. 'I . . . I messed it up. I asked a question without really meaning to. But she gave me a clue. We have to find her father. She thinks he can help us.'

'Your father?' Piper asked. 'Don't you know where he is?'

'Alice has a different father to me,' I explained. 'He's a Romany traveller, a writer like her. She hardly knows him.'

What does her father have to do with any of this? Gypsy wrote.

'Alice has a belief about her stories,' I said. 'That every story she starts has to be finished. I thought it was a superstition, but now I wonder if she was ... *afraid* not to.'

'Afraid?' Tabitha asked. 'Why?'

'Alice thinks she's cursed,' I said. 'All I know is that it's something to do with her father, but she never told me what. But now ...' I hesitated, remembering how obsessive Alice was about this. It wasn't normal, or healthy. 'I think maybe that *is* the curse, that Alice believes something terrible will happen if she doesn't finish a story.'

'Then why didn't she just finish it?' Piper asked.

'That's my point,' I told him. 'She couldn't. She was stuck and had been for weeks.'

Gypsy pushed her notepad towards me.

You were upstairs for a long time. Is that all Alice told you?

I nodded, unable to speak at first. Guilt lodged in my throat like coal dust. I coughed and stared at the box in my hands. 'I was a long time, because I was searching for this.'

'What's inside?' Tabitha asked, prowling along the table.

'I haven't looked yet. Alice told me to find it. Whatever it has inside will lead us to her father.'

I set the box down on the table. It was made of dark brown wood, beautifully varnished and carved into two halves to look like a book. I hadn't noticed this at first, for the carvings were subtle and it was so well made that the joins were difficult to see. It looked valuable, not something you'd see every day.

'Nice,' said Piper. 'Handmade by the looks of it. Probably worth a bit.'

'Probably, so keep your paws off.' I glared at him and lifted the lid. A couple of photographs floated to the floor. I picked them up. They were of Mum, when she was younger, with a baby Alice and a man who had silver-grey eyes. Alice's father.

There were other things loose at the bottom. A postcard. An ornate ring set with a pale stone. Two tiny bands with writing on. I read them, finding my name and date of birth on one and Alice's on the other. They were the little bands that go on a baby's wrist in hospital when they're born, to stop them getting mixed up with other babies.

There were two things left in the box. A long, thin tube of paper tied with silver ribbon and something squarish wrapped in a dark blue cloth. I took the cloth object out and unwrapped it. On the other side, the cloth was dotted with tiny silver stars. Inside it was a deck of cards, held together by a thin silver ribbon, but they were not ordinary playing cards, or like any others I'd seen before. They were beautifully painted with curious little pictures. The first was of a girl with a sad expression, wearing patched clothes, sweeping out a fireplace. The second showed twelve dancing girls, each wearing a little crown. I felt like I'd stumbled on some kind

174

of secret. I'd never seen Mum with these or heard her talk about them, but I was sure I'd seen this silvery-starred fabric before. Only in Alice's room, not Mum's.

'What are these?' I wondered aloud. 'Tarot cards?' I'd never seen any tarot cards before, but Alice had written a story about some once, so I knew they were supposed to be quite mystical and used to look into the future.

'Close,' said Piper. 'They're fortune cards.'

'Isn't that the same sort of thing?' I asked.

'Similar,' said Piper. 'With the Tarot, there are loads of different packs, but they've always got the same or very similar cards, like the Moon, or the Fool. Fortune cards are different, 'cos no two packs are the same. They're made for the owner alone.' He leaned in. 'See, these are hand-painted. It's a sign of how special they are to whoever they belong to.'

'But Mum's never mentioned anything like this,' I said. 'They *can't* belong to her. She doesn't read her horoscope and she gets annoyed when Alice talks about curses or superstitious stuff. She says it's all rubbish.'

Piper shrugged. 'Maybe she does now, but perhaps there was a time when she didn't.'

I thought of Mum's life before she had me. Her life with Alice's father, a life of stories and superstition and living wild; about as far as you could get from how she was now. She never spoke about it. It seemed that Alice, and the contents of this box, were the only things from that part of her life that were left.

I thumbed through the cards. At first, I couldn't make any sense of them. They were odd images, like pieces from different puzzles that would never fit together, and yet there was something familiar about them. A swan, a tower, a mirror. A black cat, a pumpkin. A strange little house made of sweets . . .

'They're all things from stories,' I said. 'It's the gingerbread cottage from *Hansel and Gretel*. And look.' I went back to the sweeping girl. 'This must be Cinderella.'

'Cinder-*what*-a?' Piper looked dubious. 'We call her Ashputtel.'

'How can these be used to tell fortunes?' I asked.

'Easy,' said Piper. 'You just have to look at what they mean. Everyone knows these stories.' He reddened. 'Even people who can't read. Take this one.' He picked up the Ashputtel card. 'I'd say it means there's gonna be hard work ahead. Unfair treatment perhaps. And the gingerbread cottage . . . something or someone that appears good and sweet at first, but turns out to be a trap. Something too good to be true.'

Or perhaps somewhere that wasn't safe. I glanced at the back door, uneasy. It was fixed now, but it had been broken through as easily as if it were made of gingerbread.

'Our mum used to love stories,' I said quietly. 'That's why Alice loves them. Lots of the books in Alice's room were Mum's. All the fairy tales and fables and myths.'

I couldn't imagine Mum ever reading those sorts of stories now. There were no books in her room, and downstairs the

176

shelves held only practical ones: a few biographies, nature books, an encyclopaedia and a dictionary: the kind of books Mum published at work. She had stopped reading anything that was 'made up' when Alice's father had left. She said that real life was enough of a story and there were too many lies in the world already.

I wrapped the cards up in the cloth again. I'd look through them properly later.

The final thing in the box was the rolled paper. I could see traces of writing on the other side, but they were too faint to read. I already knew what it was. Alice had told me about the story many times.

'What's that?' Tabitha asked, her tail curling into the box and touching the paper.

'A story,' I answered. 'Alice's father gave it to our mother when they first met.' I wondered when Mum had last read it. The ribbon around it was knotted tightly, but I could still make out a name inked on to it faintly: Ramone Silver. *His* name. I left it where it was. I felt sure Alice would have read it; she wouldn't have been able to help herself. I wasn't sure I wanted to know what it said, or that we had any right to look. I put everything back in the box and closed it.

'We should leave now,' I said. I was used to Dad being away, but without Alice and Mum – and even Twitch – the house didn't feel like home.

Gypsy packed away the tools and closed the back door, locking it and then giving it a good rattle. It stayed closed.

'Thanks,' I said gratefully.

She nodded. *Get your things together*, she wrote. *We'll go to my boat.*

I went upstairs and grabbed a few bits: my toothbrush, some money from my money box and pyjamas. I switched off the lights and took my keys from the hook by the front door, locking it after me once everyone was outside. Stepping out into the cool night air, we stood as quiet as church mice on the garden path. It was way past midnight. The streets were silent and empty.

Something slithered past my ankles. I bit back a yell, almost tripping, and looked down. Tabitha blinked up at me, her golden eyes luminous in the yellow street light. 'Are you trying to kill me?' I hissed. 'What are you doing out here?'

She jumped on to the wall, arching her back in a stretch. 'Coming with you, of course.'

'I don't remember anyone inviting you,' Piper said rudely.

'Perhaps she *should* come,' I said. 'Once whoever took Twitch realises they got the wrong cat, they could be back for her.'

'Good point,' said Piper. 'She might come in useful to bargain with.'

'That wasn't exactly what I was thinking,' said Tabitha, a little tartly. 'It's not much fun being in an empty house, you know.'

'Oh, I can imagine,' I said. 'Nobody to wait on you.'

'Precisely,' said the cat. 'It's not like I can make my own tea, is it?'

'Perhaps you should learn,' Piper muttered, skirting close to the wall, like he was used to staying in the shadows.

'I've tried.' Tabitha jumped lightly down from the wall and wound herself round his ankles in a way that suggested she was being deliberately annoying. 'Tea bags and claws don't mix.'

'Proper little madam, aren't you?' said Piper. 'Never was one for cats. I always preferred dogs. At least they'll do as their master tells them.'

'Dogs have masters,' I said, remembering something Alice had said once. 'Cats have servants.'

'I'm no ordinary cat, though,' said Tabitha. 'There is a way you could become my master if you're up to a challenge.'

'Why would you want a master?' I asked.

'I don't,' she replied. 'But rules are rules. I didn't make them.'

No, I thought. *Alice did.*

'Why would anyone want to be your master?' Piper asked. 'What's in it for them? Apart from the pleasure of your company?'

'Don't get lippy,' Tabitha replied. 'I can be pretty useful as it happens.'

'How?' he scoffed. 'Even when you *are* awake you just sit there guzzling tea.'

'I've certain talents,' she said. 'I can be eyes and ears when people least expect it.'

'A spy, you mean?' I asked.

'If you like,' she replied. 'Plus, I make an excellent party trick, or the voice of a fake ghost at a seance. No one ever suspects the cat.'

'Fake ghosts are in such short supply,' Piper said sarcastically. 'That would come in useful next time I hold a seance.' He rolled his eyes.

'And then there are the nine lives, of course,' she purred, ignoring him. 'Those are always in high demand.'

'What do you mean?' I asked.

'I thought everyone knew that cats have nine lives?' she said.

'That's just a saying, isn't it?'

'No.'

Gypsy nudged me to look at something she'd written. I read it aloud.

My papa told me about this once. Mischiefs can transfer their lives to others if they choose to, or if they're made to.

'Transfer their lives?' I repeated.

'I've saved a life or two in my time,' Tabitha said airily.

'So, if someone were about to die, you could save them by giving them one of your lives?'

'Bravo,' said Tabitha. 'Told you I could be useful, didn't I?'

She had everyone's attention now.

'What does someone have to do then?' Piper asked. 'To become your master?'

'Answer a riddle. If you solve it, I'll promise to serve you faithfully.'

'Go on,' I said. I felt excited, but anxious, too. Like I always did when solving one of Alice's riddles.

'Very well,' said Tabitha. 'Here it is:

"I'm up when I'm up
And down when I'm down
A thump when a smile
And a flick when a frown.
The opposite side
To the wife of a king
A vessel of venom that
Can kill with a sting."

Piper blew out a long breath, looking stumped. 'You actually reckon anyone's gonna get that?'

'It's perfectly solvable,' she replied. 'You haven't even tried.'

'Wouldn't know where to start,' he retorted.

I stayed quiet, thinking. I had a better chance of solving this than anyone, if I could get it straight in my head. It was more difficult than Alice's other riddles, but she'd taught me how to make them up and how to pick them apart. I just needed time, but I was determined to solve it. If the cat could save lives, then I wanted her on my side. I shivered, recalling Alice's words as she'd described Ramblebrook and Dolly.

They're dangerous, and crazy . . .

Alice had always had a talent for writing sinister characters. In the past, it was something I'd enjoyed. I'd even egged her on. The nastier the better. Now everything had changed. There was no option to stop reading, or to put the story down. It was happening and the characters were here. And one of them, at least, had killed before.

Yes, I decided. I needed to become the cat's master all right.

I took a final look back at the house as we turned out of Cuckoo Lane. Our ordinary little home where, until now, we'd lived ordinary lives. Where, up in her attic room, my sister had written extraordinary tales. And now I was walking along with a make-believe boy and a make-believe girl, and a make-believe cat who was strutting beside us with its tail in the air.

I glanced at Gypsy. She was staring at the ground. For the first time, I realised no one had asked *her* if she minded the cat coming with us, on to her boat. She hadn't made any objections, but she'd seemed uncomfortable having the cat around. *You shouldn't keep these cats*, she'd said. *You can get into a lot of trouble . . .*

One of the fortune cards had been a black cat. What did it mean? Was it lucky, or unlucky? Or did it just depend on what you already believed?

I decided I was going to have a good look at those cards later, once Gypsy and Piper and the cat were asleep. A very good look indeed.

I needed to figure out exactly what Alice had been doing with them.

14

Elsewhere

GYPSY'S BOAT WAS THE ONLY ONE ON THE water that night. It was past one o'clock in the morning when we arrived, but none of us was tired except the cat, who curled up on a cushion, opening one sleepy eye every so often.

Gypsy put some milk in a pan to warm on the stove and set four mismatched teacups on the side. The boat was crammed with books and trinkets, notes and pictures stuck on the walls. A magpie's nest, just like Alice's attic room. There were two bunk beds with patchwork quilts, a table with slide-in booth seats, and another sitting area with lots of throws and cushions that Gypsy called 'the snug'. This was next to the kitchen, and was where she sat when she was reading or writing her stories. We huddled there now, shivering into the blankets and swaying with the motion of the water.

'So what next?' Piper asked.

I took the wooden box out of my rucksack and placed it in the middle of the floor.

'I guess we figure out how to find Alice's dad,' I said. 'And we go to him as soon as possible.' I glanced at Piper. 'Once we have the missing part of the story that you took.'

Piper nodded. 'I can get it at first light.'

'And my cat?' I asked. 'We have to get her back.'

'Maybe she'll be let go once Dolly realises she's an ordinary cat,' Piper said, stifling a yawn.

I felt a twinge of annoyance. 'Or maybe she'll keep her as a hostage in exchange for Tabitha.' Everyone turned to look at the snoozing cat. I thought I saw a whisker twitch, but couldn't be sure.

Gypsy came over with a tray of cups. We each took one and she left a cup of tea by Tabitha's side, but the cat didn't stir.

I opened the box and looked through the contents. I left the fortune cards where they were, as well as the little wristbands and the rolled-up story. Instead, I took out the things I'd overlooked earlier: the photos and postcard.

I picked up the photos. There were two and they were very similar. The first showed Mum and a man I knew must be Ramone standing hand in hand on a hillside. Behind them was a pavillion with a statue of a stag on top. Mum looked so young and happy. Daisies dotted the grass. Ramone wore a white shirt that was partly unbuttoned, and his hair was long, past his shoulders. Even though the picture wasn't a close-up, his pale grey eyes were piercing and his black eyebrows were so thick they gave the appearance of a frown.

In the second photo, Mum and Ramone stood in the same place, in front of the stag, but this time they stood at a slightly different angle. Thick snow lay on the ground. In Ramone's arms was a little girl, probably no more than two years old. She was bundled up in a woollen coat, like a plump little lamb, her cheeks red.

Alice.

I stared at the two photographs. Before tonight, I'd never seen Alice's father, only heard him described by her.

'He looks just like Alice said.' I had a lump in my throat at the thought of this past life of Mum's that I was not part of, and knew almost nothing about.

Gypsy touched the postcard. I tore my eyes away from the photos to look at it. At first, it appeared to be a simple countryside scene in the sunset, but then I saw it again, a horned silhouette on the horizon.

'There it is again,' said Piper. 'What's with this stag?'

'Good question.' I picked up the postcard and turned it over. There was a National Trust logo on the back and a little printed description: *The Stag of Yonder Hill, West Maiden.*

'It must be some kind of landmark,' I said. 'I've heard of West Maiden. I don't think it's too far from here.'

I turned the photographs over. The back of the summer one was blank, but, on the reverse of the winter scene, something had been written. I didn't recognise the writing. It wasn't Mum's or Alice's.

'It's a poem.' I read it out.

> 'Where five should be four
> There once stood three
> Before there were two
> And now there's just me.
> Now five are still four
> There are no longer three
> If two should come searching
> It's where they'll find me.'

'What's *that* s'posed to mean?' Piper asked, after I'd read it a second time. 'It don't make sense. Poetry is stupid.'

'It's not stupid,' I said. 'It's a riddle. It's meant to be confusing, but there has to be an answer. Whatever it means will be linked to these pictures.'

There was something about the photographs that was bothering me, but I couldn't work out what it was. 'It's like one of those spot-the-difference games. It's bound to be something simple . . . and all these numbers in the riddle, that must mean it's something that can be counted.'

'Then that can only be the people,' Piper said lazily. 'Two in the first photograph and three in the second, after Alice had come along. Other than that, I give up.' He leaned back into the cushions, draping his arm over his face.

'So where do the five and the four come into it?' I wondered. No one answered. Gypsy traced her fingers over the edges of the postcard, her eyes glassy.

186

My own eyes were gritty and sore. I was tired now, but I couldn't stop staring at the photographs. I looked from one to the other, something still niggling at me like a pebble in my shoe. I blinked, my body tensing.

There it was. 'But why would there be five ...' I trailed off, confused.

Next to me, Gypsy sat up straighter, her eyes questioning. 'There. Look.'

Piper sat up, bleary-eyed. 'You spotted something?'

'Yes.' I pointed to the stag in the first picture, counting its legs. 'One, two, three, four. Now look at this one.' I moved my hand across to the second photograph. 'One, two, three, four ... five.'

'A five-legged stag?' Piper said.

'You can't see the fifth leg in the first photograph,' I said. 'It's the angle it's taken at. But in the winter one you can see it clearly. That's what the riddle is talking about – where five should be four.'

'There once stood three,' Piper said slowly.

'Three people. Mum, Ramone and Alice.'

And, before Alice was born, it was just the two of them, Gypsy added.

I reread the second part of the riddle. It made sense now.

'Now five are still four
There are no longer three
If two should come searching
It's where they'll find me.'

187

'And now there's just me,' I repeated. 'Just Ramone.'

'He's a slippery one, this Ramone,' said Piper. He drained his drink and leaned back again, closing his eyes. 'Why didn't he just leave an address instead of messing around with riddles?'

Maybe he didn't want to be found easily, Gypsy put in.

'He's a traveller. If he never stays in one place, maybe even he doesn't know where he'll be.' I wrapped my cold fingers round the warm cup. 'But finding him must be linked to this stag.'

No one answered. Piper lay still, his face covered by his arm. A snore escaped his lips. The cat was nearby in a tight ball, with her tail tucked over her nose.

It's late, Gypsy wrote. *We should get some rest, too.*

She got up, pulling thicker blankets from the overhead cupboards. She handed me one, then, after a moment's pause, tossed the other one at Piper. It landed in a wrinkled heap in his lap, but neither she nor I made any attempt to straighten it out.

Seconds later, she snapped out the overhead light, leaving just a little lamp on in the snug. The lower bunk creaked as she got into it, then everything was quiet. I pulled the blanket over myself, then put the postcard and photos back into Mum's box. My fingers brushed the fortune cards. A fold of the blue fabric around them fell open, revealing a spray of silver stars.

I took the cards out and unwrapped them, feeling once again like I'd stumbled on some sort of secret, or, at the very

188

least, an expensive box of chocolates that wasn't for sharing. I spread the blue cloth over my lap, intending to lay the cards out and have a good look at them, but then noticed a detail about the cloth that I hadn't seen the first time.

The stars only decorated the edges of the cloth. At the centre there were several rectangles arranged in the shape of a cross. Four more vertical rectangles were stacked on top of each other on the right side of the cloth. Each outline was numbered and had something written within it, a single word or phrase. They went like this:

    i   *The Seeker*
   ii   *The Obstacle*
  iii   *What's Behind*
  iv   *What's Ahead*
   v   *Strengths*
  vi   *Weaknesses*
 vii   *Enemies*
viii   *Friends*
  ix   *A Choice*
   x   *The Outcome*

It was a spread for a fortune telling, that was clear enough. I guessed the person who was having their cards read must be the Seeker, and, after they had shuffled the cards and asked their question, the cards were then laid at these positions on the cloth to give an answer.

As I studied the words, it occurred to me that the list also looked a lot like the sort of things Alice wrote down when she was planning her stories. I started looking through the cards. Each one was so beautifully painted. I set aside the ones I'd seen already and began studying the others. They were easier to put meanings to now I knew the cards were linked to stories. Some were obvious: two children following a breadcrumb trail, a spinning wheel, a poisoned apple, a girl in a red cape.

There were others I didn't understand: an open book full of words that were too tiny to read. Next to it was a burnt-out candle stump. Another card was almost identical, except the book was blank and the candle was tall and had only just started burning.

The next card showed a man who was rowing a boat between two places. Alice had told me this story a few times; it was in an old book of myths and legends. The only way the man could escape was by tricking someone else into taking the oars.

The final card was a story that had always frightened me. A hooded man was playing a flute, leading a trail of hypnotised rats to drown in the river. I pulled the blanket round myself more tightly, remembering what happened next. Though the Pied Piper had got rid of the town's rats, the mayor cheated him out of being paid. In revenge, the piper played a tune which lured all the town's children away with him, except one, a little boy who was deaf and unable to hear him play. The rest were never seen again, nor was the Pied Piper.

Piper.

I glanced at the boy sleeping nearby. He'd shifted in his sleep and his arm was tucked round his flute case, holding it protectively.

A coldness spread over my skin like river water.

I was now almost certain that Alice had used these fortune cards to plan out her story.

15

A Trail of Breadcrumbs

I WOKE TO THE SOUNDS OF SOMETHING BREAKING and sat up in a panic, at first wondering where I was. My head felt as though it were full of sand, my eyes gritty and my mouth sour. It had taken me a long time to fall asleep and when I finally had it was uneasy.

There was another crack from the kitchen. I looked up, aware that I was alone in the snug. There was no sign of Piper or the cat, but Gypsy had her back to me in the kitchen.

Instinctively, my hand shot under my pillow, checking the box was still hidden. It was. I'd slept with it there all night.

'Where's Piper?' I asked, getting up. 'And Tabitha?'

Gypsy nodded to the window above the sink, then turned, whisking a basin of eggs.

'They've gone out?' I stumbled to Gypsy's side. 'What if they disappear?'

Gypsy stopped whisking and picked up some chalk to write on a slate hanging up nearby. *I've been watching them. I'm not letting Piper out of my sight.*

I looked out of the window, searching the riverbank. Piper was kneeling in the grass, fiddling with something. There was no sign of the cat. I sat down at the table, chewing my thumb. A couple of minutes passed and then Piper's voice carried down into the hold, making me jump.

'Miss me?' He grinned, stepping down into the kitchen. Gypsy snorted.

'Thought so.' His smile widened obnoxiously. 'Never been so popular. I'm starting to get used to this.'

He shook a jumble of mushrooms out from the scrap of cloth he was carrying. 'Is that any way to greet someone who's just brought in the breakfast?'

'Mushrooms in February?' I said, eyeing them doubtfully. 'You sure they're not poisonous?'

Piper laughed. 'You sure you're awake yet? It was September last time I checked. Right, Gyps?'

Gypsy nodded, but didn't turn round. Piper went to the sink and began washing the mushrooms. *September?* So they'd come from another season – though they didn't know it yet – and brought some of the autumn with them.

'If they were poisonous, I'd be dead,' he replied cheerfully. 'I've been foraging for years. I know what I'm doing.'

Gypsy put a pot of tea and four cups on the table. We poured it in silence, which was broken by a lovely hiss as she threw a scoop of butter into the hot pan, then added

193

the eggs and mushrooms. Minutes later, we were each served a fluffy, golden omelette with crusty bread. I couldn't wolf it down quick enough.

I'd just put down my fork when Tabitha appeared at the window behind Gypsy with a dead bird clamped in her jaws.

'Seconds, anyone?' Piper said, stuffing another crust into his mouth.

A muffled sound came from the other side of the window.

'Did you say something, puss?' Piper asked the cat.

Tabitha nodded vigorously. A feather came loose and stuck to the glass, smeared with blood. *'Et ee in!'*

'I think she wants to come in,' Piper told Gypsy with a smirk.

Gypsy wrinkled her nose and shook her head, then put her fork down on her plate with a couple of bites still unfinished. I felt my own breakfast lurch in my tummy. I was used to seeing Twitch kill small creatures, but it seemed different with Tabitha: a cat you could speak to and reason with . . . and who'd been munching happily on candyfloss only last night.

'I reckon that's a no,' Piper called. 'It's breakfast al fresco for you, Tabitha!'

Tabitha's golden eyes narrowed, then she vanished from the window, leaping on to the roof above. Once or twice, her long black tail swung into view and a couple of feathers floated down.

When she returned to the window, her mouth was empty.

'May I come in now?' she asked coldly.

Gypsy unlatched the window.

'Hope your whiskers are clean,' said Piper, grinning.

'Of course they're clean. What do you think I am, some kind of savage?' Tabitha strolled in, bringing a cold draught with her, and jumped straight on to the table. 'Is there any tea left in the pot?'

I poured a cup for her. 'Need to wash something down, do you?'

'As a matter of fact, yes,' Tabitha replied sarcastically, dipping her head to drink. 'Nothing worse than having fleas and feathers stuck in your teeth.'

'Why didn't you have an omelette?' I asked. 'You drink tea like the rest of us.'

'Tea doesn't keep me alive,' the cat answered. 'It just helps make my situation more bearable.'

'So you don't have a choice?' I asked.

'If I did, do you think I'd choose to crunch up bones and beaks?' said Tabitha. She hiccuped, looking gloomy. 'It was a scrawny thing, too. That's the price you pay, I suppose.'

For what? Gypsy wrote.

'Having nine lives. The food is terrible and takes ages to digest,' she grumbled. 'Speaking of which—' she yawned, '—I need to do some of that now.' She jumped off the table and strolled lazily to the snug, flopping down on a pillow.

I watched her for a moment, unsettled, then went outside on deck into the frosty morning. It wasn't so much the killing of the bird that bothered me, but the realisation that I didn't really know much about Tabitha at all.

Every character in a story must want something, Alice had explained to me once. *That's what makes the story work and gives it conflict.*

Besides Gypsy, who I guessed must want to break her curse and get her voice back, and Ramblebrook, who wanted his museum, I had no idea what the others were after. Piper and the cat were still a mystery to me and, without the story itself, I only knew whatever they chose to tell me.

I didn't trust either of them.

Perhaps the pages Piper had stashed would hold some extra clues, but I knew I wouldn't be able to stop Gypsy reading them. When she did, there was every chance she'd find out the truth, about who and what she was. I considered telling her, but it didn't seem like something she'd believe. Either way, it couldn't stay hidden much longer. Once she knew, once Piper knew, what would they do?

I tried to imagine someone telling me something quite so shocking about myself. It would be like finding out I was adopted and everything in my life was a lie. Yet this still didn't compare to finding out that you yourself were a lie, entirely dreamed up by someone else.

I heard footsteps beside me and turned. Gypsy stood there, watching me with her notepad in her hand.

We're going soon, she'd written.

'To get the pages Piper took?' I asked.

She nodded, staring across the water. I gazed at her. Her skin was smooth and rosy. I searched her jawline for a small scar that Alice had from the time she'd had chickenpox as a baby, but it wasn't there. I reminded myself that this wasn't Alice, and thought of the fortune cards. The spinning wheel with its cursed spindle, the black cat, the Pied Piper.

'What happened between you and Piper?' I asked.

He betrayed me, she wrote. Her eyes clouded a little and she blinked. *It was a long time ago.*

I remember the notes Alice had written on Gypsy. They had said she'd been betrayed by a boy she loved. Surely this couldn't be Piper?

'He could still betray us both now,' I said. 'We only have his word that he hid those pages. He could be leading us into a trap.'

She frowned. *What kind of trap?*

'He could be working with Dolly. If she wanted it enough to steal it, then perhaps she wants to make sure no one else can come after it. Perhaps she wants us out of the way.'

Gypsy narrowed her eyes. *You still haven't asked me why I want the story. Why is that?*

I looked away, unable to meet her gaze. 'I just . . . it's none of my business,' I muttered.

She waited, unconvinced.

I shrugged. 'I thought, if you wanted to tell me, then you would. And . . . and I wanted you to help me. I guessed I had a better chance of that if I didn't seem too nosy.' My face burned at the lie and I rushed on to change the subject. 'I say we ditch Piper as soon as we get those pages. He'll just lead us into trouble.'

'I reckon I've been pretty helpful so far.'

I spun round, horrified.

Piper was on the steps, leaning casually against the roof. He didn't look pleased, but nor did he look especially angry, either. 'Don't worry, I'm used to it,' he said. He buttoned up his coat and blew into his fingers. 'And I only heard the last part of what you were saying, in case you're wondering.'

There was no way of knowing if he was telling the truth.

'Come on then. I'll take you to the pages I hid.' He bit off a fingernail, spitting it into the canal. 'If they're still there.'

'They'd better be,' I muttered under my breath

It was still early when we arrived in the town square. The shops were starting to open, and road sweepers were out, clearing litter strewn across the cobbles from the Summoning the night before.

We'd left Tabitha snoozing on *Elsewhere*. Gypsy hadn't been entirely happy about this, but we'd decided that a cat trailing after us – especially one that couldn't keep its mouth shut – was likely to attract attention.

'Please tell me you didn't leave those pages somewhere stupid,' I said to Piper, seeing a discarded newspaper blowing all over the place.

'They're safe,' he grunted. 'In plain sight in a way. But I'm sure they'll be fine.'

'What do you mean "in plain sight"?' I asked.

'You'll see.' He strode on, towards the library, nearing the fishmonger who was taking a delivery. We hurried past the stacked crates outside and saw that Piper had stopped a little way ahead in front of a door set back in a row of crooked buildings. He rapped on the door and waited.

'This place looks empty,' I said, peering at the painted-out windows. The uppermost one was fogged up from the inside. 'Wait. Someone's in there.'

Piper knocked again, louder this time. A light snapped on, flooding the cracked glass pane above the door. Then came the clipped sound of shoes on wood and a bolt sliding back. The door opened and there stood a man in a poorly fitting tweed suit. He had a severe nose and a neat, grey moustache.

'Yes?'

'I was here yesterday,' said Piper, scratching the back of his neck. 'I helped you carry some boxes in?'

The man peered down his nose through gold-rimmed spectacles. Though he was neat, there was something about him that seemed neglected and undernourished. The only fleshy things about him were the puffy, grey bags under his eyes. 'Oh, yes.' His eyes swept over the rest of us, then back to Piper. 'What is it?'

'I think I dropped something,' said Piper. 'A watch my grandfather gave me. It's not worth much, but it means a lot to me. Could I take a quick look around for it?'

The man gave an impatient sigh. 'As long as it *is* quick. I'm busy.' He stood aside, opening the door wider. Boxes were stacked all along the hallway. Piper stepped past him. The man glanced sternly at the rest of us. 'You'd better come in; it's cold out there. But don't meddle with any of these boxes, do you hear? There's precious work in them, not things to be touched by sticky-fingered children.'

We squeezed past him into the hallway. I caught Gypsy's look of annoyance and could tell what she was thinking: she and Piper could hardly be called children, and I wasn't exactly a baby.

'Wait here,' he told us. 'And remember not to touch anything. I'm just next door.' He vanished into a nearby room and, seconds later, there came the sounds of boxes being cut open.

I stepped past a small table piled with unopened letters, looking for Piper. He was further down the hall, scratching his head as he looked at a pile of boxes. He appeared to be counting them and I guessed he must have stashed the pages in one.

I stared round the hall as we waited in silence. It was a grand space with a high ceiling, a bit like my school, but it needed a good lick of paint. There was no carpet and everything was bare except for thick cobwebs that hung from the ceiling and windows like dusty chandeliers.

My eyes rested on Gypsy, who was crouched down and looking intently at a box on the floor. Her eyes were wide and I could see she was trying to peek inside it without making a noise and alerting the man next door. I knelt by her side.

'What is it?' I mouthed.

She pointed to something printed on the side of the box:

LOTTIE CHURCHILL'S TYPEWRITER

I shook my head, confused. I didn't know any Lottie Churchill. Gypsy finally lifted the lid and we both looked inside. There, carefully padded with bunched-up paper and bubble wrap, was a beautiful old typewriter, like Alice's. Gypsy held her hands up, using her fingers to create a heart shape.

'Love?' I whispered.

She shook her head, then, again using her hands, mimed opening a book.

'Favourite book?'

Then I got it. 'Favourite author.'

She nodded, reaching in to lovingly touch the typewriter, tracing her finger over the keys. She replaced the lid quietly, then stood up, her eyes roving over the rest of the boxes. They were less interesting, marked with letters like E–F and Y–Z. Occasionally, there were boxes that had a single name followed by the word 'only'; obviously some sort of record-keeping system. I wondered if the man was an accountant; he certainly seemed organised enough, although it didn't explain why he had an author's typewriter. Perhaps he was a relative.

I stood up, looking for Piper again, but he'd vanished out of sight. A name on a box further down caught my attention. I recognised it, but I couldn't think where from. Slowly, I edged down the hall towards it, creeping past the door to the room the man had gone into. I glanced in to see him leaning over a desk, sorting papers from an open box with his back to me.

I looked down at the box. Why did I know that name? Then it came to me in a tumble: it was the name of a well-known children's writer. She'd died long ago, but her books were still popular and there were a few in my school library as well as several in Alice's room. Carefully, I lifted the lid and looked inside.

This time there wasn't a typewriter inside the box. It was full of paper. I pulled a piece out and began to read.

Once upon a time, it began. My pulse began to race. *Stories? Typewriters?*

'You're not touching anything, are you?' the man called shrilly, still within the room.

'No,' I answered quickly. I slid the paper back inside the box and made my way back to the little table by the door. I picked up one of the unopened letters from the pile, my breathing shallow. I knew what the name on the envelope would be before I even saw it.

Mr Sheridan Ramblebrook.

16

Paper People

'RAMBLEBROOK?' I BLURTED.

I clapped my hand over my mouth, but the damage was done. Footsteps sounded nearby and then a surprised Ramblebrook appeared at the door.

'Yes?'

'Er . . . I, um . . .' I searched for an excuse. 'Did you used to . . . um . . . teach at Fiddler's Hollow School?'

'I've never taught at any school,' Ramblebrook replied. 'And I'd never set foot in this town until a few days ago.' He rubbed a hand over his moustache. 'I should be interested to know if there is someone locally by the name of Ramblebrook, though. It's an unusual surname. I've never heard of it outside my family.'

Because it's made up, I thought. Alice was fond of inventing strange names.

'You shouldn't snoop,' he added, scooping up his letters protectively.

'Sorry. I didn't mean to. I just noticed the name.'

I tried not to stare at the lettered boxes piled up everywhere. Not boring accounts after all. They must be alphabetised authors' names, and the contents had to be stories.

Unfinished stories.

'Why did you come to Fiddler's Hollow?' I asked. I wanted to get Gypsy and Piper out of this place before Ramblebrook said much more, but I also needed to know his plans. Was he intending to stay here, or just passing through? What had Alice written for him? Had she brought him here, like the others, or had he slipped through of his own accord when she got writer's block?

'Work,' he answered, looking back over his shoulder as though he were aching to get back to it. 'The rent is cheap here and it's as good a place as any.'

'So you're . . . um, sticking around for a while?' I asked.

Ramblebrook nodded to the boxes. 'Certainly. I don't want to be shifting this lot again any time soon.'

I looked down the hallway. What was taking Piper so long? Gypsy had pulled out her notebook and was writing something. Her face was alive with interest, and I knew she wanted to ask more about the typewriter and how it came to be in Ramblebrook's possession. I wished now that I had told her the truth about the story, for if Ramblebrook made any mention of the museum it could ruin everything. Mostly her trust in me.

For the first time since Alice had disappeared, I felt

something other than worry for my missing sister. I felt pity for Gypsy and Ramblebrook, and even Piper. Alice may not have fully believed in what she was doing, but all this had happened the way she'd written it. *Because* she had written it. Her characters had always been real to her, but they were properly real now, and here. They spoke, they ate, they slept. If I cut them, they'd bleed.

So what was to become of them when we found Alice? Would they be absorbed back into the story like ink sucked into paper? No longer existing except as words on a page?

Was that what it would take to get my sister back? Perhaps. I guiltily realised that I didn't care. I just wanted Alice to be all right.

What sort of work do you do? Gypsy had written. *I couldn't help but notice you have Lottie Churchill's typewriter.* She held the notebook up to Ramblebrook and he read it, then regarded her curiously, but was too polite to ask why she didn't speak.

'I'm a collector,' Ramblebrook told Gypsy. 'I collect things to do with writers. Typewriters, favourite pens, or lucky charms, that sort of thing. But mainly I collect their work, although it's of quite a specific kind.' He stopped, looking sheepish. Perhaps he'd been made fun of in the past for his bizarre interest.

What kind? Gypsy asked.

'All kinds in a way.' He was speaking more quickly now, encouraged by Gypsy's obvious interest. 'I collect stories. Stories for children, stories for adults. True stories, short stories, long stories, life stories. They all have one thing in common. They're unfinished.' A shadow crossed his face. 'Quite often due to being the last thing the writer was working on before they . . . uh, passed away.'

I realised I was holding my breath, waiting for Gypsy to make the connection, but she was too caught up in what Ramblebrook was saying to think about what it actually meant. Besides, I had two things on my side: Ramblebrook had not mentioned the word museum, plus Gypsy was looking for a *story* with that title, not a place. Thankfully, Piper appeared next to us, a shabby watch dangling from his fingers.

'Found it.'

Ramblebrook's beaky nose twitched as if scenting the lie. 'I don't really remember you having a watch,' he murmured.

'Why would you?' Piper asked. His tone had changed now he'd got what he wanted. The polite boy who'd knocked had been left at the front door, it seemed.

'I have a knack for noticing small things,' said Ramblebrook. 'And I remember now, yes. You asked me the time once or twice. Why would you do that if you had a watch of your own?' He looked panicked. 'Who are you really? What are you doing here?' He darted along the hallway, checking boxes, making sure they were unopened, then scuttled back to us. 'What have you taken?'

It was Piper's turn to look confused. He pushed the watch at Ramblebrook again. 'I asked you the time, because my watch doesn't work, see?'

Ramblebrook squinted down his nose. 'Oh.' With trembling fingers, he handed it back, then pinched the bridge of his nose with a thumb and forefinger. 'If you'll excuse me, I have to get on.'

He herded us to the door, practically bundling us on to the street. Why was he so worried? And what did he think Piper had stolen?

Gypsy was the last out. I heard a slap as something hit the floor in the hallway behind me, and turned. She had knocked a padded envelope off the table and a sheaf of glossy leaflets had slipped out of it. She bent to retrieve them and handed them to Ramblebrook. He took them, muttering his thanks, and shut the door abruptly. A couple had escaped through the door: one scampering down the street, caught by a draught, and the other under Gypsy's boot. She picked it up, and I glanced at it, my heart sinking.

On the leaflet there was a picture of a quill next to a pot of spilled ink. Below it, a line of words stretched out in a familiar phrase:

THE MUSEUM OF UNFINISHED STORIES

Gypsy stared at the leaflet, walking slowly towards the corner of Pike Street. She chewed her lip, then stopped to look back at Ramblebrook's place. She tucked the leaflet in her pocket and took out her notepad.

Had Alice heard of this museum before it came to Fiddler's Hollow?

I hesitated. 'I . . . I'm not sure. I suppose she must have.'

Gypsy looked thoughtful. *You said she based a lot of things in her stories on real life, real places. She must have researched it; it can't just be coincidence.*

'No,' I muttered guiltily. I could almost guess what was coming next.

Perhaps, if we don't get the rest of the notebook, I might find what I'm looking for in the museum itself, she wrote. *If it inspired Alice's story, there's a chance.*

Piper had stopped a short way ahead of us and was blowing into his hands.

'What's she saying?' he demanded.

I repeated Gypsy's thoughts.

He shrugged. 'We might still get the notebook yet. Plus,' he reached into his coat and pulled out a sheaf of paper, 'your voice could even be in this part.'

Gypsy strode to him, glaring, and snatched it out of his hand.

'Well, that's what you're looking for, ain't it?' he muttered. 'A way to break the curse?'

'Wait,' I said quickly. My voice had risen, giving away my alarm. What if these pages *did* say something about Gypsy or Piper? There was no way another 'coincidence' could be passed off. If Gypsy saw her name within those pages, saw herself and her life written in someone else's words . . .

She looked at me, suspicious.

I swallowed. 'Maybe I should look first . . . to make sure there's nothing . . . p-personal . . . you know? About Alice.'

'Personal?' Piper lifted one black eyebrow. 'You said it was a story. That it was all made up.'

'I know, but . . .'

'You're hiding something,' said Piper. 'I know it. Look at you, you're sweating like a pig in a butcher's shop.'

'I'm not,' I insisted, but, despite the chill wind, I felt my forehead becoming clammy.

'Read it, Gyps.' Piper folded his arms. 'Find out what he's so afraid of.'

'Don't!' I lunged for the pages, but Gypsy held the sheaf out of my reach, and I could only get close enough to see that the pages were covered in Alice's writing. There was no way of knowing what was on them. Perhaps they never mentioned Gypsy at all and I'd blown it anyway.

'Wait,' I croaked, reaching towards her, but she twisted away from me and began to run.

'Yes, Gypsy, run!' A sing-song voice rang out over the cobbled street. 'Run away and read it. You're in for a *real* treat!'

I spun round, aware that, behind me, Gypsy's hurried footsteps had frozen at the sound of her name.

Dolly Weaver had appeared on the corner of Pike Street and was staring at Gypsy. Her smiling, rosebud lips were painted red, as glossy as her neat, bobbed hair. She opened her mouth to speak again and I saw that her teeth were smeared with red. I knew it was lipstick, but I couldn't help imagining her tearing into a lump of raw, bloody meat. It was this, and those glassy eyes, that made her look so disturbing. I'd never seen eyes so lacking in warmth, or so empty. Staring at her, my tummy became a hard little ball of dread.

She walked slowly towards us.

'Dolly Weaver's the name,' she said, then flashed her red smile. A chill went through me. *Dangerous . . . and crazy.* That was how Alice had described her.

'But some of you already knew that, didn't you?' She straightened one black leather glove, then winked at Piper. 'And others I'm already acquainted with.'

Piper scowled, but placed himself between Dolly and Gypsy. 'What do you want?'

'Don't ask silly questions,' she purred. She nodded to Gypsy. 'I want Goldilocks over there to read those pages, then give them to me.'

'Why would we give you anything?' I said shakily. 'You're the one who broke into my house!'

Dolly laughed a tinkling laugh and held up her gloved hands. 'Guilty.' She reached into a little black shoulder bag and pulled something out. 'I suspect you'll be wanting this?'

'That's my sister's notebook,' I said, my temper rising. 'Give it here now.'

'I'll swap you,' said Dolly. 'Those pages, and whatever else is missing from it, in exchange for the rest.' She flicked through the notebook. 'It's a pretty good offer, given that I have the larger chunk.'

I clenched my fists. 'You've got no right to—'

'Oh, I've got every right.'

Something about the way she said it made my body tense even tighter. She *knew*.

'I reckon I can get it,' said Piper, stepping towards Dolly.

She smiled wider, but didn't move. 'I really wouldn't attempt it if I were you. It would . . . *upset* me.' She pulled off a glove and inspected her hands. They were every bit as horrible as Piper had described, her fingers caked with blood and black with something congealed round her fingertips. As I looked at them, I wondered what kind of things they were capable of. And what they might have already done. 'When I get upset, things can sometimes get broken. Fingernails . . .' She took something else from her bag and threw it. It landed at my feet, a grubby green strip of fabric. 'Collars . . .'

I picked it up with trembling fingers. It had been savagely torn in two. A few silky, black hairs were caught on the buckle.

'. . . Furry little necks,' Dolly finished, smiling like she'd just offered us a slice of warm cake. 'So, if you'd like to see that cat again, you'd better give me what I want.' She rolled her eyes. 'I'm fed up with the tiresome thing anyway. It refuses to speak. I'd be glad to give it back, or kill it.' She inspected her nails. 'Your choice. I don't mind which.'

'What do you m-mean our choice?' I stammered. I shot a warning look at Piper, afraid he might mention Tabitha on Gypsy's boat – but he was tight-lipped. I wondered what Dolly would do if she knew it wasn't Tabitha she'd taken, just an ordinary cat, who was non-magical? Would she still think she had something worth trading? And, if she thought Tabitha were valuable, did she really mean to give her back at all – or was having the rest of the notebook even more important to her? 'How do we get her back?'

'By co-operating.' Dolly pulled her glove back on and put the notebook in the bag. 'I can see you're not ready to just yet.' She shrugged. 'That's all right. I'm a patient lady. I understand that you'll all want to read those pages before handing them over, well . . . all except *you*, Piper dear.'

Piper said nothing, but his expression said more than a thousand words of hatred ever could.

Dolly laughed and blew him a kiss, then gave Gypsy a playful look. 'How are you enjoying it so far? She has quite an imagination, doesn't she, this Alice?'

For the first time since Dolly had appeared, I looked at Gypsy properly. Her eyes were darting between Dolly and the pages, but it was the story that had most of her attention and her face was a mixture of disbelief and confusion. I knew then that my fears had come true. Gypsy had seen her name.

'Are you getting it yet?' Dolly asked. 'Are you wondering how someone you've never met could know so much about you? And why it is that this person, this Alice, looks just like you?'

'What's she talking about?' Piper demanded, trying to look at the pages as if he could make sense of them. 'How could Alice have written about you if she's never even met you?'

'Don't feel left out,' Dolly cooed. 'You're in there, too, dear Piper. And me, and the pesky cat for that matter. We're all there, all just paper people. Though, admittedly, Gypsy is the ... what's the word? *Protagonist.*'

Gypsy's head snapped up, a flash of understanding in her eyes.

'What's a protag ... protagon ... ?' I began.

'The main character in a story,' Dolly said. 'So what's it like, Gypsy? Finding out your entire life is a lie dreamed up by someone else? I mean, I know how *I* feel, and I can't feel too sorry for you, not when you've got the starring role. The *heroine's* role.'

The colour had drained from Gypsy's cheeks. She tore her gaze away from Dolly and turned the page over, her eyes racing over the words on the back.

'Still,' Dolly continued, 'everyone knows that villains always get the best lines, so I can't grumble too much.' She paused and winked. 'They sometimes get a fluffy kitty, too!'

'Are you demented or what?' Piper asked. He spoke slowly, like he was talking to someone very young, or stupid. 'Do you know how *nutty* you sound? Don't listen to her, Gyps. She's two licks short of a furball.'

He put his hand on Gypsy's arm, but she shook him off.

'But hark at me going on. I promised myself I wouldn't give away any spoilers, but I just couldn't help it. I'll leave you to it now.' Dolly's voice changed, became sharp, and she looked at me. 'And, speaking of furballs, you have exactly twenty-four hours.'

'To do what?' I asked, unable to disguise the fact my voice was shaking.

'Before we meet back here and exchange our sections of the notebook, plus the cat. That's more than enough time for you to read your part of it, and by then my patience will have worn rather thin. So, if you're not here, the cat dies and the notebook is destroyed. If you try to pull any tricks or forge the story in some way, the cat dies and the notebook is destroyed. Got it?'

'How do we know you haven't already killed the cat?' I said. 'Or faked Alice's notes yourself?'

Dolly waved a hand. 'All that can be verified tomorrow. Besides, you really don't have a choice.'

'We do,' I said, more boldly than I felt. 'We don't have to do what you say.'

'Maybe *you* don't,' said Dolly spitefully. 'But Gypsy does.'

Gypsy looked up again, ashen-faced. She shook her head, but it was unconvincing to us all.

'Yes, you do.' Dolly's voice was soft. 'Because you'll want to know what happens. You'll want to know your destiny and what's written for you in the end – or at least where your story is going.'

'And you?' Piper asked and even he sounded rattled now. 'You've read most of it already. Why do *you* want these pages so badly? There's hardly anything here compared to what you have.'

'No,' said Dolly. 'But I like to have all the information to hand before I make any decisions, particularly when the outcome for me doesn't look good.' She smirked at Piper. 'Same goes for you.'

'What are you talking about?' he asked.

'The ending,' Dolly said. 'I don't like how things are shaping up. Now I know that dear old Alice hasn't finished it yet, so I'm going to give her a hand.'

'You're planning on finishing Alice's story?' I asked.

'*Finishing* it?' Dolly pouted. 'Why would I want to do that when I can live as I please here, in your world, with no rules? Anything I want to happen *can* happen. So Alice finishing the story really isn't part of my plan.'

I stared into her mad eyes, finally understanding. 'You want to kill her.'

The pouting lips stretched into a grin. 'Well, I told you I was the villain, didn't I?'

17
The Silence and the Foundling

A CHOKED SOUND CAME OUT OF GYPSY. SHE pushed the pages at Piper, who grabbed them clumsily. Tears streamed down her cheeks and she turned and ran, sobbing.

Dolly cackled, breaking the stunned silence.

'Gypsy!' I yelled, but found I was rooted to the spot, torn between running after her and getting the pages from Piper in case he was thinking about giving them to Dolly. I moved closer to him and held out my hand. To my surprise, he handed the pages to me without arguing. He was pasty-faced now, unsure of himself and everyone around him. Despite my distrust of him, I found myself edging closer. Piper might be a liar and a thief, but right now he was all I had.

'The plot thickens,' said Dolly. 'How juicy! I wonder what Alice would make of all this if she were here to see it. I think she'd approve actually.'

'How do you know she isn't writing this right now?' I said, saying it as the thought popped into my head. 'Making all this happen? She could be hiding out somewhere, writing a new version. *This* version.'

'Doubtful,' Dolly said. 'You really think if Alice were in control we'd still be here?'

'Maybe,' I said hoarsely. 'She wrote *you*. She created you. She can snuff you out just as easily.'

Dolly sneered. 'Don't kid yourself. She did the groundwork, but then she lost the plot. The story isn't Alice's any more. It's there for the taking. Anything can happen now.'

'No,' I said. 'It's Alice's and always will be. Whatever you are, it's because she decided it. So she's stronger than you. She has to be.'

'Dream on,' said Dolly. Her pale eyes glinted. 'Alice created in me what scares her. All very well when you're reading it on a page, but facing your fears for real? Not so much.'

'You don't know her,' I whispered.

'I don't need to. She knows *me*. And she knows I've killed before.'

I couldn't speak. Terror stuck in my throat like a poisoned apple.

Dolly ran her tongue over her red-tinged teeth. 'I'll see you back here this time tomorrow. And don't be late; it makes me cross. I might be crazy, but I'm always punctual.' She giggled and began walking away, her heels and laughter echoing over the cobbles as she vanished into Pike Street.

'We have to find Gypsy,' I said. 'Then look for Alice's dad. He must know how to end this and how we can find Alice.'

'And what happens if you get Alice back?' Piper asked. He was staring at his hands like he was trying to remember what they were for, as if nothing made sense any more. 'Gypsy and me . . . we just . . . disappear? Go back to being nothing, except in your sister's head? That's what Dolly said, ain't it? That we're made up. Just characters in Alice's book.'

'No,' I said. 'No stories or characters ever disappear, not really. They're always there.'

'Only when someone reads them,' Piper said bitterly.

'I don't think that's true. Alice says stories never start at the beginning. They start when something is about to *happen*. And, when we close the book, does that mean it's the end for the characters? No. They still go on, but without whatever problems they had in the story.'

'Then that must mean there's a reason for me to be in it, too,' said Piper. 'That I'm not . . . *useless*. But . . .' His face darkened.

'What?' I asked.

'Dolly said she didn't like what Alice had written for her, that the outcome didn't look good. And she looked at me and said, "*Same goes for you.*"' He was speaking quickly now, panic making his voice rise. 'What if . . . Alice is gonna kill me?'

'We don't know that,' I said. 'Dolly could be lying, trying to get you to switch sides.' *That's if Piper is even on anyone's side but his own*, I thought privately. 'And anyway the story isn't finished yet.'

'How do you know Alice isn't writing it right now?' he asked bitterly. 'You said to Dolly she could be hiding out somewhere—'

'I was bluffing. Not that she believed it.' I shook my head. 'Wherever Alice is . . . she's not writing this now. She's not writing *you* . . . any of you.'

He nodded slowly, calmer now.

'We need to get Gypsy and find Alice's dad,' I repeated. 'Where would Gypsy have gone?'

He shrugged. 'I ain't a mind-reader.'

'But you know her better than I do.'

'You think?' He chuckled and bitterness crept back in. 'I don't know anything. How can I if I'm not even real?'

'You're real to Alice – and Gypsy,' I said. 'And you're real to me now, too.'

He sniffed. 'So we have to get to the stag. How far is it? Can we make it there and back again by tomorrow?'

'I don't know, maybe. We need a map. Then we can work out how far it is and the best way to get there. And I think I know where we might find Gypsy.'

'Where?' Piper asked.

'The same place we'd find Alice if she's upset about something,' I said softly. 'Somewhere with books.'

*

We went to Chapters first, but found it closed, all the windows dark. I'd forgotten it was a Sunday, when some of the shops stayed shut.

'Let's try the library,' I suggested. 'I'm sure it's open on Sunday mornings.'

We trudged through the mostly empty streets. The bounce had gone from Piper's step. He walked now with his shoulders sloped, sometimes staring into the distance as if in a daydream, or looking around him as if seeing the world for the first time. In a way, I suppose he was.

When we stepped through the library doors, it felt cooler inside than outdoors. It was a vast building with high ceilings and never felt warm even in summer. The papery smell of books, old and new, lingered everywhere. It was impossible not to smell it and think of Alice.

We found Gypsy in the children's section. She wasn't sitting, or reading, or crying, or moving at all. She was simply standing still, staring at the bookshelves. Silvery lines of dried tears traced her face like a watermark through paper.

I hung back as Piper approached her.

'Gypsy?' He touched her lightly on the shoulder, then let his hand drop like he wasn't sure what else to do with it. She didn't react to his touch. 'Oh, Gyps. I dunno what to say.'

She didn't answer. It was clear she thought there was nothing *to* say. Fresh tears spilled on to her cheeks. Piper fumbled in his pockets, but came up with nothing. Instead, he lifted his hand again as if to wipe away her tears, but then thought better of it.

I decided to give them a few minutes and slipped away to the map section, glancing back at Piper and Gypsy every so often. With some help from the librarian, I found a general map of the area, and one of the waterways and towpaths. I took them to Gypsy and Piper.

'It looks like West Maiden is about fifteen miles from here. If we go on Gypsy's boat, it'd get us pretty close to where we need to be. We could walk the rest of the way and make it back before dark.' I paused. 'That's just to the stag. We don't know what we'll find there, or whether it'll lead us to Ramone.' I pushed the maps at Gypsy. She took them numbly, her eyes blank.

'Gypsy?' I said uncertainly. 'Can you take us to the stag?' She shrugged, followed by the faintest of nods.

'Let's go then.' I took Alice's purse out of my rucksack and checked out the maps using her library card. Then we left.

'You've been ages,' Tabitha complained when we arrived back. 'I'm thirsty. I had to drink water from the washing-up bowl.'

Gypsy filled her kettle and placed it on the stove, then stood at the window, brooding. She made no attempt to unmoor us. In the end, it was Piper who unwound the rope and got us on the move. He stayed outside, gazing into the distance. I made a pot of weak tea that no one wanted except the cat, who drank two cups, then began asking questions that no one wanted to answer.

'Is anyone going to tell me what's happened?' Tabitha demanded.

'We ran into Dolly Weaver,' I said finally.

'The catnapper?'

'Right. She wants to trade her part of the notebook and Twitch for the pages we have. We have until tomorrow to read them and work something out.'

'That's good, isn't it?' said Tabitha. She lifted her hind leg to scratch behind her ear. 'Why do you look so worried?'

'Because I don't trust her.' *And because she's threatened to kill Alice*, although I couldn't tell Tabitha this, not without giving her a reason and revealing to Tabitha that she, too, was a made-up character. A surge of panic rose up inside me. We had to find Alice before Dolly did. As much as I tried to tell myself that Alice could hold her own, and that if she had created Dolly she must be stronger, Alice wasn't evil. Dolly was ... and she'd killed before. There was also this other character, Dorothy Grimes. Where did *she* fit into all this?

I closed my eyes and took a deep breath. Getting upset wasn't going to find Alice, or save her. I reminded myself that a good detective works with facts. I thought about what Dolly had and what we did. She had Twitch as a bargaining chip and most of Alice's story.

Neither, I realised, would help her to get what she *really* wanted – and what *we* really wanted – which was Alice.

I opened my eyes, calmer now. We had more clues than

222

Dolly. I was the one who'd thought to Summon Alice. I was the one she'd told to look for her father. *Me*. I was the one who had solved the clue of how to find him. I should have seen it sooner. The best chance of finding Alice was all within me, what she'd taught me, and what I knew about her. Dolly would never have that.

There were other things on our side, too. I glanced at Tabitha. I still didn't completely trust her, but then I didn't trust Piper, either. I didn't know enough about either of them for that, but the cat was valuable – or its lives were. If the worst happened and Dolly found Alice first, then there was a way I could still save her life.

I had to become the cat's master.

'Tell me that riddle again,' I said.

'The one about the Irishman?' Tabitha asked sleepily.

I stared at her blankly.

'Oops, sorry. Wrong riddle.' She stretched. 'Ready?'

'Wait.' I tore some paper from Gypsy's notepad and took her pencil. 'Go on.'

'I'm up when I'm up
And down when I'm down
A thump when a smile
And a flick when a frown.
The opposite side
To the wife of a king
A vessel of venom that
Can kill with a sting.'

I finished writing and read through it several times. Now that it was written down, I found I could think about it more clearly, but it was a tricky one. Looking at the whole thing was too confusing – it was meant to be, but Alice had taught me how to pick riddles apart, line by line. What you had to do was think of everything you could that each clue was telling you, and find the one thing they all had in common.

'Any ideas yet?' Tabitha asked.

'Give me a chance,' I muttered. The first part of the riddle had me completely stumped. Lots of things could be up when they were up, or down when they were down. A kite, a ball, an elevator. Even a person's feelings. I moved on to the next part. 'A thump when a smile and a flick when a frown? What does that mean?'

'Tee-hee,' said Tabitha.

'Are you sure this makes sense?' I asked crossly.

'Of course.'

I grunted, moving on to the second half of the riddle. This seemed more straightforward, something I might actually stand a chance with. *The opposite side to the wife of a king?* 'The wife of a king is a queen,' I mumbled. 'But . . . the opposite side?' I looked at the final lines. *A vessel of venom that can kill with a sting.* There were lots of things that could sting. Wasps, bees, jellyfish. Some people could die from these stings. 'Queen bee?' I said suddenly, thinking of a bee flying up and down. It fitted with that.

Tabitha yawned. 'Nope.'

What else could sting? Nettles? An electric shock? I couldn't make either of those connect with the queen part. I was missing something. 'Any ideas, Gypsy?'

She didn't respond.

I sighed and slipped the piece of paper into my pocket. I'd try again later.

I took out the loose pages from my rucksack. They were crumpled now.

'Do you want to finish reading these, Gypsy?' I asked. 'I mean, before I do? As it's, well . . . about you after all.'

Gypsy shook her head and continued to stare glassily out at the water.

I leafed through the pages. This section appeared to start mid-chapter. A few pages on, it ended and a new chapter began. I flipped back to the front. Gypsy's name jumped out at me almost immediately.

The first couple of pages described how *Elsewhere* had belonged to her papa, and how they would walk down to the river from their cottage in the summer months and sit aboard it. Her papa would catch fish for supper, and Gypsy would read him her stories. Papa would also tell her about her mother, who had left them when Gypsy was just a baby. Neither of them had seen her again, and Gypsy could not remember her at all. And, though they were very happy together, Gypsy often wondered why her papa always sailed so far and seemed to be searching for something.

Unlike many others who are cursed, Gypsy's was not one she was born with, which made it all the harder to bear. When you are born cursed, it is accepted as part of your lot and you never know any differently.

Gypsy's curse was Silence, and it was bestowed on her when she was ten years old. On the day it happened, she was playing down by the river with Johnny Piper, though most of the villagers called him the Foundling Child as he had been taken in by Gypsy's family when he was small.

Foundling children were considered unlucky in Twisted Wood. It stemmed from an old folk tale told to children about a little foundling girl with red boots who turned up in the village alone one winter's night, begging for shelter. Only one family took pity on her, but in the morning they woke to find that she was gone, having slaughtered their children in their sleep and eaten them. The only traces of the girl were red, bloody footprints leading away from the house and off into the snow.

It also did not help that Johnny Piper played a flute, and, when he did, odd things happened around him: chickens laid more eggs; cows produced more milk; children would follow him in the street; and adults would often forget what they were saying or doing.

When Gypsy's papa learned of this, he forbade Piper from playing his flute anywhere except at home and in the woods down by the river. There was enough hearsay surrounding Gypsy and her father already: stories about her mother that were never too far from the tongues of the village gossips. It was said that there had been a pinch of witchery about the woman, as well as a liking for cruelty.

On this day, Gypsy's papa was painting the boat and making a few repairs. Gypsy and Piper were playing in the grass next to the river, Piper making up little tunes and Gypsy putting words to them to entertain them all. When Papa's work took him inside the boat, the two children began to stray to the edge of the woods, led in part by Piper. He was twiddling a tune to a trail of blue butterflies that swooped in time to his will, plainly bewitched.

Eventually, losing interest, he stopped playing and released the creatures from his spell, and he and Gypsy watched as they fluttered dozily away. The two children found a puddle of sunlight in the grass and sat there, plucking daisies.

'You've never explained how you do that,' said Gypsy.

'Dunno how really,' Piper replied. He put the flute away and stretched out, folding his arms behind his head. 'I just remember being taught some of the tunes by my pa, and made to play them over and over. He was pleased when I did that, because people threw coins . . . loads of coins. A lot more when I played than when he did, so I'd play and he'd collect.'

Gypsy nodded. She had heard about Piper's pa before, from both him and her papa. The story was the same, but different, depending on who told it. She wondered which version was right, for surely they couldn't both be? She knew her papa to be a good and honest man, and yet she had heard

Piper's version many times, and it never changed. It was a story he told often, because it was the tale of the last time he had seen his pa: how they had gone to a different town, and Piper had played a new tune that he'd been practising, and people had stopped to listen, dropping more coins than ever before.

Afterwards, his pa had scooped up the money and hurried them away, and, when they stood in an alleyway, counting it out, there was much, much more than Piper remembered seeing, as well as purses, wallets and jewellery. Piper's pa told him he'd done good and ruffled his hair. Then footsteps sounded at the mouth of the alley and voices shouted: 'There they are!' And Pa stuffed Piper's pockets with the purses and wallets and told him to run and to wait for him by the museum. Pa would come for him later.

So Piper ran. He knew where the museum, an enormous stone building, was, because his pa had pointed it out earlier. He waited on the steps, hiding in alcoves behind statues and ducking behind pillars when he thought anyone was looking at him. It got dark, and the museum closed its doors, and still Pa didn't come. Piper kept staring at the word MUSEUM above the doors. He knew it was a word even though he couldn't read, and he passed the time by memorising the shapes of the letters. It got darker and colder, and still no Pa.

He fell asleep at the foot of a statue and only woke when strangers came, telling him his pa was gone. He was taken to a place where children went that had no other place to go, although he kept telling them his pa would come and take him home. But, in the end, it was the Spindles who did. He never saw his pa again.

Gypsy's father's version of the tale was one only she had heard. Papa had never told it to Piper and said she never should, either. It was much the same story, except that Papa said that the money and jewellery hadn't just come to them from Piper's music. His pa had been seen pilfering the crowd's pockets while the tune held them mesmerised.

Piper's pa knew what he was doing when he sent Piper to wait for him, and was never planning on collecting him. They knew this, because the wallets and purses he had given to Piper were empty; his pa had taken everything of value and left his son penniless while he, loaded with riches, made his escape. Piper was never told this, because, Papa said, it would take away his hope, and that was something that no one should live without.

'Do you think you'll see your pa again?' Gypsy asked now.

'I used to,' Piper replied. 'But they reckon, if you're lost, the best place to stay is where you are. I've been in Twisted Wood for six years now and he's never come back.'

Gypsy said nothing.

'What about you?' he continued. 'Think you'll ever see your mother again? Would you want to?'

'What do you mean?' she asked.

He pulled up a handful of grass, crushing it in his fist. She moved out of the shaft of sunlight she was in to see him better. His cheeks looked a little pinker than usual. 'Everyone's heard the stories about her.'

'I've heard the odd whisper that she might have been a witch,' said Gypsy. 'But she'd been a traveller before she met Papa. Her beliefs were different to the people around here. She had strange little sayings, used different medicines to them. Sang different songs.' She sighed. 'She followed her own path, an older one than most people do nowadays.'

'What about the other stuff . . . about her and . . . you?'

'What about me?' Gypsy felt defensive all of a sudden.

Piper didn't answer.

'What have you heard?'

'Just . . . spiteful gossip.'

'Well, you brought it up.' She screwed up the daisies and tossed them aside. 'So you can tell me now. What do people say about her?'

'Just drop it, Gyps, please?'

'Tell me!'

'They say . . . they say she cried and cried after she had you. And that one day your papa came home and found her holding your face down in a bucket of water. She was trying to drown you.'

'That's a lie!' Gypsy leaped to her feet with wild eyes. 'You tell me who said that, right now.'

He tried to take her hand, but she snatched it away. 'Everyone. It's what everyone says. Your papa didn't tell no one, but people heard him shouting through the walls, saw him chasing her out with you clutched in his arms. You were dripping wet and blue. He got to you just in time.'

'My mother would never do that.'

'She'd done it before, Gyps. With kittens. Every one of them in a bucket of water before their eyes had even opened.'

Gypsy's breath came in short, quick gulps. 'But . . . b-but—'

'I know you've heard that story before,' Piper said softly. 'I was there in the schoolyard, right next to you, when that Fletcher kid started singing it. Remember?

"Mrs Spindle had a pail of water,

As well as a liking for slaughter.

She was first scratched and bitten

As she drowned three white kittens

Before—"'

She did remember. Piper had thrown a punch before the Fletcher kid had managed to finish. Got him right in his fat, spiteful mouth. That'd shut him up. It was funny, but she'd always been too upset thinking about the first part of the poem to wonder much about how it might have ended. The line Piper had prevented from being said. Now she had a pretty good idea of what it was, but she wanted to hear it anyway.

'What was the final line?' she asked hoarsely.

'You sure you want—?'

'Yes.'

'Before . . .' Piper swallowed. 'Before moving on to her daughter.' He reached out for her hand, squeezing it tightly.

'That can't be true. It just can't. The kittens . . . they must have been sick. She would have been doing it to put

231

them out of their misery. And the rest, that's just people being wicked. My mother wouldn't do that!'

'You never knew her, Gyps,' Piper said softly. 'You only know what you've heard from your papa. Other people say different.'

'It doesn't matter what other people say! Papa knew her best!'

'Or maybe he just knew the best side of her . . . until he saw the truth.' Piper raked his hand through his hair. 'There's never just one side to a person, or a story. Maybe you need to hear a few different versions before you can work out the true one.'

'You can talk!' she cried. 'Hoping your pa might still come back for you!' She heard his breath catch, heard the cruelty in her own words, but couldn't stop. She was hurting and she wanted someone to share it. 'Everyone knows he ditched you. He just used you to make him money and, as soon as he had enough, he was gone. So don't talk to me about what's true when you can't even see it yourself!'

She gave him a hard shove. It caught him off guard and he staggered backwards as she fled into the trees. He gave chase immediately, but Gypsy was quick and the woods were dense. With the sound of his own movements crashing in his head, it was hard to hear where she was and, within a little while, he realised she'd thrown him off the scent by tossing a stone or a stick in another direction.

He stopped running. Why was he chasing her anyway? Let her go. It would do her good to stew in her own juice.

232

He trampled on, stamping down grass, cracking twigs and snapping dandelion heads. He was way off the path by now, but past caring. He went on and on, working up a sweat, but his temper only worsened. Eventually, he stopped and sat on a log, taking out his flute.

He brought it to his lips and started to play. That would serve her right, he thought, to be brought back to him by his tune. If she were close enough to hear, she would come.

Soon someone did. He heard footsteps behind him, sensed he was being watched.

It was not Gypsy, though. It was an old woman, and he couldn't help giving her a scowl for not being who he wanted her to be.

'Ooooh, a temper, is it?' she said, craning her neck to look at him. 'What a cross little tune indeed.' She was bent over with a load on her back that looked far too much for her twiggy little legs. He hadn't seen her before. Even though she was tiny, she was made bigger by the dozens of little cages hanging off her sleeves. Some were empty; others contained small creatures, mainly birds.

'Poaching's against the law,' he muttered, angered by her observation.

'Not poaching.' She wagged a knobbly finger. 'Collecting.'

'Looks like poaching to me.'

She shook her head. 'I collect pretty things.' She took a sidestep into his path. 'I saw a pretty thing come along this way just a few minutes ago. At least she would have been pretty if her face wasn't all screwed up, and she was saying some ugly words.' She gave a mischievous grin. 'A quarrel, was it?'

'None of your business.' His anger flared up again, at the old woman, and especially at Gypsy.

'Want to get back at her?' Her eyes were sly and there was something a bit bird-like about them. Even so, he couldn't resist asking.

'How?'

'Just a little trick,' she said. 'It'll make her think twice before saying unkind words again.'

'How?' he repeated.

She untied one of the cages and handed it to him. A little green-and-blue bird sat inside. 'Play her a tune,' she said. 'The one you were playing a moment ago.'

He lifted the pipe and played. The bird tilted its head, listening. He wondered what kind it was, something not from these parts, that was for sure.

'Keep playing,' she whispered, releasing the peg from the cage door.

The bird took off through the woods, singing as it went, echoing his tune back to him. He heard it circling their heads, then grow fainter, singing all the while. Then the singing stopped and he heard a familiar sound. Gypsy's voice, somewhere within the trees.

'Don't stop,' the old woman said. She held the cage up in the air.

Gypsy's voice rang out from above, high-pitched and afraid. 'What's happening to me? Why can't I—?'

The bird swooped down and landed in the cage. The old woman slammed the door shut and pegged it, hopping from one foot to the other in glee.

'Help!' cried the bird in Gypsy's voice. 'Somebody help me!'

Piper stopped playing as Gypsy came crashing through the woods, her eyes wide and her hands clutching her throat. He dropped the flute and ran to her. It wasn't a lesson; it wasn't a harmless little trick. It was spiteful and she was scared.

'That's enough now,' he said, turning back to the woman. 'Let the bird go—'

But he and Gypsy were alone. There was no sign of the old woman, or her creatures. They had vanished, taking Gypsy's voice with them.

18

The Luck Charm

THE CHAPTER ENDED THERE. THERE WAS STILL more to read, but my head was too full of Gypsy and Piper to concentrate.

Gypsy was still standing by the window, unmoving, when I went to her side.

'I've read the pages,' I said quietly. 'I know how you lost your voice.'

Without warning, she seized a cup next to the sink and turned, hurling it at the opposite wall. I flinched as it smashed, broken china flying everywhere. Gypsy's face was no longer blank. It was alive with rage. I backed away from her, crawling on to the bunk bed and shielding myself with a cushion as she turned and grabbed whatever was to hand.

The cat zipped past, ears flat to her head and tail sticking out like a bottlebrush. 'She's gone mad!' she yowled.

I saw Piper duck down to look through the window, and heard him swear. '*Gypsy!*'

The crashing continued as he stopped the engine and brought us to a halt. He appeared in the cabin, his boots crunching over glass.

Gypsy was like a wild thing, her hair flying out and her teeth bared in a silent scream. Her cheeks were wet with tears. She lashed out with her fists and feet, not caring what she hit. Piper grabbed her, taking a couple of blows in the process, but held her tight to him to stop her beating arms.

'Stop it. Just stop now. This ain't gonna help.'

She struggled, but he held her firm, surveying the damage. She'd swept the draining board clear, breaking most of the crocks. The sugar pot lay on its side, the lid in two halves on the floor and sugar scattered everywhere. Milk dripped from the work surface.

'Do you think your papa would want to see you treating his boat like this?' Piper said. 'Well, do you?'

She glared up at him, then her face crumpled and she buried it in his shoulder and wept silently. When her sniffles had subsided, he led her to the snug and sat her down, tucking a blanket over her like she was a child, and placing the chalk and slate next to her.

Gypsy picked up the chalk with one hand and rubbed her nose with the other. She pressed the chalk against the slate.

'What's she saying?' I asked unthinkingly.

Piper scowled. 'If darling Alice had given me the ability to read, then I'd tell you.' That same bitter note had crept into his voice again, but this time I understood. Now

237

that I'd read about his past, I'd seen another side to him. He wasn't just a smirking thief. He'd been only a child, a frightened boy when the one person he had in the world had abandoned him. More than that, he had cared for Gypsy – and plainly still did now.

Reluctantly, I climbed off the bed and went to Gypsy. 'I'll do it,' I said. I sat down next to her, wary at first in case she flared up again, but Piper gave a slight nod. She was like a cork that had been popped, a match that had been struck. The fight had left her.

I read what she had written aloud.

You have no idea what it's like to find out that everything about you is a lie. That you're just a figment of someone else's imagination. She waited until I'd finished, then wiped the slate with her sleeve to make more room and continued.

We only exist because your sister put us into a story. We exist for her entertainment. For your entertainment. My mother is a monster because it made for good entertainment. Her eyes narrowed. *And probably because, if I'm the main character, to make you pity me. To get you on my side. I lost my voice to keep you turning the pages. Piper's pa abandoned him.*

All our lives are on these pages. Our private thoughts, our secrets. Things no one should have to share, but they're here for whoever reads them to see. She cleared the slate again and gestured to notebooks on the shelves. *All the stories I've ever written are no longer my own. They belong to Alice, like everything else in my world.*

I waited for Gypsy's temper to flare, but she remained

still. I tried to think of something to say that would ease her pain. 'Alice often says her characters take over when she's writing. Doing their own thing. Like the story is writing itself and the characters take control.' I gave a weak smile. 'Never like this before, though.'

Gypsy's chalk pressed against the slate so hard that crumbs of it chipped away and landed in her lap. *I envy her.*

'I think she feels the same about you,' I said.

Gypsy shook her head, disbelieving, but I rushed on. 'You're the version of her that she dreams of. The person she wishes she could be. You're beautiful—' she snorted at this, '—well, you *are* and you don't care what people think of you. You wear cool clothes and you sail around on this perfect boat, going wherever you like, writing stories that you can finish if you want to, but don't have to. Not like her.'

But she cursed me. She made my mother abandon me.

'I think your mother left because Alice's father did,' I said. 'And, with the curse, you're forgetting something.'

What's that?

'That every story and every character have problems they need to solve,' I said. 'That's the point of the story. She wrote your curse, but she would have wanted you to undo it. That's the whole point of the story.'

And if she can't finish the story? What then?

'She has to finish it,' I said. 'But first we have to bring her back from wherever she is. Her dad will know what's happened to her – we just have to find him.'

'We'd better get going,' said Piper, getting up. 'Gyps, I'm gonna need your help in a minute. There's a lock coming up.' He crunched over the broken crockery to go outside on deck.

Gypsy got up and took a dustpan and brush from under the sink, and set about sweeping up the mess. I knelt down to help her, but she shook her head.

It's my mess, she wrote. *I'll fix it.*

I sat back on my heels, watching her. She pulled her hair off her face and tied it back in a messy knot. I found myself staring at the tiny scorpion tattoo just below her ear, and remembered first reading about it in Alice's notes. I'd thought then it was a strange choice, and I still did – but now I found it suited her. It wasn't ugly, or cruel-looking. It just kind of reminded me of Gypsy herself. Waiting for an attack, ready to defend herself. Lashing out, but only when she was injured.

'Why did you get that, Gypsy?' I asked. 'The scorpion?'

She stopped what she was doing, touching her fingers to her neck. Then she took out her pencil again. *Where we come from it's a symbol of strength. A luck charm, for protection.*

'Protection?'

She nodded. *Most people choose charms for love or riches. I chose the scorpion, because it's said its sting has the power to ward off danger, even save your life.*

'Sting!' I snapped my fingers, instantly thinking of Tabitha's riddle. Of course – the sting of a scorpion could be deadly. Could that be the key? I couldn't think of how it connected to a queen, though. I took out the slip of paper with the riddle on it, trying to make it fit, but, after staring at it for several minutes, I was no closer to solving it. When Gypsy finished clearing up and joined Piper outside on deck, I went back to the snug, sinking into the cushions and puzzling over it, but still getting nowhere. I closed my eyes, thinking, exhausted, lulled by the rocking of the boat on the water. Without meaning to – or even realising I was – I drifted off. Sometime later, Piper's shout from above jerked me awake.

I scrambled to my feet, rubbing my eyes as I went up on deck. A chill breeze chased the last sleepiness away.

'Look,' said Piper, pointing ahead.

Gypsy stood at the front of the narrowboat, shielding her eyes from the sun.

There, on a hillside in the distance, stood a majestic horned statue.

'We found it,' said Piper. 'The five-legged stag.'

Twenty minutes later, we'd moored as close as we could, shrugged into warm clothes and clambered on to the path. It was just past noon, but the day didn't feel much warmer than it had when we'd started out.

'Looks a bit of a trek,' said Piper. 'It's all uphill. Come on, there's a path up ahead.'

We'd only taken a few steps when a black shape appeared alongside us.

'Nice of you to join us,' Piper grunted. We began

walking again, Tabitha moving silently through the grass beside us.

She yawned. 'I felt like stretching my legs.'

'Well, now you're here, perhaps it's time you told us a bit more about yourself,' I said.

'Why?'

'Because you've been lurking around since the start of all this, not saying much, but hearing everything. And,' I said, suddenly realising something, 'you didn't seem surprised at all when Gypsy was upset just now, after finding out she was a . . .'

'A character in your sister's story?' Tabitha said bluntly.

'Yes.' I reddened, glancing sideways at Gypsy. Her expression was stony. 'And, well . . . there's no easy way to say this, but you are, too.' I paused. 'Or had you guessed that already?'

The cat pounced on something in the grass. 'Drat. Missed it.'

'Tabitha? Did you hear me?'

'What? Oh, sorry. Well, yes, I assumed that was the case.'

'You're not shocked?' Piper asked.

'Nothing surprises me any more,' Tabitha replied. 'That's the way it is when you've lived three lives. Besides, I've heard enough to work out that, wherever I am, it's somewhere that talking cats are rare.'

I snorted. 'Not rare. Impossible.'

'Yet here I am, talking to you,' said the cat scornfully. 'So clearly not. Nothing is impossible.'

'You said you've lived three lives,' I said. 'And that you were human once—'

'Did I? I don't remember that.'

'When you said you missed soap and water,' I reminded her.

'Oh.'

'Someone must have turned you into a cat,' I pressed.

'What makes you think I didn't do it myself?' Tabitha asked. She leaped on to a tree stump and scratched it hard, her white claws gleaming like tiny talons.

'You did it *yourself*?' Piper turned to look back, his eyebrows lost in his long fringe. 'Why?'

'Because I could and it was better than the alternative,' the cat answered. 'Do you know what happens to people who can do that sort of magic where I come from? It's not pretty.'

'You mean like ... witches?' I asked.

'Oh, goody, they use that word here, too,' Tabitha muttered sarcastically.

What word would you prefer then? Gypsy scrawled. *Enchantress? Sorceress?*

'Cripes, no,' Tabitha retorted. 'None of that fancy malarkey. "Wise Woman", it was. I was happy enough with that. They'll come to you to cure their warts and their flatulence, but as soon as anything goes wrong they turn on you, quick as you like. "*Ooooh, Mother Tattle see a toad that looked at her funny!*" Or, "*Farmer Ned 'ad bad dreams about someone pinchin' 'im, an' woke up black an' blue!*" That's all it takes to get fingers waggling. And then the "witch" word starts getting bandied about.'

'People here used to burn witches hundreds of years ago,' I said. 'And that's in real life.'

Tabitha jumped off the tree stump, her ears flattened to her head. 'Real life sounds just as bad as life in stories.'

'It's probably worse,' I said. 'Anyway, why did you decide to turn into a cat?'

'I thought I'd just explained that,' said Tabitha. 'To escape.'

'But why a cat? Why not just someone else?'

She looked at me as if I were very stupid. 'It had to be someone or something that would agree to switch places with me. No human in their right mind would choose to do it, but my dear moggy was more than happy to. I'd given her a good life, you see, and witches – if we're using that word – and their familiars are bonded for life. If I died – and I would have, if they'd caught up with me – she'd have died, too, only she'd have suffered more. *Nine* times more, as they finished each of her lives. This way I'd have a chance of escaping and surviving, and she could at least go peacefully.' Tabitha gave a little sigh. 'She was a sensible thing, still on her first life as luck would have it.'

I frowned. 'Her first life? What about the other eight?'

'She still had them. They're there to get you out of scrapes, but, like I said, she wasn't scatty. . .'

'So the cat was on her first life, and you used up another two,' I said. 'That means you have six left?'

'Indeed,' Tabitha agreed, with a sly look at Piper and Gypsy. 'Plenty of mischief left in me yet.'

Gypsy fell into step beside me. Until now I hadn't been sure she was listening, but she lifted her notepad to show me something.

'Gypsy wants to know what happened to the cat, after you switched places with it?'

'The switch used up life number one,' said Tabitha. 'So, at that point, I was on the second, with seven left. We were in hiding by then. The whole town had witch fever – if they had found me, they'd have ripped me apart with their bare hands, let alone burned me. I knew it wouldn't be long before they discovered my hiding place.' She gave a sad little hiccup. 'Once she was in my human body and I was in this one, she drank a sleeping draught I'd mixed. I'd made it strong enough so that she'd never wake from it. She slipped away in her sleep. After that, I coloured the tip of my tail and one paw white with flour to disguise myself, and made my escape.'

'Poor cat,' I murmured, breathless now. I looked uphill. 'Are we nearly there yet?'

'Shouldn't be far now,' said Piper. 'Let's just hope the weather stays dry— *Yeeouch!*' He broke off, his shriek scattering birds from the trees overhead. Tabitha had leaped on to his shoulder and was hanging on with her claws as he tried to shake her off. 'What are you doing? Get— *Ouch!* Get off me!'

'I'm tired,' she complained, retracting her claws and arranging herself round his neck. 'There. Is that better?'

'No!' he spluttered. He jerked his shoulders and she landed neatly on all fours. She shook herself and glared at him.

'What?' he said. 'You said you wanted to stretch your legs.'

'They're stretched,' she said coldly.

'Try that again and you'll say goodbye to another life.' Piper rubbed his back. 'Probably by strangulation,' he muttered under his breath.

'I heard that.'

'Good.'

'How were the other two lives used up?' I asked.

'Oh, those?' the cat said airily. 'I gave them willingly.'

'*Gave?*' Piper scoffed. 'You're not completely selfish then?'

'Most of the time, yes,' said Tabitha, without a hint of embarrassment. 'In my experience, being nice doesn't get you very far. But on this occasion I owed a favour.'

'To who?'

'To someone who had saved one of my lives – or probably all of them.' She sighed. 'I'd got myself noticed, you see. Talking when I shouldn't have been.'

'There's a surprise,' said Piper.

'Don't interrupt,' said Tabitha. 'Anyway, I'd been caught by this horrible boy who was doing all sorts to try to get me to talk again. Goodness knows how far he'd have gone if I hadn't been saved. So, you see? It was a pretty big favour. It was only fair I repaid it.'

'What did you do?' I asked, unzipping my coat. The climb

was making me warm now; I could feel the blood humming through my legs.

'Same as before,' she replied. 'I switched places with a human in a tricky spot, then later on switched back again.' She sighed. 'The switching back was regrettable, but it was part of the deal. Still, there's always hope for a permanent trade one of these days.'

'You'd rather be a human?' I asked.

'Of course. Spending two-thirds of your time asleep gets dull after a while. Plus, the diet is terrible.'

'Who—?' I began, but broke off as Piper gave a shout.

'We're here.' He broke into a run, haring off ahead with Gypsy behind him.

I loped after him, my limbs heavy. A high wall came into view through the trees. Further on, on a tall stone pillar mounted above an overgrown pavilion, was the stag. A gravel road swept past it to a vast house, plainly derelict, set some way back.

'Look at this place,' said Piper, pausing as Gypsy and I caught up to him. 'No one's been here for a long time.'

Gypsy pointed, mouthing two words: *Someone has.*

At first, I couldn't see it, but then a huddled shape under the pavilion came into view.

'Great,' said Piper. 'S'all we need: some drifter in the way.'

'Looks like they're asleep,' I said as we drew nearer. The ground was bumpy and scattered with litter: signs of other trespassers. For now, though, it was just us, plus the figure under the pavilion. For the briefest of moments, I wondered

247

if it could be Ramone; after all, he was the reason we'd come here. Could it be that easy?

Piper squinted. 'Is that definitely a person? Not just a pile of old clothes?'

'No, it's a person all right,' I said. 'Look, there's a leg . . .'

I stopped walking. For a moment, it felt as though my heart had stopped, too.

'What's wrong?' Tabitha asked.

'That's not Ramone,' I whispered.

Before I knew what I was doing, I found my feet were pounding the ground, running harder than I'd ever run before.

'Midge, wait!' Piper shouted after me, but I couldn't stop, not now I'd seen that leg . . . and recognised those pyjamas. I heard the others running behind me, trying to catch up, but I reached the pavilion first, leaping into it and skidding across the marbled floor.

There were four stone benches curving round, sheltered by the roof. She lay on one, curled up on her side, her hands placed together under her cheek like a child. Her eyes were closed and her lips, pale but still pink, were slightly parted.

I was afraid to touch her, but I reached out anyway, placing my fingers on her cheek.

'Alice,' I whispered. 'Alice, wake up!'

She didn't move.

I grabbed her hand. 'Please wake up!' I was having trouble seeing for some reason, my vision kept swimming in front of me. It was only when Gypsy reached out and wiped my face that I realised I was sobbing. 'Why won't she wake up?' I croaked. 'Is she . . . ?'

Piper knelt at Alice's side and touched his fingers to her neck. 'She ain't dead. She's breathing and warm somehow.'

'Are you sure?' I whispered. 'But how? She's been gone for nearly two days . . . she must have been here all night!'

I saw it now, the slight rise and fall of her chest as she drew breath. I felt an arm round me, smelled a familiar scent that was so like Alice, but not. Gypsy had pulled me to her. 'We need to get her up,' I babbled. 'She'll die if she stays in the cold. It's a miracle she's even alive out here in her nightclothes . . . in February! We have to get her to a hospital!'

Piper brushed a strand of hair from Alice's cheek. 'She looks just like you, Gyps,' he said, his voice soft. 'It's like looking at you.'

Gypsy's face was a mask of shock – she was unable to tear her eyes from Alice. I slipped my arms round her and hugged her back.

'You're right, let's get her somewhere warm,' said Piper. He slid his hand under Alice, cradling her head, and shifted her weight into his arms. Something fluttered out of her hands and landed at my feet.

I picked it up, already knowing what it was. I recognised the pattern on the back. It was still warm from having been pressed between Alice's hands.

'A fortune card,' I whispered.

I turned it over. The image on the other side showed a

young woman in a deep sleep. She'd clearly been there for a long time, for her hair had grown long, spreading over her pillow and spilling round the room. The background showed a spinning wheel overgrown by thorny brambles.

'The curse,' I muttered.

'I thought she was called Sleeping Beauty,' said Piper.

'She is,' I said. 'But she was cursed, like Alice ... and like Gypsy.'

'Got herself in a right pickle,' said Tabitha, shaking her head at Alice. 'Even without that card, it's obvious this is no catnap. Medicine and hospitals aren't going to help her.'

'Alice was trying to break the curse,' I said slowly. 'She must have come here for the same reasons we did – to find her dad. But she was too late.'

'Juicy,' said Tabitha, curling her tail into a neat loop. 'Plot twist or what?'

'All this time I thought Alice was *in* the story,' I said. I remembered the coal dust on her face when she appeared after the Summoning, and the coal dust on the paper I'd found on the hearth. 'Unless ... unless she *is* in the story in a different way.'

'What about when she popped up in my cup of tea, hmm?' Tabitha said. 'Was she here, there, or in the story? She can't have been in all three.'

'But she must have been, don't you see?' I said. 'Her body was here – she must have come to this place straight after she left home. But her mind ... that's in the story.' I looked at the fortune card. 'Like a dream she's stuck in. The Summoning couldn't bring both parts of her back – only the strongest part. Her mind. That's why she appeared as a reflection.'

'So where's Ramone?' Piper asked, throwing up his hands in annoyance. 'We've come all the way here and there's no sign of him.'

I searched the grounds, but there was no one else in sight. 'I don't know. We must be missing something.'

I stepped off the pavilion and jogged a few paces to get a better look at the stag, the first proper look I'd taken. There were two letters cut into the curved stone walls of the pavilion, W and S. Initials of whoever had once owned the house, I supposed. And it was then that I noticed something else.

'It doesn't have five legs,' I said. 'We were too busy looking at Alice on our way up to it that none of us noticed. But look.'

Piper came to stand beside me. Gypsy and Tabitha stayed where they were, Gypsy cradling Alice on the stone seat.

'How many does it have then?' Tabitha asked.

'Four,' said Piper. 'Plus an extra lump of wood that's been added in, like a support or something. From a distance, it looks like a fifth leg.'

I gazed at the stag, unable to stop feeling disappointed. I'd wanted it to be true, that once there might have been such a creature as a magical, five-legged stag. I stayed silent for a moment, thinking. It was exactly the sort of thing Alice would put into a story, only she'd invent some wonderful tale behind the reason for the fifth leg.

'We're still no closer to finding him then,' Piper said angrily.

'What about the house?' I said, desperate. I turned to it, searching its boarded-up windows for a sign someone could be in there, but it seemed unliveable in – except perhaps for foxes or rats, or people who had fallen on very hard times.

Piper made a scoffing noise, drawing his coat further round him. 'No one's in there.'

I stared at Alice. 'Ramone Silver, where are you?' I whispered.

As the words left my lips, a gust of icy wind chilled my cheeks, and Alice's hair whipped across Gypsy's face. At the same moment, a thin, creaking sound came from above us. I glanced up.

The stag was moving, swinging wildly to face the other direction. I ducked, thinking it was going to topple and fall, but it settled in place as the wind died down.

Piper pointed to the letters carved into the stone and began circling the pavilion. I followed, and soon it became clear: W and S. Not initials, but simple directions. West and south, followed by east and north.

'It's a weathervane,' I said. 'And it's pointing north.'

I felt a weird fluttering in my tummy and my heart began to thud. A bit, I thought, like the hooves of a stag pounding the ground. 'So north must be where we have to go to find Ramone Silver.'

19

Story Born

WE PUT ALICE ON THE BOTTOM BUNK BED back on *Elsewhere*. Gypsy brushed the tangles out from her hair, and placed Alice's hands on her chest over the blanket that covered her.

'Now she's a proper Sleeping Beauty,' Piper murmured.

I stared at Alice. She was so still that it was hard to see that she was even breathing, or any sign of the pulse that fluttered faintly in her neck. The only indication that she was alive was her eyes. Under her closed lids there were occasional movements, as if she were dreaming.

'Or Snow White,' I added. Only this time it was not a bite of poisoned apple that kept my sister from waking up.

'Does Alice have anyone ... a boyfriend?' Piper asked.

'I don't think so,' I answered. 'There was someone she liked ...' I hesitated. 'He looked a lot like you. But she's always been so shy.'

I looked at Gypsy. Her lips were pressed in a thin line.

I turned back to Piper. 'You were thinking about those stories, weren't you? Snow White and Sleeping Beauty were both woken by a kiss of true love.'

He shrugged. 'It was just a thought. But if she has no one—'

Hope stirred within me. 'There *is* someone, though. There are different kinds of love. It's worth a try.'

'No point if you ask me,' said Tabitha, blinking sleepily. She'd curled up on Alice's feet at the bottom of the bed. 'Even if we do find Alice's father, how can he love her if he barely knows her?'

'I wasn't thinking of Ramone,' I said. 'I was thinking of me. No one could love Alice more than I do.' I stroked Alice's cheek, then bent over and kissed her on the forehead.

'Wake up, Alice,' I said softly. 'I need my big sister back.'

There was the tiniest of twitches around Alice's mouth, like the start of a smile, but it vanished before I was sure it had even been there. She slumbered on.

'Any more bright ideas?' said Tabitha.

'No.' I gave her a cold look. 'But if *you* have any feel free to share them.'

Gypsy went up on deck to steer. We were heading north and, though none of us had said it, we all knew that it could only be a matter of hours before we were forced to turn round and go back if we were to make Dolly's deadline.

'*I've* got an idea.' Piper took out his flute.

'What are you doing?' I asked.

'Speeding things up.' He walked to the steps to go up on deck. 'If he's anywhere within earshot, I can bring him to us.' He vanished outside, leaving me alone with my sleeping sister.

Moments later, a lilting tune carried down from above.

I sat down at the table, closing my eyes. Piper really could play. I'd never heard anything like it. It was more powerful than what he'd been playing the day I met him – the tune Alice had been humming. This was richer, and I couldn't imagine wanting to ever stop listening. I followed the tune, every note of it, in my mind. Followed Piper through the canal waterways, through the streets, through the seasons: bright, spring daffodils; cool water washing over hot sand; filling my pockets with smooth, brown conkers; the smell of the air just before it snows. The tune was painting all of those pictures, erasing any sense of where or who I was . . .

My eyes snapped open to a light creaking sound. I turned my head, dazed. The music had stopped and so had the boat. All I heard now was the ticking of the little clock nearby. I looked at it . . . and did a double take.

What had felt like a few minutes had been over an hour.

I leaped up and went outside. Piper and Gypsy stood by the tiller, gazing across the water. There was a bridge behind us and another narrowboat. A solitary figure stood on it, staring straight at us as he moored. I squinted through the sharp sunlight, trying to make out his features. His hair was shaggy and grey, resting on his shoulders, and thick, grey bristles covered the lower half of his face. His clothes looked old and grubby.

'What's he staring at?' I asked.

Gypsy nodded to the boat, her eyes wide.

'Is that him?' Piper said. 'Is that Ramone Silver?'

Gypsy tugged at my arm, pointing to something she'd written.

Look at the name of the boat.

'Can someone tell me what I'm missing?' Piper demanded.

'The name of the boat is the same as Gypsy's,' I told him. '*Elsewhere.* Alice must have taken the idea for the name from there.'

The man hopped off his boat and crossed the bridge. He walked with a slight limp, as if one of his hips were troubling him. His boots thudded on the wooden boards and then crunched up the towpath. He stopped by the boat, shielding his eyes from the sun. His face was brown with deep lines, but his eyebrows were black and, beneath them, silvery grey eyes that were exactly as piercing as Alice had described.

'Well, well,' he said, revealing a crooked bottom row of teeth. His gaze was fixed on Gypsy. 'I thought that was you.'

Gypsy stared back at him, silent.

He rubbed his hand over his beard. 'It was the name of the boat that caught me to start with, then I saw you. It's been what . . . ? Five years now? You've grown up, but I'd still know your face anywhere.' He sighed impatiently, but there was something else mixed in, too: sadness. 'You need to stop looking for me, Alice. You know your mother doesn't like it. You belong with her, not me. Go home.'

'She's not Alice,' I said. 'Her name is Gypsy.'

'I think I know my own daughter—'

'Good,' said Piper. 'Then maybe you'll know how to help her.'

The man rolled his eyes. 'Alice, what's going on here? Who are these kids? Why are the three of you out here alone and, more importantly, are you going to stop gawping and actually *speak* to me?'

'She can't speak, because she's NOT Alice!' I yelled.

'Who do you think you're talking to?' he snapped.

'I know who I'm talking to,' I said. 'You're Ramone Silver, Alice's father. I'm Midge, her brother.'

His expression softened and he nodded. 'Alice told me about you. I can see it now. You look just like her.'

'Like Alice?' No one had ever told us we looked alike.

'No,' he replied. 'Like your mother.'

His eyes swept over Piper from head to toe. 'And you're a . . . friend of Alice's, are you?'

'Not really.' Piper shifted from one foot to the other, using his sleeve to polish his flute. 'Can't say we've met, not properly anyway.'

'None of you are making any sense,' said Ramone. 'So, if you're going to waste my time, I'll leave now.' He turned away from us.

'His name is Piper,' I said quickly. 'And he's a character from one of Alice's stories. So is Gypsy.'

Ramone froze, then slowly turned back. '*What?*'

'A story Alice couldn't finish,' I said. 'You know what I'm talking about, don't you?'

His face had gone as grey as his beard. 'Are you telling me the truth?'

'We can prove it,' I said. 'Please. We don't have much time and we need your help. Alice is this way.'

He stepped aboard shakily and followed Gypsy down the steps. She led him to Alice's side. He stared at her, wide-eyed, then looked back at Gypsy. He opened his mouth, then shook his head and closed it again without saying a word. Finally, he turned back to Alice. I waited for him to touch her, to talk to her, to *anything* . . . but he was paralysed with shock.

'Help her,' I pleaded. 'She said you'd know what to do!'

He rubbed his chin with one hand, unable to take his eyes off her. They were stormy, troubled.

He knelt, taking her hand. 'Alice? It's me, your . . .' He broke off. 'It's Ramone.' He looked up at me. 'What is this, a fever? How long has she been like this? Where's your mother?'

'Away, working,' I said, in a small voice. 'Alice was supposed to be looking after me, but she was having trouble with this . . . this story. She said she was stuck. Then she went missing and these people kept showing up. When I saw Gypsy, I thought she was Alice at first, like you did. It was only when I found Alice's notebook that I realised the truth about the story.' I hardly paused for breath.

'But why isn't she waking?' Ramone shook Alice's arm.

'You mean y-you don't know?' I stammered. 'But that's why we came looking for you. We thought you'd know how to break the curse!'

He laughed, but it was a choked, angry bark of a noise. 'How can I do that when I can't even break my own?'

'But it must have happened to you surely?' Piper said. 'If you're a writer, too, then you must have had this before. Why else would Alice have told us to find you?'

'You don't understand,' Ramone said. 'Alice's curse . . . it's different to mine, as mine was different to my grandfather's.'

'*Your* grandfather?' I asked.

'It happens in threes, changing from one generation to the next. Always the firstborn.'

'Tell us,' I pleaded.

'It began . . .' He hesitated before continuing. 'It began with my grandfather. He wasn't a good man. He was a con artist, a swindler. An excellent liar, too. He told tall tales to captivate large audiences for money. He had no patience for the written word; he spoke his stories, making them up as he went along. Word soon reached the ears of a wealthy Romany traveller. My grandfather was persuaded to meet him.

'The traveller explained that his elderly mother, who had a great love of stories, had recently gone blind and was no longer able to read. However, she didn't wish someone to simply read to her, she wanted her own stories. They offered my grandfather a position as her storyteller, for a great deal of money. He accepted, of course, and regaled the old lady for weeks, months on end, with his never-ending supply of tales.

'Now this little arrangement suited my grandfather down to the ground at first. He was handsomely paid and the old woman was a good audience, for she enjoyed his stories no matter what he served up from the darkest corners of his imagination. He had heard talk that she had once been a powerful worker of Romany magic, but this didn't bother him.

'Over time, the old woman became ill and it was plain to see that she didn't have long to live. It was at this time that two things happened. My grandfather was told that he should prepare to find other work. Being stubborn and greedy, however, he decided he would keep going as long as possible and squeeze every last penny from the family. He told a new and exciting story that evening, but ended it at a point where the character might easily have another adventure. The old lady, being as much a glutton for stories as he was for money, insisted he continue the next night with another story about this same character, which he did. The same thing happened the following night, and the one after, and soon the old woman was so caught up in the adventures that my grandfather did not even bother to fully end them each night, but began framing each one as a chapter in an ongoing tale.

'The old woman grew weaker, but clung to life until it was clear that the story was the only thing keeping her going. Still he refused to finish it, despite instructions from her son to end her suffering, for the old woman overruled him. Then came the time when she begged for the end, and still he told her, "*Just one more night.*" And then she finally knew that he had no intention of finishing the story. Perhaps he himself didn't even know how it ended.

'The old lady had just enough fire left in her to get angry. And just enough anger to summon up a dying wish, which was to be a curse. She told him:

> "*The First shall have no ending*
> *One story it will be.*
> *The Second's tales are only told*
> *When birthplace he can see.*
> *The Third will know no peace until*
> *Their every yarn's complete.*
> *As long as blood and ink still flow*
> *The curse will then repeat.*
> *Only one who's story born*
> *Can see these words unspoken.*
> *To stop a cursed heart beating*
> *Is the only way it's broken.*"

'So you see,' Ramone continued, 'that it's been true for three generations. After the Romany woman's death, my grandfather had no more stories. Just the one he'd been telling when she died. He couldn't finish it, no matter how he tried, and it plagued him until the end of his days. From him, it passed to me—'

'What about your own father?' Piper asked. 'Surely, it would have gone to him first?'

'It was my mother's side actually,' said Ramone. 'Luckily for her, she wasn't a writer but a painter. It skipped her and came to me.'

'So you were the Second?' I asked. 'Something about your birthplace?'

He nodded. 'I can only write whenever the five-legged stag is in sight. It's where I was born, on that hill. My mother had tried to get up to the big house for help, but I arrived before she could walk any further.'

'What happens if you write anywhere else?' Piper asked.

'Nothing. I've tried, believe me. It's just not possible. Pens dry up, typewriters jam, or I just plain can't think. If that stag isn't within viewing distance, I can't write a word.' He paused, his breath ragged. 'And a writer I am, through and through.'

And Alice is the Third, Gypsy wrote. *Who must finish every story she begins.*

'Yes.' Ramone lowered his head, almost shamefully. 'I tried so hard to discourage her from telling stories, but she chose to do it anyway. So all I could do was insist that she must finish every story she began, even if I couldn't tell her what would happen if she didn't. I didn't know myself.'

'Well, now you know.' I gestured to Piper and Gypsy. 'You should have tried harder! *This* is what happens. Characters come out. People who aren't just paper, people who are real and have feelings—'

'And not just people.' The cat sat up and yawned. 'I'm here, too, you know.'

Ramone jerked backwards. 'Did that cat just . . . ?'

'Yes, I did,' said Tabitha. 'And who might you be?'

'Alice's father,' said Ramone, recovering himself. 'And it's no good saying I should have tried harder.' His eyes remained fixed on the cat. 'I did all I could to stop Alice from writing. I encouraged her to draw instead, or be creative in other ways, but still she always, *always* came back to stories. So I deliberately lost her work. Pretended to be so bored that I fell asleep as she read it out. Even told her . . . told her it was no good once or twice.' His face flushed with shame. 'All it did was made her try harder. Someone who is born to tell stories always will, no matter what. It's like telling a lion it can't roar, or a cat not to—' He broke off in alarm as Tabitha made a horrid noise and coughed up a slimy mass of black fur at the foot of the bed.

'Cough up a hairball?' said Piper.

'Beg your pardon,' said Tabitha. 'Better out than in, though.'

Ramone glared at the cat. 'As I was saying, I tried to stop Alice from writing. When that didn't work, I cut her off, even though it nearly killed me to do it. I've always thought that if she isn't near me then she might have a chance—'

'Hang on.' My cheeks felt hot. 'That's why you left in the first place?'

I wondered if somewhere, somehow it was possible that Alice could hear all this. I didn't know if that was a good or a bad thing. All these years, she had just wanted to know her father and had been pushed away. We both had Mum, but I had Dad, too, and, even though he loved Alice and she loved him, I guessed now that it hadn't been enough for her. My heart hurt at the thought of the pain Alice must have felt and kept to herself.

'You left Mum and Alice because you thought it could stop the curse?'

'Yes.' His eyes clouded. 'I thought that she stood the best chance if I wasn't around her . . .' His voice faltered. 'I would have lived with my curse, stopped writing even, if it meant I could stay with them. But I could see it was still passing to Alice, whether I continued to write or not.'

He paused again, squeezing his eyes shut. 'Your mother brought her to see me a few times, but I did my best to keep my distance. To hide any feeling for them. When Alice was older, she came looking for me a few times, mostly just watching from a distance. But once she spoke. That's when I told her about the curse. All I'd said before was that if she was going to tell stories then she must finish them, that only poor writers left stories unfinished, left their characters unfulfilled. I'd never mentioned the curse until that last time she came. I hadn't wanted to frighten her. So I told her, and then I told her to get away from me.'

'But she told me about that day!' I said. 'Dozens of times: how you spent the day together, telling stories, catching fish in the river which you ate for supper, and your promises to see her again. Promises you broke!'

Ramone shook his head in bewilderment, his face a mask of pain. 'None of that happened. Not a word of it.' He reached out as if to touch Alice's cheek, but then withdrew his fingers.

'She came looking all right. I was so happy to see her, my girl . . . so happy . . . but I couldn't let myself show it. I took her on the boat, sat her down. She was shivering and hungry; she asked me to light the stove, but I . . . I refused.' He was nearly whispering now. 'I said I had to save wood for when it became properly cold. I gave her water while I drank hot tea, gave her cold beans from the tin as I told her about the curse . . . and then I asked her never to look for me again. I walked her to the nearest town and phoned your mother to come and collect her. That was the last time I saw her, and that's exactly how it happened.'

My throat tightened as I stared at my sleeping sister. 'You're saying that she . . . made it all up?' I couldn't bring myself to say the word 'lied'. I didn't want to think of Alice in that way.

'She told you a story,' said Ramone sadly. 'The version she wanted it to be.' He studied Alice's face. 'I wrote a story about a girl named Alice once.'

'The one you gave Mum when you first met her?' I asked.

'You know about that?'

'Alice told me. Then, when all this happened, I found it.'

'Your mother kept it all these years?' Ramone finally looked away from Alice and up at me. His grey eyes were clouded with pain.

I nodded. 'I didn't read it, but I think Alice might have.'

'I'd puzzled over the curse all my life,' he said. 'And I'd tried and tried to find out what "story born" meant, without success. When Alice came along, I hit on an idea. I thought, perhaps, that if she was named after the girl in the story I wrote for your mother, and if I could influence her to become like that character – the one I'd imagined – then it might mean she was "story born".' He shook his head. 'It was a weak idea. She was nothing like that character. The only similarity was the name.'

He smiled faintly. 'Alice was too strong for that. She was always going to be her own person. It's only now I know what "story born" really is.' He looked at Gypsy and Piper and the cat. 'You.'

'But, for the curse to be broken, then that means one of them has to . . . has to . . .' I faltered, unable to say what I really knew.

'Yes.' Ramone's voice was grave. 'One of them has to take a life – either mine, or Alice's. Obviously, there's no way I'd allow Alice to die, so it has to be me.'

'Huh?' Piper's eyebrows shot up. 'Don't look at me! I've done some dodgy stuff, but I've never killed no one!' He looked to Gypsy in alarm. Her expression mirrored his, and she shook her head violently.

'You can count me out, too,' Tabitha drawled. 'I draw the line at rats. Besides – the curse is the whole reason we're here. Without it, we're nothing, just paper and ink.'

'So where does that leave us?' I asked. 'We're as stuck as Alice is! There must be another way?'

'There is,' Ramone said quietly. 'We stop writing, for good.'

I shook my head. 'Alice will never stop writing. Even if she did, what if she has children someday? The curse would still go to them, wouldn't it?'

Ramone's silence answered me. I thought of Dolly Weaver. She wanted Alice dead and was prepared to do it. There was a chance, the smallest chance, that the curse could be broken that way – and then, if I became master of the cat, I could bring Alice back by using one of Tabitha's lives ... but I couldn't voice that thought, or even bear to keep thinking about it. It was just too huge a risk. If it went wrong, Alice would be gone for ever.

'What I don't understand is why Alice is in this dream state,' Ramone muttered. 'It makes no sense if her characters are here to pester her and give her no peace as the curse claims.'

Quickly, I told him about the balled-up paper I'd found on the hearth. 'She wrote herself into the story. And I think it's linked to the fortune cards.'

'Fortune cards?'

I showed him the Sleeping Beauty card. 'Alice was holding this when we found her. I have the rest in the pack over there.'

He recoiled from the card as if it might bite him. 'What on earth was she doing with these? They were your mother's!'

'I – I think she was using them to plot the story,' I said, scared by his reaction. 'The way the cards can be read to tell a fortune could also be a story outline. And some of the characters, too.' I glanced quickly at Piper. 'The Pied Piper . . . a black cat. It's like she took some of the ideas straight from the pack.'

'This is bad,' Ramone murmured. 'Fortune cards are an old, deep magic. They shouldn't be meddled with.' He scratched his shaggy head, lost in thought.

The card began to feel damp in my fingers. I placed it on the floor, not really wanting to touch it. 'Are you saying the cards have made things worse?'

'They certainly haven't helped. Tell me, has anything like this happened before? Has Alice ever spoken about not finishing a story?'

'Last year,' I said. 'She saw people – characters. They were following her. I thought she had a fever at first, but then I saw one of them, too.'

'What happened?'

'She destroyed the story and they went away.'

'Destroyed it?' Piper's eyes were wide with alarm. 'Then what would happen to us? It'd be like we never existed—'

'Destroying the story isn't the answer,' Ramone interrupted. 'Not this time. Not with Alice like this. It won't bring her back.' He nodded to the fortune card. 'Not now these are involved.'

'What makes you so sure?' I asked.

'Because the cards are made to play out in sequence.

They have to be seen through to the end.' He paused. 'The way the cards were made to work together means the characters will be drawn together, too. Like cards in a pack, or magnets.'

I thought of how Dolly had approached Piper to steal the notebook. She couldn't have known who he was at that point, and hadn't known until she'd got the notebook in her possession and read it. Then, out of everywhere Piper could have stashed the pages he'd ripped out, he'd found his way to Ramblebrook. What Ramone said was true: the characters had been drawn to each other, like the story was telling itself. Quickly, I filled Ramone in on all this, and everything else that had happened.

'So what do we do about the missing notebook?' I asked.

'Forget it,' said Ramone. 'It's worthless. You have something far more valuable.' He gestured to Gypsy and Piper. 'The characters themselves. What can the notebook tell you that they can't? They know what they want. Now you have to figure out how to get it.'

What about Alice? Gypsy wrote. *Isn't she the one who has to finish this?*

'Not any more.' Ramone stared at the fortune card. 'It was Alice's story to begin with, but by not finishing it she brought you here. She made it real. Here, now, all of us . . . this *is* the story.'

I felt as though my heart were galloping away from me. *Us? We were the story?*

'But it's not just us,' I blurted out. 'There are other

characters, too. A man named Ramblebrook, who collects unfinished stories for a museum, and another character in the story notes ... a writer in some sort of hospital for the criminally insane. She's called Dorothy. From what we've read, there's a story of hers she wants to get back. I think ... I think Ramblebrook has it.'

'But she was in a secure hospital?' Ramone asked, frowning.

I nodded.

'Then perhaps we needn't worry about her just yet. But we have to be wary ... she must have some part to play.'

'Ramblebrook seemed pretty harmless,' said Piper. 'A bit nutty perhaps, but not exactly dangerous.'

Perhaps it's not him that's dangerous, Gypsy wrote. *But what he has.*

'What do you think he wants?' Ramone asked. 'What's his goal?'

'To set up this museum,' I said. 'It's all he cares about.'

'And presumably he doesn't know that he's part of an unfinished story himself,' said Ramone. 'Interesting. How about you, Gypsy? And Piper? What is it that you two want? What will finish your stories?'

Gypsy mouthed two words. *My voice.*

'I want to help Gypsy,' said Piper. 'And for her to forgive me – it's my fault she lost it.'

'Guilt is a heavy burden,' Ramone murmured, taking Alice's hand again. 'That leaves Dolly Weaver and the cat here.' He looked at Tabitha expectantly. 'Well?'

270

'Yeah,' said Piper. 'What about you, puss?'

'To be human again,' the cat replied huffily. She narrowed her eyes until all that was visible were two golden slits the size of a couple of grains of rice. 'And not to be called "puss", if you don't mind.'

'Fair enough,' said Ramone. 'And Dolly?'

'We don't know,' I said. 'Whatever's written about her is in the section she has. She told us she's the villain, and that the ending Alice was planning for her wasn't one she was going to let happen. She said she didn't want Alice to finish the story, that she'd be better off here. In our world.' I stopped, noticing that Ramone's grip on Alice's hand had tightened. 'Dolly wants to kill Alice.'

Ramone swallowed noisily. 'Then she must think Alice still has some control over the story.'

'You just said she doesn't,' I said. 'That the characters are in control now.'

'They are.' Ramone's voice was quiet, but I could hear the fear bubbling beneath the surface. 'For as long as Alice is in this dream state. If she wakes up and starts writing the story where she left off, then it becomes hers again. She takes control. Dolly knows our aim will be to save Alice. She won't want to risk that.'

'So, if Alice never wakes up, that'd suit Dolly, too,' I said.

'It seems that way,' said Ramone. 'Which means that, if Dolly can't get to Alice to kill her, then she may try to kill us instead.'

20
Cat Burglar

A SHOCKED SILENCE FILLED THE AIR, SO STILL
that the water lapping at the sides of the boat
was the only thing that could be heard. Then
everyone began talking at once.

How do we keep Alice safe? Gypsy wrote.

'How do we stop Dolly?' said Piper.

'And get Twitch back?' I asked.

Ramone held his hand up for silence. 'I'm thinking,' he
said. 'But one thing's for sure. Alice isn't safe on this boat,
or even mine, with it having the same name.'

'We can't take her home, either,' I said. 'Dolly's already
been there once. She could come back.'

'We need to take Alice somewhere that Dolly can't get
to her. Where could we take her? Who do you trust that
wouldn't ask questions?'

I stared at him helplessly. 'There isn't anywhere.'

'We'll keep her on my boat then, and at least one of us

must stay with her.' He rubbed his chin, brooding. 'You know, it's odd that Dolly has offered you the notebook, plus the return of your cat, in exchange for such a small section. It's too . . . generous.'

'You think she's planning something?' I asked.

'Why would she be decent enough to do a swap on the one hand, and on the other openly admit to wanting to kill Alice?' Ramone's expression darkened. 'It makes no sense.'

'She must be plotting something else,' said Piper.

'Sorry to interrupt,' said Tabitha, 'but is anyone else hungry?'

'No,' I snapped. 'Do you ever think of anything but your tummy?'

'Ouch,' said Tabitha. 'That was . . . catty.'

Piper rounded on her. 'Why don't you keep quiet unless you've got anything useful to say?'

'That doesn't usually stop her,' I said. 'But, thinking about it, you haven't said much.'

Yes, Gypsy added. *Why is that?*

'Because I've been listening,' Tabitha answered. 'Besides, it would have been almost impossible to get a word in between all your yapping.' She yawned. 'But, now you ask, I do have something to say.'

'Let's hope it doesn't involve tea,' I muttered.

Tabitha ignored me. 'I was going to say that if you no longer need the notebook, then there's no need to meet Dolly as planned.'

'Yes, there is,' I said at once. 'She has our cat, and she

said she'd kill her, too, if we don't show up. Or had you forgotten that?'

Tabitha sighed. 'No.'

'No?' I spluttered. 'So you just don't care!'

'I do care,' she said. 'Which is why I'm offering to be your replacement cat.'

'There's an offer you *can* refuse,' said Piper. 'Although . . . she might have a point.'

'About *what*?'

'About not going to meet Dolly. Perhaps we could hide – follow her back to wherever she goes and see where she's keeping your cat. Because you know something? Ramone's right. She's almost made it too easy. How do we know she isn't planning something like that herself? She could follow *us* if she even thinks we know where Alice is.'

'We could.' Ramone shrugged. 'Depends how much your cat means to you.'

'I'm not letting Twitch die,' I said. 'And if we're going to get rid of Dolly it'd work best if we don't make her suspicious by not showing up.'

'Get rid of her?' Piper asked. 'You mean . . . kill her?'

I nodded slowly, shocked at myself.

How? Gypsy wrote. *None of us are killers.*

'I know that. So we've got two options. The first is to wake Alice up and get her to finish Dolly off.'

'Tricky, seeing as we don't know how to wake her,' said Piper.

274

'And, even if we manage to, there's no way of knowing if she'll have an ending to the story,' Ramone added. 'What's option two?'

'We get Dorothy Grimes to kill Dolly.'

'The girl in the hospital?' Ramone asked, bewildered. 'But you said you hadn't encountered her yet.'

'She don't sound like someone you wanna mess with,' said Piper. 'She sounds nuttier than Dolly.'

'That's why we need her,' I said. 'She'll do our dirty work for us.'

What makes you so sure? Gypsy asked.

'I've been wondering how Ramblebrook fits into all this,' I said. 'I'm convinced he has the story that Dorothy Grimes wrote. Dorothy wants it back badly. She'll do *anything* for it. So, if we get to it first, we have something to offer her in return for getting Dolly out of the way.'

'But Dorothy's in a secure hospital,' Piper said.

'She was in the part I read,' I said. 'But who knows what could have happened in the part Dolly has? No matter how secure the hospital, Alice would have found a way to write Dorothy out of it. She's here, I'm sure of it.'

'Then we've gotta get the story from Ramblebrook,' said Piper.

Saying what? Gypsy wrote. *How do we get him to give us the story without telling him what's going on?*

'Easy,' said Piper. 'Nick it.'

'Is stealing your answer to everything?' the cat asked.

He shrugged. 'From the sounds of things, half the stories

275

in the museum weren't Ramblebrook's to take. I ain't got a problem with stealing it back.'

'It's not stealing if the story really belongs to Alice,' I said. 'Just like all the others in the museum.' I felt pleased with myself until I caught sight of Gypsy's face. She looked as though I'd slapped her.

What I'd said was true ... but without meaning to I'd reminded her that all her stories were Alice's, too.

We arrived back in Fiddler's Hollow by late afternoon. The street lights were on now and the pavements were wet from a light rain, reflecting orange. Piper moored Gypsy's boat and came inside, slicking his damp hair off his face with one hand.

'Ramone's just behind us. There's no one on the towpath. We should move Alice while it's clear.' He glanced at the sleeping figure on the bed, then his eyes went to Gypsy. 'Unless ...'

Gypsy looked at him questioningly.

'What is it?' I asked.

'I think I know a way to hide her.'

'How?'

'By having her and Gypsy switch places.'

'Switch? You mean—?'

'Trade clothes, shoes, jewellery ... the way they do their hair. Everything. All the while Alice is like this, she wouldn't be able to defend herself against Dolly. She couldn't run. But if Dolly thought she was *Gypsy* then she'd have no reason to attack her.'

'But equally she would have reason to attack Gypsy,' said Tabitha. 'If she believed Gypsy was Alice.'

'She'd have to get past me first.' Piper looked to Gypsy. 'And Gypsy's in a better position to defend herself than Alice is at the moment. What do you reckon?'

Gypsy stared at Alice and nodded.

'You're forgetting something,' I said. 'If Gypsy does bump into Dolly, her cover could be blown if Dolly speaks to her. How would Gypsy answer?'

'She wouldn't. She'd run.' Piper held Gypsy's gaze firmly. 'Right?'

A conflicted look passed over Gypsy's face, deepening the worry that was starting to build inside me.

'I think it's a brilliant idea.'

I turned at the sound of Ramone's voice. He'd come on to the boat and was standing at the top of the steps, listening. 'The best way to hide anything is in plain sight.'

Gypsy took off her necklace and moved towards Alice.

Piper nudged me. 'Come on, Midge.' He looked at Gypsy. 'Meet you outside when you're . . . when you're Alice.'

We moved out into the cold: Ramone, Piper and me, stamping our feet to keep warm and not saying much. A low mist crept off the water and curled round our ankles. I was damp, tired and dirty. I hadn't slept or washed properly since Alice went missing.

I turned at the sound of footsteps on the deck.

Gypsy stood awkwardly, like a child forced to put on an ugly school uniform. Her face was scrubbed clean of make-up and she'd brushed her hair out so that it hung round her face. It was only her eyes, green and more thickly lashed than my sister's, that were different.

'That's the Alice I remember.' Ramone held his hand out and helped her on to the path. She clambered down, unsteady in Alice's shoes. Even the way she held herself was different. She no longer stood tall and proud. She huddled, slouching into herself. It had taken me a while to look at Gypsy without seeing Alice. Now all I saw was how different they were.

'And Alice?' Ramone said hoarsely.

Gypsy pointed to the window. One by one we peered in. A single lamp glowed inside the boat, falling on the figure on the bed. But the figure was no longer Alice. She lay on her side, resting her head on the inside of her bent arm. Her other hand was on the pages of an open book lying next to her. From this angle, it was impossible to see her eyes were closed, and that she wasn't just reading.

'I'll stay with her,' Ramone said.

Tabitha leaped on to the roof of the boat, startling us all. 'Me, too.'

Piper stepped back from the window. 'No, you're coming with us.'

'I'm tired!' the cat complained.

'How can you be tired?' he demanded. 'All you do is sleep!'

She yawned widely. 'I'm awake now. Just about.'

'Well, you can stay awake, because you're coming with us. We might need you as a lookout. If anything happens

278

and we need to get word to Ramone, you'd be the best person, sorry . . . cat, for the job.'

'Fine,' she snapped. 'But tomorrow I sleep all day, and someone buys me a sardine from the fishmonger's.'

Piper rolled his eyes. 'Whatever. Let's go.' He turned to Gypsy. 'Ready?'

She nodded, wrapping Alice's baggy cardigan more tightly round herself. 'I hate these clothes.'

'Better get used to them,' Piper replied. 'Besides, they're only . . . what did you say?!'

'I . . . My voice . . .' Gypsy's hands flew to her mouth. 'It doesn't sound like . . . like me.'

'It's Alice's voice!' I said, dumbfounded.

The beacon in her eyes was quickly snuffed out. 'Oh. I thought . . . I . . .'

'It's because you're wearing Alice's clothes,' said Ramone. 'And because she's in yours.'

'This happened just from trading clothes?' I asked.

'I wondered if it would,' said Ramone. 'It's not just from the clothes. The story, the fortune cards: there's magic all around us. Even without all that, clothes are powerful. We use them to express ourselves. They carry our scent. They become part of who we are. The old Romanies believed you should never wear the clothes of someone who'd died, that it would bring bad luck.'

Gypsy pulled a thread from the cardigan, wrapping it round the tip of her finger. 'So, when we switch back, I won't be able to speak again.'

He nodded. 'Alice's voice will return to her.'

'We'll find a way, Gyps,' said Piper. 'I'll get your voice back somehow, I swear.'

She touched her fingers to her lips. 'At least if we bump into Dolly I won't need to run now. There's nothing to tell her I'm not Alice.'

'Don't sound so happy about it,' said Piper. 'She wants Alice dead.'

We left Ramone on the boat and walked under the glowing street lamps, not speaking. The cat slunk along beside us in a huff, keeping to the shadows. Her mood lightened following a few quick pounces and the doomed squeaking of some small creature. As we neared Pike Street, she jumped on to a low wall beside me, humming a tune.

'Cats aren't supposed to hum,' I reminded her.

'Whoops. I keep forgetting.'

'And stop talking.'

'*You* stop talking,' she replied. 'I'm only answering you. There's no one around but us anyway.'

It was true. The streets were empty. We'd passed a handful of shopkeepers closing up, but now there was no one to see or be seen by.

I stared up at Ramblebrook's place. Every window was dark. For the first time, I saw that the ground-floor ones had bars over them, like many of the other nearby houses. 'It looks like Ramblebrook has left for the night. How are we going to get in, though?'

'There's gotta be a back way.' Piper beckoned us further up the street. 'Look, here's a cut-through.'

We followed him into a narrow alley next to the fishmonger's and skulked along it until we got to the other side. We found ourselves in another wider alley that ran along the back of the buildings. Here the stink of fish crates was overpowering.

We clambered over boxes and crept past bins, disturbing a scavenging fox.

'This one.' Gypsy pointed. 'This is Ramblebrook's.'

Piper blew his fringe out of his eyes. He went to the door and rattled it, then knelt to look through the keyhole. Pulling a book of matches from his coat, he lit one and held it up. 'The key's in the lock on the other side.' He surveyed the rest of the windows. 'Up there. One of the fanlights is open. Bingo.'

Piper reached over and tickled the cat's chin with his finger. 'Be a dear and make yourself useful, would you, puss?'

Tabitha's ears flattened. '*Me?*' she yowled. 'I'm no good at climbing.'

'Then this is your chance to practise,' said Piper. 'That window is the only way in, and you're the only one who'll fit through it.' He pointed to an old brick outhouse. 'If you get on the roof, it's only a bit of a climb up the ivy to the window.'

'You mean the roof with the huge hole in it, which looks as if it could collapse at any minute?' Tabitha asked. 'No, thank you.'

'I wasn't *asking*,' said Piper. 'You've lazed around, napping and demanding tea and not doing much in return—'

'Except cough up hairballs,' said Gypsy.

'And get Twitch catnapped,' I added. 'And talk when you're supposed to be keeping quiet.'

'Yeah,' said Piper. 'It's time you earned your keep.'

'All *right*,' Tabitha snapped. 'Anything for a bit of peace!' She glared at Piper. 'Can you at least lift me on to the roof?'

He scooped her up, smirking, but it was wiped off his lips as she flicked her tail in his face. She skidded over the roof tiles clumsily, avoiding the hole. Within it, rotten beams sagged inwards like curled-up spiders' legs. A slate slipped out from under her, smashing on the ground. She froze, then continued, each step a little steadier. Where the roof met the wall of the main building, ivy reached up it like the rigging of a ship. She stood on her hind legs, tail flicking from side to side, then hooked herself on to it, slithering through the stems.

Finally, she made it to the window ledge, shaking herself and spitting out an ivy leaf. 'What do I do when I'm in?'

'Go to the back door,' said Piper. 'See if you can get the key and if there are any other bolts.'

She hooked her paws over the lip of the window and scrabbled with her hind legs against the glass, her behind wiggling until she'd squeezed through and vanished. Something was knocked off the other side of the sill as she landed, smashing.

'Useless,' Piper muttered. 'Worst cat burglar ever.'

We waited. Slow minutes passed, with no sign of movement from inside.

I started to pace. 'What if she's in trouble? There were so many boxes stacked up in there. What if one's fallen on her?'

'Death by unfinished stories,' said Piper. 'Now that's a way to go. Doubtful, though. She's probably come up against a door she can't get through.'

'What then?' I asked.

Piper went to answer, but was stopped by the sound of scratching on the other side of the door.

He knelt by the keyhole. 'Puss?'

'Who else?' came the muffled reply.

'Are there any bolts? And can you get the key?'

'One bolt, but it's not across the door. I think I can get the key out.' More scratches and scrabbling followed, then a metallic *ping*.

'Got it?'

'Yesh. In teef.'

'Good. Now get back here.'

She appeared at the window far more quickly than it had taken her to make it to the back door. When the furry black head emerged from the window above, Piper was already in place as the key dropped and landed in his hand.

He jammed it in the lock. There was a soft click and the door opened. Piper went in first and the rest of us followed into a large room that contained only boxes. There was no furniture and no curtains; yellow light from outside filtered through, casting shadows on the walls. The room was plain except for an old-fashioned fireplace that had a stack of newspapers and a basket of logs on the hearth. I looked at it longingly.

'It's colder in here than it is outside.'

'It's an old place,' said Gypsy. 'Probably hasn't been used in a long time.' She flicked the light switch. The bare bulb overhead snapped into life.

'Is it safe to have the lights on?' I asked. 'What if we're seen from outside?'

'We ain't got much choice,' said Piper. 'We can't work in the dark, and the quicker we find this story the quicker we can get out. I'll go upstairs and keep a lookout at the front in case we do attract any attention. Tabitha, you come and keep watch at the back.'

For once, Tabitha did as she was asked without argument and the two of them slunk out of the room, each as silently as the other.

Gypsy and I set to work, searching for boxes labelled with 'G'. We found just one, which Gypsy began rifling through.

'Make sure everything is put back the way it was, so Ramblebrook doesn't know anyone's been looking through all this stuff,' I said. 'If we don't find it tonight, we might have to come back. I'll check the rest of the place.'

I left Gypsy and went to the hallway. There was one door between the room behind me and Ramblebrook's office, and he had scrawled *Room One* on the door in chalk. I pushed it open to find a wide space with bare floorboards and a damp smell. There were no boxes. I moved on.

Ramblebrook's door was closed. I turned the handle and it opened soundlessly. I peered round it, half afraid he'd be waiting there in the dark, but there was no one inside. Nor were there any boxes, just paperwork laid out neatly on the desk. I leaned over it, holding one of the pages into the stream of light coming through the bare window. It was a handwritten plan of the museum, splitting the rooms up into sections:

Room One – Reception, History of the Museum
Room Two – Office
Room Three – Unknown Writers
Room Four – Published and Well-known Authors
Room Five – Writers' Belongings
Room Six – Temporary Exhibition Space

I put it down. There was other paperwork, stuff about funding and Arts Councils that I didn't understand. I had a quick look in the desk drawers, but there was only stationery. I peered over the other side of the desk – and froze. On the floor in front of the fireplace was a thin mattress made up with blankets and a pillow. Next to it was a large suitcase.

'I think we've got a problem,' I said.

'What?' Piper called down immediately.

'Wherever Ramblebrook is, he probably won't be long. All his clothes are here and he's obviously sleeping here, too.'

A frantic scuffling of papers came from the back room.

'Then let's hurry up,' said Gypsy.

I left the room, remembering to close the door behind me, and went up the stairs. I felt jittery now. What if Ramblebrook came back and caught us? What would he do?

It was cooler upstairs, and the grubby carpet gave way to a polished wooden floor. I tried to keep my footsteps quiet, but each one had its own little echo. At the top, it opened out into another hallway. Piper stood at the opposite end of it, silhouetted against the window.

He glanced my way, then looked back through the window. 'All's clear.'

I nodded. 'I'm glad I'm not alone up here.'

Piper flicked at a cobweb. 'It's pretty creepy. But I've been in worse.'

'It's not just the building.' I stared through the door to the room facing the front. Boxes hulked in surly piles, like a square-shouldered army. 'It's everything that's in this place.'

'The stories?'

'There's something . . . wrong about collecting them. It feels sort of . . . *haunted* in here. Like these stories are all ghosts that can't rest, because Ramblebrook won't let them.'

'At least someone cared enough to keep them. Some things are just . . . thrown away.' Piper stared out at the empty street. 'You'd better keep looking.'

I crept into the room nearest, the one stuffed with boxes. I went to the closest pile, stubbing my toe on something jutting out of the floor. I lost my balance and kicked something loose on the floor – a dropped coin.

'Ouch!' I steadied myself on the stacked boxes.

'What's the matter?' Piper asked.

I wiggled my sore toe and winced. 'I caught my foot on a nail sticking out of the floorboards.' I listened as the coin rolled a little way before landing somewhere out of sight. *Heads or tails*, I thought automatically, and something shifted in my head. Almost immediately I realised what it was: the heads side of a coin was, of course, the Queen. *The riddle!* I pushed it from my thoughts. Right now I had to focus on finding Dorothy Grimes's story.

Looking at each box carefully, I quickly discounted the first eight stacks. Ramblebrook's labelling made it easy work. Then, in the ninth, I found it.

'It's here,' I said. 'Grady to Grimshaw. Dorothy Grimes's story has to be in this one!'

I ran to the stairs and called down. My voice carried easily through the echoing spaces and, within seconds, Gypsy had raced up the stairs and stood next to me.

She lifted the box down and, with her thumbnail, made an incision in the tape holding the lid on, slitting it from end to end.

She pulled the lid off. 'Midge, turn the light on.'

I flipped the switch, but nothing happened. 'The bulb must be broken.'

287

'Here,' said Piper. He fished his matches out of his coat and tossed them into the room. Gypsy caught them and struck one, holding it over the box and going through its contents with her other hand.

'Grimes, Grimes, where are you, Dorothy Grimes?' She flicked through the neatly packed files, each one with a printed label displaying the name. 'Granger, Graves ... Griffin, lots of Griffin ... Grimshaw ... wait, there's no Grimes.'

'There *must* be,' I said. 'Unless Ramblebrook's made a mistake – but he doesn't seem the type.'

'Check again.' Piper had left his post at the window and was leaning on the door frame, staring at Gypsy. 'Maybe he put it in the wrong place.'

Gypsy struck another match and held it up, carefully checking the box again.

She looked up. 'There's nothing here by Dorothy Grimes.'

'But there *has* to be,' I insisted. 'Why else would Alice put her in the story? It doesn't make any sense—'

My mouth dried up at the unmistakable sound of a key rattling in a lock downstairs and the front door swinging open.

21
Nine Lives

THE FRONT DOOR SLAMMED AND FOOTSTEPS crossed the hall. A light snapped on and papers rustled.

'We have to get out,' Gypsy whispered.

'How?' I asked. I fumbled with the lid of the box, replacing it before lifting the others back on top. 'Our only way out is through the back door. We'll never get past without him hearing us!'

Piper took a quick look into the hall, then crept back to us. 'We'll have to create a distraction. The room where Tabitha got in has a key on the outside of the door . . .' He frowned. 'Where *is* that cat? I haven't seen her since we got up here.'

'Wherever she is, I hope she has the sense to hide,' I said.

Piper nodded. 'There's a cupboard in that room. If I can hide in it and draw Ramblebrook into that room, I'll lock him in and we'll escape.'

'But we can't just leave him locked in,' Gypsy said. 'He could be stuck there for days!'

'He won't die. He'll easily be able to call for help from the window.'

'But the story—' I began.

'There *is* no story, not by Dorothy Grimes.'

I nodded, bitter that my idea had failed. 'Fine.'

'All right then,' said Piper. 'Now hide, just in case he comes into this room first.'

Gypsy and I crouched behind the boxes. Piper took a step towards the door . . . then tripped, lost his balance and fell. He hit the floor with a whack and rolled on to his back, swearing. His flute case clattered to the floor.

'Caught my toe on that bloody nail!'

Boots thundered into the downstairs hall, followed by a growling voice. 'Who's there?'

Piper's face was pinched with pain. 'Hide!'

Footsteps clumped up the stairs, each one a kick, a threat. I crouched next to Gypsy behind the boxes, peering through a tiny gap. My fingers met something cold on the floor: the penny I'd kicked earlier. I picked it up and slipped it in my pocket. We needed all the luck we could get. I saw Piper roll himself behind the door, clutching his knee. I felt sick. From the look on his face, Piper wouldn't be running anywhere just yet.

Ramblebrook had reached the top of the stairs, breathing heavily. 'Who's in here?' he demanded again. His boots slapped across the wooden floor, moving away from us. A door creaked at the opposite end of the hall. He was in the room with the open window.

'He'll come in here next,' Piper mouthed. 'I'll stall him and you can escape!'

My chest felt tight from being too afraid to breathe. Ramblebrook's shadow appeared before he did, looming in the doorway and stretching across the floor. He moved into view. Light spilled across his sharp features as he turned to see Piper sprawled across the floor.

His face twisted in surprise. 'You again! What are you doing in here?'

Piper lunged for him, wrapping his arms round Ramblebrook's legs. 'Run!' he yelled.

'What?' Ramblebrook roared. He turned, losing his balance, and fell, hitting the floor hard. Piper grabbed at his ankles, but cried out as a swift kick from Ramblebrook snapped his fingers back.

'Go!' Gypsy yanked me out from behind the boxes. We fled, brushing against Ramblebrook, who was already clambering to his feet.

'What's the meaning of all this?'

His voice echoed off the walls as we raced to the stairs. Gypsy leaped for the steps, taking them two at a time. Footsteps pounded behind me and fingertips brushed against my hair. My eyes bulged as my collar was seized from behind and I came to a halt like a dog on a choke lead. I grabbed at the banister, coughing and gasping for breath.

Ramblebrook twisted me round to face him, his beakish nose almost touching mine. 'Got you!'

'Midge!' Gypsy shouted, frozen on the stairs like a cornered animal deciding whether to fight or run.

'Let him go,' she said. 'Please. It was just . . . a dare. A silly game. We haven't touched anything and we won't bother you again.'

Ramblebrook twisted my collar more tightly. 'Now why don't I believe that? Could it be because you were all here earlier today, sniffing around? See, what I think is this: you saw something you fancied was valuable and decided to come back and steal it.' He shook me, making me bite my tongue. My eyes watered and I tasted metal. 'Is that it, boy?'

Gypsy ran at him, delivering a swift kick to his shins. 'Let him go, you bully!' she cried.

Ramblebrook staggered back, but kept hold of me. I touched my fingers to my mouth. They came away red. Behind me, Ramblebrook gasped, releasing me.

'Did I do that . . . ?'

'Yes,' I mumbled, wiping blood on my trousers. 'You did.'

'I . . . I never meant to hurt you . . .' He blinked, then pulled a crumpled tissue from his pocket. He pushed it at me with cold, fumbling hands. 'Here.'

I pressed it to my mouth.

'No one's ever called me a bully before.'

'Well, that's what you are.' Piper emerged from the front room, limping towards us. 'You shook him like a dog with a rabbit.'

'You're trespassing,' Ramblebrook said, his voice hollow. 'I was angry. I – I panicked.' He sagged against the wall. 'Oh, go,' he said. 'Just . . . go.'

I edged to the top of the stairs, not taking my eyes off him. Piper came after me, his head bent, hair across his face.

We'd taken only a couple of steps when Ramblebrook spoke again.

'You may as well tell me what you were looking for,' he said. 'I know you were after something.'

'We told you,' Gypsy said icily. 'It was for a dare.'

He gave a wry smile. 'Then can you explain why two of the boxes in the room you were in were not in the places I left them?'

'No.' Gypsy nudged me forward. 'We're leaving, right now.'

'Wait.'

Something in Ramblebrook's voice made us pause. He leaned over the banister, eyes sweeping over us. 'I didn't pay much attention to you earlier, but now I look at you all I see there's something going on. You're like three little ragamuffins, with those dirty clothes and frightened faces. Tell me what it is.'

'Why?' asked Gypsy.

'You're obviously here for a reason,' Ramblebrook answered. 'Perhaps I can help you.'

'Why would you want to?' Piper asked suspiciously.

'Because there was once a time when I could have helped

someone and didn't.' His face reddened and, for a moment, he looked young, like a schoolboy that had been hauled in front of the head teacher.

Gypsy and I exchanged looks, then glanced at Piper. He shrugged, and eventually Gypsy nodded, although it was accompanied by a meaningful look which said, *Don't tell him everything.*

'We were looking for a story written by someone called Dorothy Grimes,' I said. 'I thought it was here. But we must have made a mistake.'

Ramblebrook's eyebrows crouched over his hooked nose. 'Grimes ... Grimes ... why do I know that name?' He trailed off, his expression changing, becoming grave and then a little frightened. 'Yes. I know the one.'

'Then why couldn't we find it?' Gypsy asked, unmoving. 'We searched a box in that room. According to how you've organised them, it should have been in there.'

Ramblebrook nodded, stroking his chin. 'My dear, if you know about that story, then you must know that I'm not supposed to have it. For that reason, it's kept somewhere ... a little safer.' His eyes darted over each of us. 'May I ask why you want it?'

For a moment, no one answered. I took the tissue away from my mouth. It had finally stopped bleeding. 'We think she's looking for it. We wanted to get to it before she did.'

'Looking for it?' Alarm crept into his voice. 'How can she be when she's been locked up for life?'

'We've got reason to believe she's escaped,' said Gypsy.

'And we need her to do something for us. The story is our bargaining chip.'

'You mean blackmail?'

Piper shrugged. 'Same thing.'

'I see,' said Ramblebrook. He adjusted his glasses. 'If that's the case, then I think the best thing I can do is get rid of it before anyone comes to any harm.' He paused. 'You *do* know who Dorothy Grimes is, don't you? You must have read about the awful things she's capable of? You don't want to get mixed up with her.'

'We don't have a choice,' I said. 'Please – you said you wished you'd helped someone once. That's what we're trying to do now. Let us have the story.'

Ramblebrook chewed his lip. 'Are you sure you want to read it? It's dark. Disturbing. In fact, it'd probably give you nightmares.'

'Please,' I repeated. 'Someone's life depends on this.'

He stared at us a little longer, then finally nodded. 'Very well. Follow me.'

He led the way to the room at the back, the one through which Tabitha had got in. He stopped by the darkened doorway. One by one we joined him outside. I hung back, suddenly on edge.

'This room is empty.'

'It isn't.' He pushed the door wider, pointing.

There in a dark alcove were several boxes, plus a large safe. They were so well tucked in that I'd missed them the first time I'd looked.

He flipped the light switch, before realising that there was no fitting, just a tangle of wires hanging from the ceiling. 'Bother,' he muttered. 'That should've been fixed.'

He walked towards the safe, his shoes clipping the bare floorboards, and dug into his pocket, removing a set of keys. 'It's kept in the safe, for obvious reasons.'

We filed into the room and stood by him in silence as he fumbled with the keys. 'You can take it downstairs and read it . . . if I can ever find the key. I need some light . . .' He shuffled back to the door, still fumbling.

Piper had gone ahead of us and was kneeling by the safe, his fingers on a large dial. 'Hang on.' He stood, his voice sharp. 'Why would you need a key for a combination—?'

The door slammed shut and the key turned, locking us inside the dark room, with Ramblebrook on the other side of the door.

'. . . lock,' Piper finished, and kicked the safe with all his might.

Gypsy ran to the door and pounded it with her fists. 'What are you doing? Let us out!' She turned to Piper, speaking urgently. 'Piper, your flute. Could you play something? *Make* him open the door?'

'I could if I still had it, but I dropped it back in the other room when I fell.' Piper booted the safe again, then turned his back to the wall, his head in his hands. 'I can't believe I fell for such a simple trick,' he fumed. 'I *knew* I should have waited outside.' He limped to the door, rattling it. 'Open this door before I kick it down!'

'I doubt you've tried kicking down a door of solid wood before,' Ramblebrook hissed on the other side. 'It'd take you most of the night. Now you tell me exactly how you know about that story, because, as far as I was aware, there were only two people in the world who knew it was here, one being me and the other being the person I got it from.'

I went to the door and stood next to Gypsy. 'Do you mean Dr Rosemary?'

There was silence. Then, 'How on earth would *you* know about Dr Rosemary? Who are you children? Who sent you? You're not coming out until I get answers!'

'You want answers?' I shouted, losing my temper. 'Well, you won't like them.'

'What do you mean?' Ramblebrook said, sounding rattled now.

'I know things about you, Ramblebrook. I know how you've stolen lots of these stories for your museum, and the reason it all started.' I slid my rucksack off my shoulders and unzipped it, reaching for the section of the notebook I'd had from the start.

'What are you doing?' Gypsy mouthed.

'Bluffing,' I whispered. 'There's a chance I might be able to get him to let us out.' I leafed through the pages and found what I was looking for: a name. It meant nothing to me, but everything to Ramblebrook.

'Don't lie,' he blustered. 'No one knows that! Only me.'

'You started to collect unfinished stories because you felt

guilty,' I said. I tried to keep the nervous squeak out of my voice. 'About what happened to Georgie Squitch.'

A strangled sound came from the other side of the door. 'How . . . ? Who told you that name? Who . . . ?'

'Someone who knows a lot about you,' I said. 'And Georgie Squitch. And how you blamed yourself for . . . what happened to him.' I held my breath, waiting and afraid. I *didn't* know what had happened. Alice hadn't revealed that, but, if I could convince Ramblebrook that I knew, perhaps he might be persuaded to let us go.

Another gasping noise came from Ramblebrook. I realised he was sobbing. 'Who else knew?' he babbled. 'All these years . . . I thought I was the only one. I . . . I tried to tell someone once. My mother. But I couldn't do it. I couldn't bear to see the disappointment on her face, to have her know that about me.'

I looked at Gypsy in dismay. Her expression had softened now. Whatever he might have done, Ramblebrook's distress was difficult to listen to. Only Piper looked unmoved.

'No one else has to know,' I said. 'Just let us go and we won't say anything.'

He appeared not to have heard, weeping softly on the other side of the door. 'If only I'd opened the gate,' he muttered, sniffing. 'If only I'd been brave and not a coward. He could have been saved.'

I scanned the story again with difficulty. The light was so faint it was hard to read. I searched for some clue, something in Alice's writing that would get him to talk more, but found nothing. I stayed silent, but to Ramblebrook it must have sounded like an accusation.

'I had no choice,' he said, defensive. 'Anyone else in school would have done the same.'

'Would they?' I asked.

'Everyone knew he was being bullied. No one did a thing. They were too scared it would make them targets, too.' He'd stopped crying now and spoke more quickly. 'I can't have been the only person who was in their garden that evening. I can't have been the *only* person who heard them chasing him down the alley.'

'But you could have saved him,' I pressed, remembering some mention of a gate. 'You could have let him in.'

'Everything could have been so different,' Ramblebrook murmured. 'If only I'd let him in and got him away from them. Or if I'd at least gone into the alley and delayed them, just by a few seconds . . .' He faltered. 'If . . . if the train at the end of my street hadn't been going past just as they chased him on to the track. All those "ifs".'

I closed my eyes. Georgie Squitch had been chased into the path of a train, and Ramblebrook had lived with the guilt of knowing he could have been saved . . . if only Ramblebrook had been brave enough to open his gate and offer Georgie an escape.

'They'd emptied his bag out in the alley,' Ramblebrook continued shakily. His voice was far away now, as if he were lost in his memories. 'Thrown his belongings around. I picked them all up after they'd gone. That's how I found his stories, dozens of them in his school books. I stayed up half the night reading them; brilliant, they were. And then there was the unfinished one. I was desperate to know what happened next. I decided then and there I was going to be Squitchey's friend, no matter what.' He hiccuped. 'But, of course, it was already too late for that. I found out at school the next day that he'd been killed. Him . . . and the two cretins chasing him. So you see? It wasn't just one life but three I could have saved.'

'You can still save a life now,' I said. 'Help us! Give us the story and let us go.' I pressed my ear against the door, trying to get some clue as to what Ramblebrook's next move might be. All I could hear was his breathing, fast and panicked.

'Who else knows what I did?' he demanded. 'Who told you this?'

Gypsy's eyes were wide. She shook her head, warning me to say no more. I nodded. I already knew that Ramblebrook wouldn't be able to handle the truth. He was so eaten up with the guilt of what he had done that there was no way I could tell him about Alice, even if it was to try and make him see that she had written everything for him. The discovery would crush him and possibly put us in worse danger. There was no telling how he might react or lash out.

'I . . . I can't tell you,' I said finally. 'But we know you didn't mean for it to happen. It was an accident, a horrible accident. Whoever was chasing Georgie was to blame. *They* were the ones who made it happen.'

'Yes, they made it happen.' Ramblebrook's voice was

faint. 'But I let them. Sometimes doing nothing is the worst thing of all. That's why I have to think carefully about what to do next with you.'

I stared at Gypsy and Piper, stricken with fear, as Ramblebrook's footsteps shuffled away from the door. The stairs creaked as he went down them.

'He's *keeping* us here?' I mumbled. 'But he can't . . .'

'He's keeping us for now,' Piper said, glowering. 'He knows he's gotta let us out sooner or later, but at the moment we're stuck.'

'Piper's right,' Gypsy said quietly. 'The only way we're getting out of here any time soon is if we can escape.'

I turned. She had opened the window and was leaning out, her breath puffing in the cold air.

'How far down is it?' I asked.

'Too far to jump without breaking any bones.'

'What about the roof below, that the cat climbed on to?'

Piper joined us at the window. 'No, the roof's unstable. There were tiles slipping even when the cat walked over it. If one of us tried it, the whole thing would cave in. We could be killed.'

'Wonder what happened to Tabitha?' said Gypsy. 'Did you see her at all after you came upstairs?'

'No. She went into this room and I stood at the front window. I never saw or heard nothing from her after that.'

'Maybe she got out when Ramblebrook came back,' I said. 'She could have gone back to Ramone for help.'

Piper looked unconvinced. 'Or she could've just saved her own skin.'

'We need another idea.' I scanned the room desperately. 'Something that would force Ramblebrook to open the door.' My eyes rested on the safe. 'Perhaps there's money or valuables in there. If we could get into it and start throwing the money out of the window, he'd come in to try and stop us and we could overpower him.'

'Bingo.' Piper's eyes glinted. 'Well done, kid!'

Gypsy eyed the safe doubtfully. 'How are we meant to get into it? We can't possibly guess the combination.'

'Forget the safe.' Piper grabbed the topmost box from the pile in the alcove. 'We've got something Ramblebrook values above everything else.' He put the box on the floor, pulling it open. The musty smell of old paper hit my nose.

'Stories,' I whispered.

Piper pulled out a handful of papers.

'Ramblebrook!' he bellowed. 'You'd better get up here and open this door!'

'What are you going to do with them?' I asked.

Piper began heaping the stories on the hearth. 'Whatever it takes.' He nodded to the other boxes. 'Help me empty these.'

Gypsy shifted the next box and I took the one after, staggering under its weight. It slid out of my grasp as I went to put it down, landing on its side. In the dim light, I could just see a single letter printed on its side: *W*. I began pulling the stories out in handfuls. Some typed, some handwritten.

Some just a page or two, others that were much longer novels but a few chapters incomplete.

Had Alice thought of every single one of these stories? It seemed impossible. There were just too many, even in these few boxes. And it wasn't just me thinking it.

'Alice came up with all these?' Gypsy asked. 'How? Just . . . how? It's enough to drive someone mad.'

'Maybe that's why all this happened,' I said, my voice shaky. 'Maybe that's exactly what happened.' I thought of my storytelling sister asleep on the boat and my eyes suddenly stung with tears.

Piper took out the book of matches.

I stared at him in alarm.

'Ramblebrook!' he called again. 'If you wanna save your stories, you'd better get up here!'

'You're really going to burn them?' I asked.

His eyes gleamed triumphantly. 'I will if he don't let us out, but I'm betting he's gonna open that door pretty soon.'

Gypsy pressed her ear against the door. 'He's coming.'

Piper stuffed the pages into the grate, a match held at the ready. I stared at it, almost longingly. It was so cold in the room. My gaze drifted over the stories I'd pulled out and scattered over the floor. So many stories, so many names. All these imaginary people . . .

. . . and one very *real* one.

I sat up straighter, staring at a folder that had slid almost into my lap. With shaking fingers, I picked it up. There was no mistaking the name written at the top.

I opened it up. Inside was a story called *Nine Lives*. The edges of the pages were grubby, smeared with inky black fingerprints and something else that was dark, but not quite black. I started to read.

Once upon a time, there was a little girl called Dorothy Grimes who lived in a special hospital. She had been sent there, because she did something bad and the doctors thought that her head was all wrong, but Dorothy did not agree. She thought her head was perfectly fine, thank you very much, and she said so many times to her cat, who was a rather special cat, but we will come to that in a moment.

The cat was one of Dorothy's favourite things, but not her absolute favourite. No.

Her absolute favourite thing was writing stories, which were also special – but we will come to that in a moment, too.

One day, a little while before she went to live in the hospital, Dorothy was thinking about something. She poked the cat, who was asleep, and said, 'Names are important, don't you think?'

'Eh?' the cat replied, because this cat was one of those rare cats that could talk. (This was one of the reasons she was special, but there were more.)

'Names,' Dorothy repeated. 'Pay attention.'

'I was asleep,' the cat said grumpily. 'Is this important?'

'Yes,' said Dorothy. 'You know, considering I saved you from being tortured, it's as if sometimes you don't even like me at all.'

'Who said liking you had to come into it?' the cat retorted. 'Anyway, spit it out.'

'You're cute when you're grumpy,' Dorothy said, giggling. 'Where was I? Oh, yes, names. If my stories are going to be famous one day, I'd better think of another name for myself, hadn't I?'

'What do you mean?' the cat replied. 'What's wrong with the name you already have?'

'Grimes is not a name for an author,' said Dorothy. 'It sounds like a chimney sweep. Like dust and dirt and unwashed things. I want another name to go on my stories. A pen-name. What's the proper word for it? A pseudonym.'

'Fair enough,' said the cat. 'What do you want instead?'

'I've been thinking about spiders' webs and all the work that goes into them. And how people say lies are like webs. Well, stories are like that, too. So I've decided on Weaver.'

'Dorothy Weaver,' said the cat. 'Like it.'

'No, no, not Dorothy,' she snapped.

'You don't like Dorothy, either?'

She scowled. 'It gets shortened to Dot, or Dotty.

Dotty means mad and I've had enough of people saying that.'

'So what will your first name be?'

Dorothy took down a doll from the shelf and stroked its long, golden hair. 'I think I like Dolly.' She picked up her scissors and started to snip, snip, snip. Chunks of yellow hair fell in her lap. 'A dolly can be whatever you want it to be. You can dress it how you want, and make it say and do what you want. A bit like a character in a story.' She pressed the blade of the scissors into the doll's eye, gouging. There was a soft pop and it rolled out on to the floor.

'Yes, Dolly it is.' She smiled, crushing the glass eye underfoot. 'Dolly Weaver.'

'Excellent choice,' said the cat. 'Now do you think I could have a cup of tea?'

22

Turncoat

I SLAMMED THE PAGES DOWN. THERE WAS NO NEED to read the rest. 'Piper, start burning the stories now!' I hissed. 'We're in trouble!'

'What is it?' Gypsy asked.

I held up the folder, displaying the name on the front.

Her mouth dropped open. '*Dolly Weaver?*'

'It's a pen-name,' I said. 'The pen-name of Dorothy Grimes. Dolly Weaver *is* Dorothy Grimes!' I pointed to the stains on the edges of the paper. 'Look, it makes sense now. Dolly's gloves – she was hiding the state of her hands . . . she's a writer. The stains on her fingers are ink. Our plan can't work. And that's not the worst part.'

Ramblebrook hammered on the door, cutting me off. 'What are you hollering about?'

Gypsy glanced fearfully at the door. 'What is it, Midge? What else does it say?'

'The cat, Tabitha.' I felt a stab of betrayal as I said her

307

name. 'She's *in* this. She's Dolly's — I mean, Dorothy's cat! She must have been working against us the whole time, listening and spying and feeding information back!'

'And now we're trapped in here and the cat's gone,' Gypsy said, horrified. 'She knows Alice is on my boat, with only Ramone to protect her . . . She hasn't gone to fetch help at all . . . she's gone to take Dolly to Alice!'

Ramblebrook thumped the door again. 'What are you whispering about? I know you're up to something in there!'

'We've got to make him open the door,' I said. 'We have to get back to Alice now!' Papers rustled around us, a few floating into the far corners. 'And I've got to solve that riddle. If Dolly gets to Alice before we do, I need to be master of that cat.' I pushed the story into my rucksack and pulled out the riddle, reading through it again, but still it was no clearer. Nettles . . . bees . . . scorpions.

A vessel of venom that can kill with a sting . . .

Which one was it? What was I missing?

'What are you doing in there?' Ramblebrook demanded, his voice rising. 'That sounded like paper crumpling! You'd better not be meddling with my work!'

'Oh, we're meddling all right!' Piper shouted. 'We've opened up all your boxes and, if you don't let us out, we'll start on the stories one by one!'

'What?' Ramblebrook growled. 'You'll start doing *what?*'

Gypsy strode to the door. 'Burning them.'

'You wouldn't dare!' he raged. 'You'll put everything back in those boxes at once, do you hear me?'

'Make us!' Piper crowed. 'Open the door. I'll count to ten, then the first story goes up in smoke!'

'Don't you dare!'

Piper put his hand on his chin and spoke in an exaggerated voice. 'Hmm. I don't think he believes us. Let's see . . . what's this one?' He picked up a couple of loose pages from the floor.

I leaned closer, reading the title aloud. '*The Silver Cage.*'

'Are you fond of *The Silver Cage*?' Piper called.

'By T. M. Winter,' I added.

'By T. M. Winter? Because it's about to vanish for ever!'

'Put that back this instant!' Ramblebrook cried.

'One, two, three, four . . .'

'I'm warning you . . .'

'. . . five, six, seven, eight . . .'

'If you've so much as wrinkled it, I'll wring your neck!'

'. . . nine, ten.' Piper sighed. 'I don't think he's gonna open the door yet, do you? And it's *so* cold in here.'

There was utter silence as Gypsy and I waited, unsure whether he would carry out his threat. On the other side of the door, I sensed that Ramblebrook was hardly daring to breathe. The hiss of the match being struck was oddly loud. Even Ramblebrook heard it.

'No!' he wailed.

Piper held the flame to the paper. It was dry and brittle with age, and the flame took hold easily.

'Whoa!' He threw it into the grate and stepped back from the orange glow. A curl of grey smoke spiralled up the chimney. The pages blackened and fell to ash.

'One story gone,' I said, oddly sad about it. 'Are you ready to let us out?'

There was no reply, but we could hear that he had begun to pace.

'Good,' said Gypsy. 'You got his attention. Burn two stories this time.'

I picked up a handful of stories from the hearth and looked at the top two.

'*Never Gone* by Woody Wickens, and *Les Chats . . . Les . . .*' I squinted in the faint light. 'I can't read this one.'

Gypsy took it from me. '*Les Chats Formidables*. It means *The Great Cats* in French and it's by—'

Ramblebrook stopped his pacing. 'No!' he howled. 'Not that one!'

'Then open the door!' Piper yelled. 'Let us go and we'll stop!'

There was a roar of rage as Ramblebrook grappled with his decision. Then the pacing began again, faster this time. Piper stuffed the two stories into the grate and threw the match. The words charred and vanished into black.

'Another two gone,' Piper declared. 'How many more are you willing to sacrifice?'

The pacing continued, along with the horrid scraping sound of something sharp being dragged over the walls, scratching and gouging in anger.

The key.

'Keep going,' said Gypsy, her voice low. 'He's going to cave, I can feel it . . .'

She seized another stash of paper and began reeling off titles, too quickly for me to even take them all in, and with each one she threw it on to the flames.

'The Mischief Spell . . . gone!' she shouted. 'The Yellow Tree House – gone! Three Sisters . . . The Witch in the Bottle, The Tale of Spinney Wicket . . . gone, gone, GONE!'

'Enough!' Ramblebrook flew at the door, jamming the key in the lock. 'Enough, I say!'

We huddled together as the lock clicked back, and then the door was thrown open, sending a freezing draught into the room. It lifted the pages, scattering them further into the corners.

Ramblebrook stormed in, halting as he took in the scene. He lifted his hands to his head and a horrible sound groaned out of him. A loose leaf of paper wrapped round his leg, like it was trying to comfort him. He staggered to the fireplace and dropped to his knees, weeping and pulling at the burning pages with his bare hands.

'What's he doing?' Gypsy said. 'He's crazy if he thinks he can save them!'

Piper shoved us towards the door. 'Just go,' he hissed. 'All we need to think about is saving ourselves and Alice.'

We fled the room, thumping down the stairs. Then Piper stopped in front of me, turning back up the stairs.

'Piper, no!' Gypsy caught his hand. 'Where are you going?'

'My flute. It rolled out somewhere in that front room when I fell before.'

'Forget the flute!' she cried.

'I can't, you know I can't.' He pulled away from her and limped on to the landing.

I hesitated. 'I'll get it; you can barely walk. Go and I'll meet you downstairs.'

'No . . .'

I pushed past him, racing along the landing to the first room we'd been in. It was darker in here; the vast amount of boxes blocked what little light there was from the bare window. I knelt, feeling around blindly, my fingers gathering grime and dust. Then they brushed something smooth and cold. I wrapped my fingers round the flute and scrambled out and across the landing to the top of the stairs.

Something, fear perhaps, made me glance into the room where Ramblebrook was. What I saw rooted me to the spot.

He was on his hands and knees and, having removed his jacket, was swatting at the burning papers with it in an effort to put them out . . . but he'd only spread the flames further. Glowing embers had drifted to the moth-eaten curtains. The bottom of the fabric was smouldering, and already I could see dark, toxic smoke leaking away from it.

He looked so broken, so pitiful, that I couldn't help feeling sorry for him.

'You have to get out.' I coughed as something bitter caught in my throat. 'The flames are spreading and this whole place is full of paper. You can't save it.'

I sensed he'd barely heard me over the crackling of the flames, but his eyes flickered in my direction. All I saw in them was madness; the look in them told me all this paper meant more to him than his own life.

Then Gypsy was next to me, tugging me away, breathless. 'Leave him. He has time to get out if he'll only make the choice.' She urged me towards the stairs and I almost stumbled, wheezing as fumes invaded my lungs. We clattered down the stairs, to where Piper waited by the open front door. As I stepped outside and tasted the sweet, fresh air, I took one final look back at the stairs, willing Ramblebrook to come down them, but all that followed us were scraps of fiery orange paper, floating into the night like burning confetti.

'Run,' said Piper, grimacing. 'I won't be far behind you.'

We raced to the end of Pike Street. Before I turned the corner, I looked back at Piper. He was true to his word, keeping up well, but we'd still beat him to the boat. Behind him, orange light lit the upstairs window of Ramblebrook's place. I turned away, my breathing ragged and my throat sore. I couldn't think about him now.

The moon sailed above us, half clouded, unmoving, making everything seem slower, though speed had never been more crucial. Each time my feet pounded the ground, all I could think was *Alice*.

Alice, Alice, Alice. Please be all right.

'I told you ... that cat ... would bring bad luck!' Gypsy panted.

I didn't have the breath or energy to answer her. Even if I had, there was no point. I recalled how Alice, when I'd summoned her, had been trying to tell me the truth about

Dolly, and I'd prevented her by interrupting. I'd brought my own share of bad luck upon us. Now I had to make things right. I thought of the riddle again and of things that could sting. A hornet? Cold wind or rain on your face? Surely I'd thought of everything that could sting by now? Bees, nettles, scorpions . . .

Gypsy's hair flew back, showing her tattoo of the scorpion, its tail up and ready to strike.

I slowed, but my heart raced faster. A scorpion could kill with a sting, delivered by one swift blow from the stinger at the end of its . . . *tail.*

I went back to the other part of the riddle, remembering the rolling coin with the Queen's head. *Heads or tails?* The opposite side to a queen wasn't just a king, it was *tails.*

But how did it fit with the rest of the riddle? I dug it out of my pocket.

I'm up when I'm up and down when I'm down . . .

I thought of an animal, how its tail would be up when it was happy and down between its legs if it was sad. Now the next part finally made sense, too. *A thump when a smile and a flick when a frown.* Dogs thumped their tails to show they were in a good mood, whereas a cat would flick its tail if it were annoyed.

I ran harder, catching up with Gypsy. Jubilant energy pulsed within me. I had it, I was sure of it! One word . . . and that turncoat of a cat would have to do whatever I said. Though I was bursting to tell someone, I kept it to myself. The only way I could be completely certain of saving Alice's life – if it came to it – was to make sure I was in control of the cat. Me and no one else.

A low mist hung over the water when we reached the canal, and had oozed on to the towpath. Gypsy slowed to a walk and held her finger to her lips as we approached *Elsewhere*. I glanced back at the path. Somewhere along the way we'd lost Piper.

The narrowboat swayed lightly on the water. Gypsy crept to the window, squinting.

'The lamp's been turned off,' she murmured. 'I can't see anything.' She eased herself over the side and on to the deck, reaching for the door. It opened soundlessly and a chill ran over my skin.

'Surely Ramone wouldn't have left it unlocked . . .'

Gypsy threw the door wide open. 'Stay there.'

'No.' I climbed on to the boat. 'It's safer if we stick together.'

Gypsy didn't argue. 'Then just stay behind me.' She reached inside and I heard a switch click a couple of times, but the boat remained in darkness.

Her voice trembled as she called out. 'Ramone?'

Silence.

She swallowed loudly. 'There's a switch to the backup generator in the kitchen cupboard. I'm going in.' She went down the steps slowly, feeling her way to the bottom. I tried to get a glimpse of the bed where we'd left Alice, but I could barely see a thing. Gypsy slipped into the darkness, then cried out, stumbling against something.

She landed somewhere on the kitchen floor with a grunt.

Something like a sob came out of her, and then there were the sounds of things being tossed aside as she rummaged in a cupboard.

'What was that?' I asked, my voice high-pitched with fear.

'I tripped ...' Gypsy's voice shook, muffled inside the cupboard. 'There's something ... some*one* on the floor ...'

Not Alice, please *not Alice,* I begged silently.

There was a sharp *snap,* then a dingy light flickered on overhead.

Ramone lay sprawled on the floor. His wrists and ankles had been tightly bound with rope, and there was a bump the size of an egg on his forehead. His lips were parted slightly, swollen and smeared with red. On the floor, a short distance away, part of a broken tooth lay in a few droplets of blood. He must have landed on his face as he fell. The blood glistened, fresh and wet.

'Is he ... dead?' I asked.

Gypsy leaned over him. 'No. He's breathing.' She touched his shoulder lightly. 'Ramone? Can you hear me?'

He didn't move, but a whimper escaped his lips.

'Wake up. It's Gypsy.'

But it was not Ramone who answered. A childlike, sing-song voice on the other side of the boat began to chant.

'*Mrs Spindle had a pail of water, as well as a liking for slaughter ...*'

For the first time since the light had come on, I looked towards the bunk. It took all my self-control not to scream.

316

Alice was still on the bed where we'd left her. Only now she wasn't alone.

'*She was first scratched and bitten as she drowned three white kittens before moving on to her daughter!*'

Dolly Weaver ran her ink-stained fingers over the coat of the black cat on her lap and then grinned back at us.

'Surprise!' she said.

23

The Master of the Cat

GYPSY LUNGED FOR THE KITCHEN DRAWER, frantically looking for something. She slammed it shut, empty-handed, then searched the drainer next to the sink. A dish clattered on to the work surface, then fell to the floor and smashed, narrowly missing Ramone.

'Looking for this?' Dolly withdrew a large kitchen knife from beneath a cushion next to her and smiled. Light flashed off the blade.

'Please, Dolly,' I said. 'Don't hurt Alice.'

Dolly rested the blade flat against Alice's cheek. 'So long as I get what I want then no one will get hurt.'

Gypsy took a small paring knife from the drainer and crouched by Ramone, reaching for his bonds.

'No, no, no!' Dolly wagged her finger playfully. 'Daddy stays there.'

Gypsy stopped, but remained where she was. 'You've tied

the ropes too tightly; his hands are turning blue. At least let me loosen them.'

'No. This won't take long. And you can put that knife down.'

Gypsy stood slowly, but held on to the knife.

'Please don't make me cross,' Dolly said sweetly. She stroked Alice's hair, then lifted a strand, slicing it clean away. She threw it on the floor.

I gasped. 'Leave her alone!'

'Each time you disobey me, I'll cut away a little more of Alice.' She ran the knife down the tip of Alice's nose. 'After her hair, maybe I'll take her tongue.' She smiled at Gypsy. 'Speaking of which, you seem to have found yours, although my furry little friend here tells me it's only temporary . . . while you're walking in her shoes, wearing her clothes. That's . . . *interesting*.' She looked at each of us in turn. 'Just the two of you? Where did your little crook of a friend go?'

'Ran away,' Gypsy said flatly. 'Decided to save his own skin.'

'Hmm,' said Dolly. 'How curious. I wonder which way Alice would have gone with him in the end?' She tilted her head to one side, studying Gypsy like a bird watching a beetle. 'And don't think I haven't noticed you still have that silly little knife.'

Gypsy placed the knife in the sink and stepped away from it. 'What are you talking about? Which way Alice would have gone about what?'

319

'With Piper. She couldn't quite decide what to do with him.' Dolly paused. 'Whether to let him live, or die.'

'How do you know?' I asked.

'Because it's in the notebook,' Dolly replied. 'Still, it's out of Alice's hands now, thanks to my friend here.'

'Yes, your furry little friend has been very helpful, hasn't she?' I said bitterly. 'You wormed your way in from the start, didn't you, Tabitha? Feeding information back to *her*.' I thought back to the first time I'd seen the cat. 'No wonder I found you in Alice's room. It makes sense now. You were looking for the story even then, weren't you?'

The cat gave a slow blink. 'Don't take it personally,' she said, almost apologetically. 'I really didn't have much choice.'

'You knew this was all a story from the start,' I said. 'You *and* Dolly. How?'

Dolly ran her eyes over Gypsy, her gaze lingering on Alice's clothes. 'I didn't know *right* from the start,' she said. 'But then I got lucky. Very lucky. I had the pleasure of meeting Alice. From there, it all unravelled.' She sniggered. 'A bit like Alice herself.'

I stared at her, confused. 'You met Alice? When? How?'

'I was trailing that idiot Ramblebrook,' Dolly said. 'He has something of mine, you see.'

'Your story,' I said. 'Yes, we know about that, *Dorothy*.'

'Oh, you figured that part out, did you?' Dolly clapped her hands. 'Bravo!' She beamed. 'So, obviously, following Ramblebrook brought me here, and I was just plotting how I was going to get him out of the way when, quite by accident, I saw Alice.'

'Saw her?' Gypsy asked. 'But she would have been a stranger to you. I don't understand.'

Dolly waved the knife dismissively. 'She *was* a stranger.'

'Watch it,' said the cat. 'You nearly took my whiskers off.'

'But of course,' Dolly continued, 'I wasn't a stranger to Alice.' She smiled faintly. 'I don't know how long she'd been following me when I spotted her. But, when I did, the look on her face was just, well . . .' She sighed dreamily. 'Incredible. I've never encountered fear like it . . . and, believe me, I've seen a lot of that. But this was different. Like she knew everything about me, every wicked thing I've ever done. Which, of course, she did – although I didn't know it then. That look . . . it was delicious. Like a drug, especially when she saw that I'd noticed her.

'So I approached her. And she freaked out, right in the middle of the town.' Dolly gave a hoot of laughter. 'Made a proper scene, bashing me with her notebook, telling me to leave her alone and that I was a character in her story. I must admit, it was a thrill.'

'You *liked* hearing that you were a character?' Gypsy asked, aghast.

'No, silly!' Dolly snorted. 'I didn't believe a word of it – not then. I was excited, because after years of people saying *I'm* mad, I'd finally found someone who seemed to be stark raving . . . *cuckoo, cuckoo!*'

'Alice isn't mad,' I said angrily.

'Shh,' said Dolly. 'I'm getting to the good bit. So, like I said, she hits me and this notebook goes flying over my shoulder. And I see the sheer panic in her eyes – she's afraid I'm going to get it before she does. So that makes me *want* it. I reach it first, and just get a quick look in it before she snatches it off me. But it's enough to get me interested, because I see my name – my *real* name – and Tabitha's, and Ramblebrook's. And I'm wondering how this crazy girl got our names and so, at the very least, I want to know what she's writing about.

'So I send Tabitha after her. And what do you know? There's a cat that looks just like her, making it so easy for Tabby to slip into the house. To watch and listen. And to hear enough to convince me that *maybe* this girl is telling the truth . . . or enough to convince me that I need to see that notebook. When I did, that's the point at which I knew that she was telling the truth . . . and that I had to get rid of her.'

Get rid of her? Dolly spoke about Alice like she were nothing more than a used tissue to be thrown away. I glanced at the door. Was Piper coming? I thought Gypsy had been bluffing when she'd told Dolly he'd left us to save himself – but what if she was right? And, even if he did come, was there anything he could do when Dolly had a knife to Alice's throat? Was there anything any of us could do, aside from keeping Dolly talking?

'How did you escape from the hospital?' Gypsy asked. 'I'd love to know how Alice wrote you out of *that*.'

'I used the cat,' said Dolly, with a little laugh. 'We switched places. Clever, or what?' She tickled the cat's ears. 'I knew she still had a few lives left. I went into the cat's body and she went into mine. Her on the outside and me still trapped in my room.'

'Hang on,' I said. 'Surely if you went into Tabitha's body and she went into yours, your body would still be in the prison—'

'Hospital!' Dolly trilled.

'—and the cat's body would still be on the outside,' I finished.

'All right, clever clogs,' said Dolly, inspecting her nails. She pushed her cuticles back with the knife, then picked skin from the blade. 'Tabby, be a dear and explain the science bit, will you?'

Tabitha lowered her gaze, almost like she was ashamed. 'It's not science,' she said. 'It's magic. You're right, though – that's how it normally works. It's the souls that do the moving – the bodies stay where they are. But, with a bit of witchery, using mirrors and the moon while the switch takes place, it can be the *bodies* that exchange places, rather than the souls.' She sounded wistful. 'As I did with my own dear familiar.'

'So there we are,' said Dolly. 'Happy?' She winked. 'If not, then tough. It's not like Alice is going to be rewriting any of this. I think she got a bit stuck on the logistics of that part. Anyway . . . where was I? Oh, yes. Cat, me, abracadabra and so on . . . Dorothy Grimes nowhere to be seen and a black cat in her place! Oh, it was brilliant. The faces of the wardens the next morning were an absolute hoot! They had to let me go, of course, for as far as they knew I was just a cat. I was taken to an animal sanctuary, meowed pathetically and got adopted by a nice old lady. It wasn't difficult to get away from her at all.'

'And then you met up with the cat ... well, the cat in your body, and switched back,' Gypsy finished.

'Exactly.' Dolly beamed and tickled Tabitha's ears. 'We're a great team, aren't we?'

The cat stretched lazily, then stood up and moved, settling on the end of the bed near Alice's feet.

I glared at Tabitha. 'You betrayed us for *her*? Do you actually even like her?'

'No one said I had to *like* her,' Tabitha said gloomily. 'I just have to do as she says.'

'Unless someone else becomes your master,' I said.

'Tut-tut.' Dolly pouted at Tabitha. 'You haven't been trying to escape me, have you? Giving these people riddles, to try and find a new master?'

'For all the good it's done me,' the cat muttered, flicking her tail again.

The answer to the riddle was on the tip of my tongue. Dare I say it and risk Dolly losing her temper? Besides, what good would it do to be the cat's master now? After her betrayal of us, I didn't want anything to do with her.

But she could save lives ...

Perhaps I'd need her after all before the night was over.

If, I reminded myself, she'd been truthful about having any lives left.

'What do you want, Dolly?' Gypsy said tersely. 'You want the missing part of the notebook? We'll give it to you. You want the story that Ramblebrook stole? We have it.'

'Give them to me.'

I opened the rucksack and took them out, placing them on the bed before backing away.

Dolly brushed aside the pages of the notebook and picked up her story, grinning broadly. 'Thank you.'

'Where's my cat?' I asked. 'You said you wouldn't hurt her.'

'I haven't.' Dolly was distracted, scanning the pages of her story and smiling broadly. 'I never had your silly little cat. I just wanted you to think I did – it gave me more power over you.'

'You had her collar.'

'I tried to grab her,' Dolly admitted. 'But she was too fast. The collar came off in my hand. So I figured I'd bend the truth a little. I needed another reason for you to come back, just in case you realised the notebook was worthless.'

She slid her hand beneath the cushion under Alice's head and withdrew the rest of the notebook, tossing it on the floor.

I made no move to pick it up. 'So where is she?'

'Probably still skulking in the back garden,' Tabitha said sheepishly. 'She tried to come back in once or twice, but I chased her off.' She looked thoughtful. 'Even cats don't like talking cats apparently.'

'So you never wanted the other part of the notebook?' Gypsy said.

'No,' Dolly answered. 'I wanted you to lead me to Alice – the notebook was just an excuse. The story changed when Alice brought us here. She may have created us, but now we're the ones in control.' She brushed Alice's hair away from her sleeping face. I shuddered as her fingertips wormed over my sister, the skin around Dolly's nails chewed and bloody, inky and stained. She looked up at Gypsy, licking her shiny, red lips. 'Let's keep it that way.'

A faint creak behind us caught my attention. Then slowly, so slowly it was only noticeable to those of us who were standing, the boat shifted very slightly with the weight of another person. Someone who was trying to be quiet.

Piper.

'What do you mean, "let's keep it that way"?' Gypsy asked.

Dolly shifted position. Alice's head rested on her lap, like a child sleeping on its mother, but there was nothing tender about it.

'You *want* her to wake up?' Dolly sneered. 'You know what'd happen to you if she does?'

'She'll finish the story,' said Gypsy. 'And we'll go back to where we were before.'

'Exactly,' said Dolly. 'You'd go back to being Gypsy Spindle, searching for her voice. Think about it! You could stay here, wear her clothes, speak with her voice. Would it be that much of a sacrifice to give up being Gypsy Spindle and be Alice instead?'

Gypsy's eyes glimmered with unshed tears.

'What's she ever done for you?' Dolly whispered. 'Except cause you misery? Everything that's happened to you is because *she* made it happen. She took your mother away from you. Then she took your voice. Why not take it back?'

'Gypsy, don't listen to her!' I pleaded. 'She's poison!'

Unthinkingly, Gypsy touched her throat. Her lips.

'You could do it.' Dolly moved closer. 'You *could* be her. You'd be doing her a favour. After all, you're the best version of her. The version she wants to be.' She slid the knife across the bed, the blade between her thumb and forefinger, the handle pointing towards Gypsy, just an arm's length away. 'All you have to do is make sure she never wakes up . . .'

The blade glinted hypnotically, so shiny that Dolly's blackened, bitten fingers were reflected in it.

'Could you kill her?' Dolly whispered. 'Do you have the courage to take control of your destiny? Do you have the guts, Gypsy?'

A tear spilled over Gypsy's cheek.

Dolly sneered. 'No, I didn't think so. You're too weak.'

'No,' Gypsy said, through clenched teeth. 'I won't do it. Not because I'm weak, because I'm anything *but* that. I'm stronger than *you*. And the reason I'm strong is because of what I've been through. It's made me what I am. Killing

Alice would be your way. Becoming her would be the easy way. But I'm not Alice. I'm Gypsy Spindle and I always will be.'

Dolly's fingers closed round the knife blade, her eyes narrowing. Red droplets oozed out of her clenched hand, seeping into the blanket beneath. 'Oh, stop being so honourable, it's boring!' She rolled her eyes. 'I could envy you, Gypsy. I'll admit, I did at first. Knowing you were the good girl, the heroine, the one everything would come right for in the end. You even got the fairy-tale name, while I got plain old Dorothy Grimes. I was always going to be the bad one, who came off worse. But you know what? It's better than being a sap. So you sit back like a good girl and wait for your voice to be given back to you, Gypsy. *Dum-de-dum-de-doo!*' she sang goofily, before her face changed again, becoming a snarl. 'I don't envy you any more, I pity you. If you'd only had the guts, you'd have learned that it's *far* more fun being bad.'

She released the blade of the knife, now smeared with her blood, then grasped the handle, raising it high. A bead of red dripped off its point, landing on Alice's heart.

'No!' I yelled. 'We gave you what you asked for! You said you wouldn't harm Alice!'

Dolly's mouth twisted into an ugly grin. 'I'm a writer. That makes me a good liar.'

I rushed at her in fury, but was brought to the floor as Piper came crashing into the boat and landed on me hard, knocking the air out of my lungs.

'Stay away from her,' he gasped, rolling off me to his feet. 'She'll kill you!'

'Oh, pipe down,' she said with a cackle ... and plunged the knife into Alice's heart.

The scream that left my mouth was a noise I hadn't known a person could make. I tore myself away from Piper's grasp and ran towards Alice, shoving Dolly aside and cradling Alice. She hadn't moved, hadn't woken, hadn't anything. Her face was peaceful, as if she hadn't felt a thing. But she didn't need to do anything. I was screaming enough for the both of us, like it was my heart that had been cut in two. I reached for the knife still buried to the hilt in Alice's chest, wrenching it out.

'Leave it!' Piper rasped, too late. His voice was weak.

I blinked tears away, confused. Why would he say that? Surely he must know I couldn't leave the knife in Alice's chest ... and then I saw why.

A dark stain spurted over the sea-green dress she wore, spreading with each dying beat of her heart. I'd made it worse.

I stood up, looming over Dolly, my hatred for her overpowering me ... and saw that something was happening to her. She had slumped back, one hand over her heart. A dark, wet patch bloomed beneath her fingers. She lifted them away to look at them and they came away black.

Not blood. *Ink.*

A groan sounded from behind us. I whipped round, crying out.

Piper and Gypsy lay on the floor side by side, a black pool stretching between them. Gypsy's mouth moved wordlessly, one hand holding Piper's. Her other hand fluttered at her chest, pulling at a flap of wool in Alice's cardigan. It peeled back in a neat slice, but on the other side were words, black on white – like paper. Piper rolled over, his face grey. He placed his hand over Gypsy's heart, as if he were trying to patch the tear up. There was a dry, hollow sound, like paper being torn.

He coughed, spraying ink droplets into the air. They hit Gypsy's face in a fine mist. 'Hang on, Gyps,' he whispered. 'You're not getting rid of me that easily.'

They were dying.

'No!' I shouted. There had to be a way ... Alice's story couldn't end like this. *Alice* couldn't end like this! But as I looked at her face, draining of colour, I knew I was losing her.

I ran to the kitchen and found the paring knife, cutting Ramone's bonds and shaking life back into his fingers. 'Wake up,' I pleaded. 'Ramone, we need help!'

His eyes flickered in his head, still struggling to focus. 'Alice ...' he muttered, rolling on to his knees before collapsing once more.

I skidded back to Alice, tripping over my rucksack. A tangle of items flew out; the fortune cards scattering across the floor. One landed at my feet: the Black Cat.

Nine Lives.

With a jolt, it hit me. I could still save them. I opened

my mouth, ready to utter the riddle's answer ... then froze as Dolly heaved herself up, gasping. For the first time, I saw that Tabitha was barely moving, too, her fur slick with ink.

'Are you ready, Tabby?' Dolly grimaced, her teeth tinged with black. She cast her eyes over Alice, then Piper and Gypsy. But, unlike them, her expression was not one of shock, or hopelessness. It was one of victory. 'Do it now. Save us.'

In a flash, I understood.

'You *knew* this would happen,' I whispered. 'You knew that, by killing Alice, none of you could survive. That you only exist as long as Alice does.'

'Close enough.' Dolly reached towards the cat. 'I thought perhaps just one would die with her; the one who did it. That's why I tried to convince Gypsy to finish her off, even though I guessed it ... guessed it might not ... work.' She paused, wincing. 'But I was prepared for this and how to save myself. I win, Gypsy.' She turned to the cat. 'What are you waiting for?'

Tabitha dragged herself to her feet pitifully. She turned to me, her golden eyes burning into mine, then bowed her head. 'Forgive me.'

A spasm went through her, like an electrical current, jerking her limbs. When she stilled, she remained weak but stood more easily. She'd saved herself, using up a life. She looked at Dolly, and a second spasm took hold, this one more forceful.

Dolly sat up slowly, touching the sliced fabric over her

331

chest. Already I could see that any wound she'd had was healed. Another of Tabitha's lives had been spent.

'Tail!' I yelled.

Dolly's eyes widened. 'No,' she whispered in horror. 'No, you can't . . .'

'The answer to the riddle is "tail",' I repeated. 'Which makes me your new master.'

'Stop!' Dolly moaned, but before the word was even on her lips the cat had hauled itself to my side. Dolly lunged for the knife once more, but she was weak and I was faster. I snatched it, running to the steps, and threw the knife as hard as I could out over the water.

'You annoying little swot!' Dolly hissed. 'I'll kill you all with my bare hands when I've regained my strength.' She fell back, sinking into the pillows and cursing.

'Tabitha,' I said urgently. 'Save them! Save them all: Alice, Gypsy and Piper. Hurry! They're almost gone!' The boat swayed violently and an odd sound reached my ears with each movement. Not a creaking exactly, but a crackling. Like paper being twisted.

Something dripped on me from above. I looked up, finding that the roof of the boat was no more than paper, leaking ink. I crouched by Gypsy and Piper, touching their faces. Their skin crackled under my fingers, translucent, black and white. Words ran beneath the surface like veins. I turned away, unable to watch. In that moment, they were more real than they'd ever been.

I crawled to Alice's side, slipping on the fortune cards.

Alice's story, jumbled into a mixture of images: Sleeping Beauty, the Pied Piper, the Black Cat . . .

'Midge?' A voice croaked.

'Alice!' I cradled her head. Alice's eyes were open, blinking slowly. Tears spilled down my cheeks, and I hugged her and hugged her and hugged her. She kissed my wet face, then lifted her hand, rubbing sleep from the corners of her eyes, trying to sit up.

'Steady,' I told her. 'Take it slowly.'

Dazed, Alice crawled over to Piper and Gypsy. They were huddled together, weak, but steadily growing stronger, life flooding back into them. Behind them, Ramone's legs twitched. He stirred with a low moan and rolled on to his hands and knees.

'Midge,' Alice said. 'You're Tabitha's master now. She has one life left.'

'I know,' I said.

'Do you remember what she wants?' Alice asked.

I nodded. 'She wants to be human again.'

Alice nodded, her eyes hard as they rested on Dolly. 'Do it.'

'Tabitha,' I said. 'Use your final life to switch places with Dolly. You'll take her body and she'll be in yours.'

'What? No!' Dolly protested, her glassy eyes bulging in shock.

'Yes,' said Alice. 'This is how it ends.'

With a scream of fury, Dolly dragged herself up and flew at Alice, grabbing for her throat . . .

333

But Alice did not move, or even flinch, and Dolly staggered and cried out as Tabitha sprang at her. I saw the cat's body convulse again, but this time, so did Dolly's. As I watched the air between them rippled like heat rising off a road on a hot day, and I knew the switch had taken place. The cat rolled away, hissing, and Dolly – or rather, Dolly's body, for it now had Tabitha in it – held up its hands and looked at them in awe.

'It's done,' she whispered. 'No more claws!'

A split second later, a sleek, black cat hurled itself at Alice, hissing and scratching, and spewing out venomous words.

A swipe of Alice's arm sent the cat rolling away from her, unsteady on its four unfamiliar legs. 'You'll pay for this!' it yowled. 'You haven't seen the last of me!'

'Perhaps not.' Alice's voice was soft. 'But you can't hurt anyone again.' She turned to Gypsy and took her hand. 'I owe you a voice. And I'll make sure you get it, I promise. Your happy ending will come, Gypsy. I just got a little lost on the way.'

'Alice?' Ramone had dragged himself to her side. 'Alice, I'm sorry. All this is my fault . . .'

'It doesn't matter now.' Her voice was gentle as she met his eyes. 'It's done.'

I clung to her, marvelling at how strong she felt. How tall she stood.

Like Gypsy.

My boat, Gypsy mouthed suddenly, looking down.

Water was pooling round our feet. The floor was buckling and fading before my eyes. Fading to white, with dark lines looping in a familiar scrawl. Alice's handwriting.

And it wasn't just the boat. Piper and Gypsy and even Tabitha were fading, their skin thinning and paling . . . just like paper.

'You're going back,' I said gently. 'Back into the story.' I took Gypsy's hand. It crumpled in mine. I placed it in Piper's and he pulled her into his arms.

'Don't be scared,' he told her, even though his own eyes were afraid. 'The story don't end when you close its pages . . . right?'

'Right,' I said. 'You'll still be real somewhere.' And I cried then, because I would miss them, both of them . . . and even Tabitha. Even though they would go on, not just in the story but in my heart.

'We need to get off the boat,' Ramone said. 'We don't have much time; it's going fast now.' He tugged Alice's sleeve, but she hesitated.

'I'll never forget you,' she told Gypsy. She reached out, touching Gypsy's face. 'Goodbye.' She gazed through watery eyes at Piper. 'You, too. Look after her.' She sniffed and lowered her eyes. 'I mean, I know you will . . .'

Water gushed into my shoes as the floor of the boat gave way.

'Go, now,' Ramone urged, pushing Alice and me to the steps. 'There's no time!'

We crawled through the collapsing boat, the smell of

canal water seeping up into our clothes, our hair, weighing us down.

'Swim!' Alice gasped, tearing a chunk from a sunken wall and pushing me through it. I emerged, spluttering, joined seconds later by Ramone and Alice. Together the three of us swam clear of the mass of paper and words that was *Elsewhere*, and dragged ourselves out of the stinking water.

As it slipped beneath the surface, something that might have once been a black cat skittered down the towpath ahead, but by the time my eyes caught up with it I saw that it was nothing more than a scrunch of faded paper carried by the breeze.

We stood there, shivering, until the water was still. Fortune cards dotted the surface like water lilies, arranging themselves into some new story.

But it wasn't ours.

'Once upon a time, there was a girl called Alice,' she said quietly, breaking the silence. 'She told stories, like her father. But she never really knew him, even though she longed to know that he loved her, and for a happy ending.' She stopped, her voice breaking. 'I came to find you, Dad. Please don't tell me to go away again.'

'I won't, Alice,' Ramone murmured, his eyes glistening. 'You'll have your happy ending this time. You'll see. We'll write it together.' He pulled her close and kissed her on the forehead. 'This is only the first chapter.'

Ever After . . .

EVERY MINUTE OF EVERY DAY A STORY IS BEGUN.
Some of these stories are published and sold in
bookshops all over the world, and some may never
be finished, instead gathering dust at the bottom of drawers
or under beds, forgotten.

What is a story? It might be a memory, of an event or a
person. Perhaps a relative we never met, who exists only in
photographs and the memories of those who knew them.
It could be a fairy tale, like the ones you and I have both
known for ever; the stories that everybody knows of witches
and of gingerbread cottages, and fingers pricked on the
spindles of spinning wheels . . . warnings to stay on the
right path. Or it could be a sister weaving her own tales to
tell to a lonely younger brother.

Sometimes true and sometimes made up.

Sometimes a little bit of both.

It's often said there are two sides to every story. The version you hear depends on who is telling it. What they remember, or what they choose to leave out.

What they want you to believe.

If Alice had told this tale her way, it would still be about what happened when she was unable to finish one of her stories and went missing, and how I found her, only with certain differences. In Alice's version, perhaps, the statue of the stag really would have five legs, or maybe the old derelict mansion would have been a castle, surrounded by a forest of brambles.

This is not Alice's story, though. It's mine, so I have told it the way only I can.

As for Alice and me, we went on to have many more adventures, and Alice wrote many more stories. She still does and they're better now than ever. Sometimes she finishes them and sometimes not. It doesn't matter now, because the curse is broken. Maybe one day you'll read them, or perhaps you have already, although you might not know it, because she uses a different name for her books. A secret name that only her family knows.

I will end this tale by saying that stories, like gossip, or curses, have the power to harm. As our mother taught us: *Be careful what you believe in. If you believe you are cursed, then you are.*

But stories have the power to heal, too. If you believe in luck, and that you will succeed – whatever monsters come your way – then you can. As Alice once wrote: the problem with monsters is that those of our own making are the most terrifying of all.

Yet, if we created them, we also have the power to overcome them.

Acknowledgments

It would not have been physically possible to write this story without the generosity of my family. I'm grateful to my mum, sisters Theresa and Janet, and Nicola for helping out and looking after Jack in order to give me time to write.

My wonderful agent, Julia, to whom this book is dedicated: you pepped me up and calmed me down as required during moments of gloom, missed deadlines, and worries that this, too, could end up as a tale unfinished. You always have the right words – a magic all your own.

I'm indebted to my editor, Rachel Mann, whose wisdom made this story work even when I feared I might well end up as mad as Alice. It takes great skill to balance knowing when to heighten the tension and when less is more, and you have it in bags.

Thanks also to my copy editor Jane Tait, whose careful attention caught many errors and added a layer of sparkle.

Last but not least, thanks to the lovely Cat Healy who named Gypsy's boat with a word that is very much hers: *Elsewhere*.

THE MAGICAL WORLD OF
MICHELLE HARRISON'S AWARD-WINNING
THE THIRTEEN TREASURES

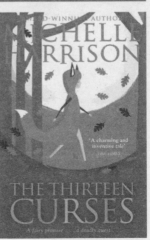

Fairies . . . but not as you know them . . .

© Charlie Hopkinson 2008

Michelle Harrison is a full time author who lives in Essex. Her first novel, *The Thirteen Treasures*, won the Waterstones Children's Book Prize and is published in sixteen countries including the UK. It was followed by *The Thirteen Curses* and *The Thirteen Secrets*. Michelle has since written *Unrest*, a ghost story for older readers and *One Wish*, a prequel to the *Thirteen Treasures* books. *The Other Alice* is her sixth novel.

Michelle's path to becoming a writer was inspired by stories told by her sisters as she was growing up, one of which was so vivid it prompted her to dig in the garden looking for evidence of a dead fairy. (She didn't find anything.) Since becoming a published author she still does strange things like asking people to shut her in the boots of their cars – all in the name of research, of course – like Alice.

Michelle has a son called Jack and two black cats. She suspects one of them is a mischief, but hasn't caught her drinking tea ... yet.

For more information visit Michelle's website: www.michelleharrisonbooks.com or find her on Twitter: @MHarrison13